September

k. m. higginbotham

Printed in the United States of America

Cover Photo by Kate Higginbotham

First Edition, 2018

ISBN-13: 978-1541367692
ISBN-10: 1541367693

To Meredith,
for the love of September

September

september

1

waffle house is always a good idea

September was leaving.

Jack said it's more like September was just passing through anyway, but that's not the way I saw it. In my mind, September would have been here forever. I would ask her out and we would move out of this seemingly never-ending friend zone she'd put me in when we met. It was a cliché scenario: the pretty new girl and me, the hot guy that every girl wanted. I had no interest in anyone. That is, I didn't before September.

I'd had it planned from the moment she walked through the door the first day of senior year. I would introduce myself, get her to tell me a few things about herself, and bam! I'd be in. It would be no time before I'd secured the boyfriend slot.

I didn't have much opportunity to execute that plan. Before I even opened my mouth to speak, she put me in my place. Apparently, she'd overheard my conversation with Marcus about a few of the cheerleaders. She lectured me on the importance of not treating a girl like a trophy piece, and I didn't listen to a word. All I could do was watch her. The way she talked with her hands when she got aggravated amused me. That lecture, the first of many, had me hooked.

1

"How many days until she leaves?" I asked Jack for the hundredth time.

Jack Evans has been my best friend since first grade. We're practically brothers—we've spent almost every holiday together since we were seven. As kids, we were absolutely inseparable. Even though we've grown up a little, our friendship has remained rock solid.

"A month," Jack snapped. "She leaves after Thanksgiving, on December 1st. If you don't quit asking the same question every ten minutes, I'm going to hit you."

"Be my guest," I sighed, resting my chin on the desk. "Maybe it'll wake me up from this nightmare."

The next thing I knew, the palm of Jack's hand came down *hard* on the back of my head, ruffling up the back of my clean-cut brown hair.

"Ouch!" I shoved him with the hand that wasn't nursing my throbbing head. "I didn't mean literally!"

"You need to wake up," he grumbled. "I'm sick of seeing you look like a lost puppy. Just talk to her about it already."

Marcus snorted, pushing his thick, black hair out of his eyes. "Like he has the guts for that. He knows he'll get rejected."

"What makes you think I'll get rejected?" I asked him.

"Dude, she's the only one who's ever rejected you multiple times," Marcus pointed out. "You asked her out *a week* after she moved to Oregon."

"And?"

"I think he's trying to say that September still doesn't like you." Jack slapped me on the shoulder. "I don't think she's interested in anyone, to tell you the truth."

The bell rang through the loudspeakers on the walls, and the chaos of fourth block change began. Marcus got up so fast that he almost flipped the desk.

"Where are you going?" Jack called after him.

"The lunchroom!" he yelled back. "It's chicken nugget day!"

I laughed, scooping my books up from the floor. We started towards the door. "Does he even have first lunch?"

Jack shook his head, combing through his blonde hair with his fingers. "Nope."

As we stepped into the corridor, the thick, wall-to-wall traffic of the students thinned. Jack led me through the hallway as the sophomores pushed the freshmen out into the middle of the walkway and the seniors and juniors pressed against the walls to stay out of the way of the chaos.

"Where are you headed?" I asked Jack as we approached our lockers.

"Home," he responded, a grin growing on his lips. "Cora's coming home from college today, and I want to be there when she pulls in."

Cora is Jack's older sister. If you saw them side by side, you'd know it immediately. They might as well be twins, they look so similar. We used to cause all sorts of trouble for her growing up, but she was a great sport, either playing along or letting us do what we wanted without interruption. Despite the physical distance between them, Jack and his sister grew closer than ever while she attended college.

"Tell her I said hey, okay?" My locker popped open after a few seconds of turning the dial, and I swapped up books before slamming it closed. The sound of metal hitting metal made every freshman in the hallway flinch.

"Will do. You still coming over tomorrow?"

I shook my head. "Nah, man. I'll let you two catch up."

"Thanks. I'll text you soon, then." He flashed me a smile before moving into the flow of hallway traffic disappearing from sight.

I had a calculus class to get to, but I wasn't particularly worried about it. I leaned against a bank of lockers—all plastered with Homecoming posters—and scrolled through the Twitter mentions and text messages on my cell phone—some from numbers I didn't even

3

recognize. I deleted every one of them, uninterested. I liked to keep a small friend group; I didn't need any jocks or frats to stretch it.

"Hello."

I glanced away from my phone to find a small, skinny, blonde girl standing to my right. She was cute, with glasses and a pretty face, but nothing memorable.

"What can I do for you?" I glanced back down at my phone.

She stuttered before pushing out a coherent sentence. "You're, um… You're Reed Davis, right?"

My eye quickly fluttered up to wink at her before returning to my phone screen. "The one and only."

She sucked in a breath before speaking again. "Um, I was wondering… If, I don't know… Well…"

She rambled on about something that had to do with Homecoming—the only words I really caught were "um" and "uh." Looking up from my phone once more, I caught a glimpse of September's dark reddish-brown hair further down the hall.

"Sorry," I interrupted, standing up straight and pocketing my phone, "I have to go. Nice talking to you."

I moved around the girl and jogged towards September, reaching her with just a few strides.

Today, her hair was pulled up in a ponytail. She wore a heavy-knit sweater and jeans and carried her books against her chest. September lived for sweater weather; she always had sweaters hanging at the front of her closet, waiting for the temperature to drop below fifty.

I opened my mouth to speak, but before I could get a word out, she held up a hand and looked over my shoulder.

"Did you do that?"

I turned around to see what she was talking about. The small girl from before stood next to my locker, looking at the ground. Her shoulders shook slightly back and forth.

"I don't know what you're talking about," I defended, holding my hands up as I turned back to September. "I didn't say anything to her."

"You obviously did something—she's *crying*. Haven't we had this conversation before?"

"*What?*"

"I'll be right back." She shoved her books into my hands and side-stepped around me. I barely caught her mumbling as she purposely bumped against my shoulder. "Why am I always cleaning up after you boys?"

After she trudged off towards the crying girl, I noticed Marcus, who had just stopped behind her carrying a disposable lunch tray of about fifteen chicken nuggets on top of his books.

"Got to the front, did you?" I nodded at his tray. He grinned through a mouthful of food, swallowing before he spoke. *How in the world does he keep from choking?*

"First one in line. Convinced Mrs. Debbie to give me extras."

I shook my head. "You're an animal."

"So are you." He snickered, nodding for me to look behind me. I turned around.

September leaned against my locker, talking to the small girl from earlier. She had an arm around the girl's shoulders.

"I didn't do anything!" I groaned.

As if on cue, September looked up and shot me a glare. I took a step back, just to be safe.

September was a force to be reckoned with.

"Oh," Marcus called, "you're in for it. She's after you, man."

"Shut up," I muttered, turning back to him. The bell rang again, and the few students left in the hallways cleared and rushed towards their fourth block classes.

"Great, Davis. You've made me late to class for the third time this month," September complained as she approached, taking her books back from the stack in my hands.

"What did you say to her?" Marcus asked September, still looking at the girl who now walked in the opposite direction. "She seems better."

"I apologized for Reed." She jabbed at my ribs with her elbow.

"Hey!" I exclaimed, wincing at the sharp prod. "Watch it!"

"I told her that Reed doesn't understand girls, and then I told her that she could do so much better. Reed doesn't deserve her."

Marcus snorted. "Well, you're right about that."

"Guys, I'm right here!"

"You shouldn't be." She pulled her phone from her pocket and checked the time. "Get to class, Davis. You've skipped too many times this month."

"Who are you, my mother?"

"No, but I do have her number. Would you like me to ask her what she thinks?"

Marcus laughed. "She's got you in a corner, man."

"You too, Marcus Holmes. I know your lunch code."

Marcus's smile faded as his eyes grew wide. "I'll see you after school, Reed."

September seemed satisfied as Marcus whirled around and sprinted down the hallway towards the staircase.

"Why are you still here?" Her trademark quirked eyebrow and playful smile were now directed at me.

September's long, dark auburn hair trailed down her shoulders and cascaded in waves like a waterfall to her waist. Her bold hair color suited her.

I realized how quiet it'd suddenly become. When I looked around, I noticed we were the last two left in the hallway.

I grinned down at her. I had five inches on her, but her attitude and personality made up for the difference in height between us. Although lean from cross country, I had muscle built up from both working on cars and working out in the gym. My toned torso and arms made me appear much bigger than her, and though I towered over her, she remained unfazed.

"You don't scare me as much as you scare Marcus, September."

"I don't scare you?" She stepped closer, a mischievous glint in her eye. I decided to take another step back.

"I didn't say *that*," I reasoned jokingly. "I said you don't scare me *as much*."

She laughed, taking one last step forward to wrap an arm around my waist. "You're something else."

We walked together down the hallway, my arm around her shoulders, our footsteps making the only sound. As we walked, I glanced over at her, suddenly remembering what had me in such a terrible mood that morning.

"When do you leave?" I knew perfectly well when she was leaving; I just felt like it wasn't real.

A frown crossed her lips.

"I've told you a billion times. I have another month."

"Thirty days, then."

"Sure, Reed, if you want to get technical. Thirty days."

I didn't respond. She looked around as if she were missing something.

"I haven't seen Jack today," she said. "Where's he gone? He didn't *actually* get to class on time, did he?"

The smile returned, tugging at the corner of my mouth. "Cora's home. He left early to go meet her."

"Oh, that's great!" She grinned at me and adjusted the books at her side. "I'm glad he's getting to see her. Not having her around has been a big change for him."

"He gets away with skipping class and I don't?"

"He has a better reason."

"You didn't even hear mine!"

She put a hand on her hip. "Let me hear it, then."

I cleared my throat and raised an eyebrow at her. "Would you believe me if I told you that I just wanted to see you?"

She used the smile she'd given me so many times before—the one that said, *Nice try, Reed.* "Not good enough. Get to class, Reed. I'll see you after school."

School droned on and on, and as usual, I paid no attention to any of my classes. I always got my assignments from the school's top student, Hannah Stephens, anyway; she was always more than willing to explain it to me and show me how to work every problem all on one convenient piece of paper, ready to turn in. In return, I occasionally introduced her to one of the guys on the cross-country team. She desperately wanted the "taken" status, so I obliged.

When the last bell rang, I bolted up before anyone else. I strode down the row to the first desk and snatched the paper lying on Hannah's desk before swinging the door open and breaking into a run, anxious to beat the afternoon traffic. I ignored the yells that echoed from classrooms when I breezed past, my sneakers squeaking against the floor tiles as I made my way to my locker. With a quick look at the list Hannah had made out at the top of the sheet, I grabbed the books I needed and shoved them into my backpack.

As I swung the metal door closed, Marcus approached me. In place of his tray of chicken nuggets, he held a can of soda.

"Have you seen September?" he asked, smacking on a piece of gum. *Ugh—gum and soda. Gross.*

I shook my head. "No. The bell only rang a minute ago, and her class is on the second floor. How could I have seen her?"

He shrugged. "She left class early. Someone came in to hand her a blue slip, and then she picked up her stuff and left. I figured you'd have already ditched calculus—you usually have by now."

"I wish. I knew September would've roasted me for that one, though. She thinks I need more math help."

Marcus snorted. "That's because you do."

"Whatever. Do you know where she went?"

"No, but before we go looking for her, can we get something to eat? I'm starving."

"Dude, you ate two hours ago."

"And?"

I rolled my eyes, pulling my phone from my pocket as we walked through the hallway. We had no trouble getting through the crowded hallway—everyone tended to move out of his or her way for us. Mark high-fived a few people and yelled "Bye" to a few others as we walked past. He tended to be more social than Jack, September, or me. It didn't hurt that he was a starter on the basketball team, either.

The cool November air hit me as we ventured into the parking lot, headed towards my car. Fall was coming to an end; I could feel it. A few more weeks and no doubt we'd have below freezing temperatures and probably some snow.

The sight of Charlotte, my faded red 1975 Scout 2, brightened my mood.

I loved her; Jack, Marcus, and I had so many great memories in that car, from drive-in movies during sophomore year to road trips the summer before senior year started. September even had a thing for Charlotte—she always asked to drive it when we were together. Charlotte was a mess, but she was my mess.

As soon as Marcus and I were in the car, I turned the key in the ignition and pushed the heat all the way up. Charlotte took about fifteen minutes to warm up, twenty if the temperature dropped lower than forty. It had been cloudy and windy all week, so she felt like an icicle by the time we got to her after school. As Marcus threw his books into the back seat, I dialed September's number. My eyes sent daggers at him as he tossed his backpack, then his binder, then the soda can he'd been carrying, now drained of all substance, into Charlotte's back seat. He caught my stare, giving me a sheepish smile as he patted the leather seat.

"Sorry, Char," he whispered.

"Hello?" September's strained voice came over the receiver.

"Hey." I tucked my seatbelt over one shoulder, balancing the phone under my ear on the other. "Is there a reason you skipped class?"

She scoffed. I could imagine her rolling her cocoa-colored eyes. "As if. I checked out during the last twenty minutes."

"What for?" I asked.

"Well, aren't you nosy," she teased. "Dad called and sent me a note. We're packing today, and they're leaving in a few days."

My heart dropped to my stomach. "You're leaving in a *few days?*"

"Hold your horses, Reed. Don't freak out yet. I said *they're* leaving, not *we're* leaving. Dad wants to go early and get things set up at the new house; I'll stay to finish some stuff here and go straight over after Thanksgiving. They've already got a buyer for the house and everything."

My lungs filled with oxygen again. "Alright. So you're going to be home by yourself?"

"I am. For three weeks, at least."

"Well, at least you aren't leaving yet," I remarked, relieved. "What're you doing right now?"

"Trying to balance a box of vintage china on my hip and a cell phone in the other hand," she answered. "Did you call just to check up on me, or can I get back to packing?"

"No, actually." I looked over at Marcus. "I was going to ask if you wanted to go get food, but Mark and I will come help you pack first. Then we can all go together."

"Sounds great."

After the call ended, I slid my phone into the cup holder before shifting the gears into drive and pulling out of the parking lot.

Greenville sat just a short drive away from Cascade Locks in Oregon. It was a small town but had plenty of character. Our sports teams were climbing the ranks and gaining some popularity. Downtown was growing pretty rapidly, filling up with shops and restaurants. We still had plenty of evergreens, though—that was my favorite part.

"I love how you offered my services without asking me," Marcus commented. "I *totally* wanted to carry around boxes today."

"If I hadn't offered, you would've gone, anyway. You'd be walking home if you didn't."

"Whatever." He turned up the radio, reclined his seat, and propped his feet on the dash.

Tiny water droplets hit the windshield, and a thin sheet of rain fell as we drove the familiar route to September's neighborhood and turned in the subdivision. The house she lived in—and would soon no longer live in—was small but just the right size for its occupants: just her mom, her dad, and her. September's mother had a thing for Autumn Joy flowers—which I'd never heard of before they moved to Greenville—and they were planted in thick bushels along their front porch and under the windows. We could always spot her house from the intersection down the street by the bright salmon-pink color that almost jumped at us from afar.

Charlotte rolled steadily into the driveway before stopping silent as I parked and pulled the key from the ignition. Marcus jumped from the car, running towards the front door and pressing the doorbell about fifty times. I shook my head, closing my door and then Mark's before following him.

September leaned against the doorframe, barefoot with her dark red-brown hair tied up high on her head. "Mark, we have to sell this house. I'm sure the next owners would like an intact doorbell."

He threw an arm around her shoulder and ruffled her hair. She swatted his hand away. "You took too long to answer. And I'm hungry."

"*Excuse me* for having to balance the Leaning Tower of Never-Ending Boxes," she remarked sarcastically. "Are you here to help or what?"

"I am," I said, holding up a hand, "but I think Mark is just here to clean out your pantry."

"Marcus Holmes, if you eat all my food again, I will come kill you in your sleep."

He held his hands up in defense. "If you two would hurry up and get packing and stacking, we won't have this problem, and no murders will be committed."

She grinned, reaching over to grab my hand and tugging both of us inside.

September wasn't exaggerating when she told us that she had balanced a tower of boxes. It wobbled in the corner of the room as the door fell closed behind us.

"Don't you think it'd be better to make multiple stacks?" I asked, looking up at the tower. "That way you could reach them all."

"If I did that, I'd lose floor space," she reasoned. "Plus, it took me an hour to get them like that, and I'm proud. If you knock them over, I'll knock you over."

"I won't knock them over, then."

She led us from the living room back to her bedroom where the windows were open and her desk, once littered with schoolwork, photos, and drawings, sat empty, the drawers yanked out and the top covered in a dusty film. The clean spaces showed the shapes where papers had laid for months unmoved. She had rolled up her multi-colored carpet and leaned it against the wall, and her closet gaped open. Half the hangers on the rod were bare, and two open boxes sat at the end of her bed.

"This is sad." I stepped into her room with my hands in my pockets. "It's depressing and empty."

"Like your soul," Mark snorted.

"Well," September said, inspecting the room, "I guess it does look a little lonely."

"How are you going to stay here by yourself for three weeks?"

She shrugged. "It's not like I haven't stayed on my own before."

"Can you guys hurry it up?" Marcus leaned his head against the wall in agony. "I'm so hungry."

"You're always hungry. You're a bottomless pit."

"I have a high metabolism!"

I moved to the boxes on her bed. Each one contained clothes, neither full. "What can I put in these, Em?"

"Anything summery." She moved beside me, picking up one box and setting it on the floor before separating clothes from hangers, folding them neatly, and stacking them in the cardboard container. Mark plopped onto the bed, making the boxes shake. I caught one before it fell off the bed.

"Mark, why don't you do something productive?" I asked.

"Nah, man." He scooped out his phone, turning it sideways to play a game. "I'm supervising."

September rolled her eyes, an amused smile sliding onto her lips. We exchanged a look before continuing to pack up her clothes.

"Dad says that the house he picked is nice," she said, making conversation. "It's supposed to be just outside of Cambridge, in a little place called Wicken."

"That's cool." I hid my discomfort with a smile. "What're you going to do in the UK?"

"Finish high school online, then more school. I'm supposedly already getting a bit of a scholarship from Cambridge since Dad's jumping straight into the semester to teach."

"That's great. You'll probably end up with a full ride, with your grades."

"I don't know how scholarships work over there, but I hope so. I don't want to be paying off student loans for the rest of my life."

We finished filling one box with clothes. I picked it up and moved it to the floor, leaning against her bedframe.

"Are you going to miss us?"

She scoffed. "What kind of question is that?"

"I just want to know."

"Maybe not you, Reed," she joked, "but I'll *desperately* miss Jack and Marcus."

Marcus pumped his fist in the air, his eyes still focused on his phone. "So, can I get some food?"

She shot him a glare. "Don't even think about it."

He lowered his fist. "Joking."

"I'm serious, September." I moved a little closer to her. "Will you miss Greenville?"

"Reed, you know I will." She reached out took my hand. Her hand was warm. "I'll think about it every day. Why are you so worried?"

"I don't want you to forget about us, that's all." I shoved my free hand into my pocket. Life had been better, more interesting since she'd moved here, and I feared it didn't mean anything to her—or it wouldn't—after a few months in England. There would be 5,000 miles between us and many more important things to think about on her end. Why would she want to remember little Greenville in a place like England?

"How could I forget you?" She gave my hand a squeeze. Without warning, she stepped forward and wrapped her arms around my waist. "You're an idiot, Reed Davis, if you think that I'd let go of Greenville that easily."

Just don't let go of me.

"The sap is so thick in here that I can't breathe, guys," Marcus whined. "Can you stop with the mushy gushy stuff?"

"You'll miss her too, Mark." I shot him a look. His eyes flickered up from his screen, and he raised his eyebrows in a challenge.

"I'll have to think about it. Can we *please* go get food now?"

I laughed, looking down at September, who smiled back up at me. I ruffled her hair before reluctantly letting go to miss her swatting hands.

"Call Jack; see if he and Cora want to come. Let's get out of my house before Mark decides to go tear my pantry apart." She slipped on a rain jacket and grabbed some shoes. "We'll have to finish this another time when Mark isn't here."

"Hey, I'm a great helper!"

I rolled my eyes. "Sure."

September watched me expectantly. She opened her palm and held it out.

I frowned. "What?"

She didn't answer. She kept looking at me.

Sighing, I fished my keys from my pocket and dropped them into her open palm. "Don't push her, okay? She's been having a rough week."

"She'll be fine. She drives better for me anyway." September skipped from her bedroom back to the living room. I heard the front door swing open. "Hurry up, you two!"

Our booth at Greenville's local Waffle House consistently sat clean and empty for us in the corner of the restaurant. We made appearances at least twice a week and even had a permanent seating arrangement; I always sat at the window, across from Jack and next to September, and Mark sat across from Em. The restaurant thermostat felt like it had a permanent home at -25 degrees; whenever we went in there, we had to bring jackets, even during the summer.

We laid claim to the jukebox with every visit. When we ate, we brought change to line up a great playlist. We never played the current hits—we always picked songs that deserved some attention and usually voted on one new one to hear.

"What'll it be?" Terra, a stout, middle-aged woman with cropped black hair, worked afternoons and late shifts during the week. She knew our orders well. "The usual?"

"Not sure yet. I think we'll wait until Jack and Cora get here." I offered her a smile.

"Cora's home?" Her eyes twinkled with excitement. "I'll bring over an extra chair for her."

"Thanks, Terra."

She winked before leaving us to find a chair.

"I wonder if they have Waffle Houses in the UK," September wondered aloud, crossing one foot under her leg. "I don't know if I could live without one."

"They have to have at least one." Mark leaned forward on his elbows and crossed his arms. "I refuse to let you go if there isn't at least one in the entire country. You'll just have to stay here."

"Gladly," she agreed.

Mark grinned. "Besides, if you stay, you'll still get to see me."

"Like I enjoy seeing your ugly face every day."

"Ouch!" he exclaimed, holding his hands over his heart like he'd been hurt. "My ego!"

September giggled. "Maybe that'll take you down a notch."

I rested my arm across the back of the booth seat, leaning back and cracking my neck out of habit. The bell above the door rang, and in strolled Jack, followed by his older sister.

The Evans siblings had the same feathered, dirty blonde hair and the same pale blue eyes. We hadn't seen Cora in almost six months, since she'd stayed at her university for the summer, but clearly either Jack had grown or she had shrunk; he towered over her by a few inches now.

"Cora!" September sprang from her seat, meeting the siblings between the door and the booth. She threw her arms around Cora's neck, causing her to stumble into Jack, who steadied both of them. She laughed as she hugged September back.

"Oh my gosh, you kids have changed so much in a few months!" she exclaimed, letting go of September and looking at all of us. Marcus and I stood from the booth to hug her.

"We're only two years younger than you, Cora." Marcus slung an arm around her shoulders. "I don't think you have the right to call us kids."

"How are you, Cora?" I hugged her around the neck. "How's college?"

"Oh, you know. It's the hardcore party life."

Jack snorted. "You don't party. You study."

"You don't know what I do." She waved him off.

Terra cleared her throat; she'd come back with an extra chair. We moved out of the walkway and back to our booth where we slid in to our spots, with Cora occupying a chair at the end.

"How are you?" Terra asked. "My, my, it's been a while."

"I'm great, thanks for asking."

Terra's contagious smile made me feel a little warmer. "Alright, kids, what'll it be today?"

"The usual," September and I said simultaneously. Cora glanced at us in amusement before turning and telling Terra her order.

When Terra had all our orders, Jack reached into his back pocket to retrieve his wallet, pulling out two one-dollar bills. He handed one to me and one to September.

"Music's on me today," he said.

"Any requests?" I nodded towards the machine.

"Something that isn't overplayed," Marcus answered.

September slid out of the booth, leading me across the tile floor to the touchscreen jukebox against the wall. We inserted our money and started selecting songs.

"I'm going to miss this," she said, dragging her finger across the screen and flipping through albums. I glanced at her, but I didn't say anything.

She turned to look up at me. "There are too many things we've done here that I'm going to miss. I wish I could just relive some of them."

"Then do it," I suggested, looking back at the screen and picking a couple of songs.

"What?"

I shrugged, picking the last few songs and turning to walk back towards the booth. "Make a list of stuff you want to do before you leave. You have almost a month left, right?"

She thought about it for a minute. "I mean, I suppose that'd work."

"You suppose what would work?" Jack asked as we slid back into the booth.

"September's going to make a list of everything she wants to do before she leaves," I said, my voice monotonous. September's departure consumed most of our conversations now; I couldn't help but feel annoyed every time it came up.

"That's a great idea," Jack said, nodding. "Let's make one now."

Marcus opened up his napkin and spread it on the table. "Anyone got a pen?"

Cora nodded, pulling out her pocketbook and unzipping it. She rummaged around for a pen and tossed one to Mark.

"Alright," he said, uncapping it and scribbling in a corner to start the ink flow. "What's at the top?"

"I want to come here another time before I leave," September said. "*Right before* I leave."

"Gotcha." Mark's scribbly handwriting, barely legible, scratched out two words that vaguely resembled *Waffle House*. "Next?"

"We should take her back to the drive-in again," Jack offered. "It's been awhile since we've done that."

Marcus wrote *drive-in* under *Waffle House*.

"September," Cora cut in, "do you not have any *girl friends* to hang out with?"

September shrugged. "Not outside of school. There are too many drama queens at Greenville High."

"You poor soul. You have to hang out with these losers all the time."

"Hey, now," Marcus protested. "You hang out with us too."

"Only when forced. Jack is the one who dragged me along."

Jack snorted. "Liar. You *asked* to come."

She ignored him. "In all honesty, I don't blame you. I had friends when I went to GHS but only one or two that I could stand outside of school. I don't know how you put up with these three."

September grinned, nudging me with her elbow. "I manage."

"Let's get back on task, ladies," Marcus said, tapping September's hand with the pen. "What next?"

"I want to take her shopping before she leaves," Cora said.

Marcus wrote *shopping* on the list. "Man, your list is lame. You could do this stuff any day. You should do something more exciting, like skydiving while blindfolded."

"We're not making a list of exciting feats, Mark," September said. "These are memories I want to make, not death wishes."

A grin broke out onto Jack's face as he took the pen from Marcus and slid the napkin in front of him. "How about we go to a concert?"

19

"Yes!" September exclaimed, clapping. "Making Midnight is coming near here on tour!"

We found Making Midnight while browsing the Waffle House jukebox, searching for new music. We heard one of their songs on a late night after seeing a movie, and we were hooked. They didn't have a huge following, but we didn't care. It meant cheaper concert tickets for us.

"I'll look for tickets tonight," I offered.

"Great!"

I glanced at September as she talked excitedly about the concert, worrying whether it would be on a school night or how many tickets would be left this late. I couldn't help but smile, despite my bitter thoughts. I loved how she used her hands when she talked.

"We should go hiking," Marcus suggested, taking the napkin and pen back from Jack. "We've only been on the trails once this fall."

"It's getting cold really fast," September pointed out. "We should go next weekend before it's too cold to go."

"Add it," Jack said. "Add a movie marathon, too. That's one thing none of us have done."

Marcus added everything to the list.

"I also want pictures with everyone," September said, "to keep with me in the UK."

"That's a great idea!" Cora said. "I have an old Polaroid camera back at the house. You can borrow it until you leave if you like."

September's smile couldn't grow any wider. "Thanks!"

"Here you are." Terra slid our plates onto the table. Another girl helped her pass out drinks.

"Thanks, Terra," I said.

"No problem. Eat up, kids. This one's on me."

"You don't have to do that," September argued.

"Please," Terra said, "let me. Cora's just come home and you're leaving soon. It's my treat."

"Thanks," Jack said, flashing a smile. "It means a lot."

"Be quiet and stuff your face," she said, waving us off as she returned to the counter to serve new customers.

Gladly, we all shifted our attention to our plates and ate, occasionally slipping into conversation. Cora told us stories about college while we intently listened.

"I don't think I'm missing out on much," Jack teased, leaning back in his seat once he finished. "It sounds like a horror story, if you ask me."

"Seriously," I chimed in. "I don't think I'm ready for that sort of commitment."

"You're not ready for any commitment," Marcus snorted. I kicked him hard under the table. His face drew together, and he pursed his lips as he bent down to rub his sore shin.

"Apparently the next two years won't be quite as bad," Cora said hopefully. "All the older students seem so much happier than the freshmen and sophomores."

"So, it's basically high school," September said, popping her knuckles.

"Close enough."

"I'm actually looking forward to college," she admitted. "Hopefully Cambridge will be a good fit."

"Let's stop talking about school," I interjected. "It's depressing. Can I enjoy my weekend, please?"

September rolled her eyes, shooting me a look.

"Well, I'd love to stay and chat all day," Mark drawled, standing up and stretching his arms, "but I've got a job to get to."

"*You have a job?*" Cora's jaw dropped open in disbelief. "When did this happen?"

Jack laughed, his lips curling into a smug smile. "His dad made him find a job a couple months ago. He's been working at the little restaurant on the corner of 10th and Forest."

"Guthrie's Diner?" she asked, turning to Marcus. "The one that's always full?"

"The one and only," Marcus confirmed, slipping his jacket on over his shoulders.

"What? Do you all of a sudden know how to cook your own food?"

"I'm learning, actually," he said matter-of-factly. "Guthrie is teaching me how to cook. I'm on cleanup duty until then, though."

I laughed. "At least he's doing *something*."

Marcus rolled his eyes. "I do more than you guys give me credit for."

"I'm sure," Jack said, sliding out of the booth after Marcus. "Do you need a ride to your car?"

Marcus nodded. "That'd be great."

Cora stood up, then September, leaving me the last one sitting in the booth.

"I'll catch you guys later," Jack said, waving before leading Marcus and his sister out of the restaurant.

September sat back down on the opposite side of the booth as we watched our friends exit the parking lot. I pulled the ink-covered napkin towards me and read through the list again. Neither of us spoke as the music played quietly in the speakers.

"So," she said, breaking the silence, "when were you going to talk to me about this?"

"About what?" I asked indifferently.

"Come on, Reed. I know you better than that. You're upset with me."

"What makes you say that?"

"For starters, you've only made a few thousand comments on anything related to me moving. I mean, really? You even had to make Cora feel bad about college?"

"I didn't say anything to Cora," I objected, sitting up. "Leave her out of it."

"Don't make this harder than it should be. I thought you knew you could talk to me about anything."

"I know that we can talk." My expression deadpanned.

"Do you?" She raised an eyebrow. "Then why didn't you tell me you were angry? That you were upset?"

"I didn't want to make you upset."

"But you don't care how other people feel? Why am I the only person whose emotions register with you?"

"You aren't the only one who registers; you're just the only one who matters."

She sighed. "Reed, just tell me how you feel. Be honest."

I allowed my shoulders to slump as I leaned further back into my seat. "I don't want you to leave. I don't want things to change around here. Is it a crime that I don't want you to forget us? I don't want—"

"How about you stop with the 'I don't want's' and give me something I can actually work with?"

I ran a hand through my hair, turning to the window.

"Can you just promise me that for now we'll keep all this talk of leaving on the down low?" I asked. "I feel like I'd be a much happier person."

"Fine," she said. "We won't talk about it if that's what it takes for you to stop acting like a two-year-old."

"Good."

"You do know that it's happening either way, don't you?" she asked. "I won't talk about it, but you can't be in denial until the end of the month. Accept it and move on."

"That's easier said than done," I muttered.

"Just try. For me."

Reluctantly, I nodded, looking at my hands before meeting her eyes. She offered me a weak smile, one that almost screamed an apology. I ignored it.

"Are you ready to leave?" She folded the napkin and slid it into her jeans pocket. I nodded again, exhaling loudly as I moved to stand.

After throwing a couple of tens on the table for Terra— —*no way* was she paying for all our food without me leaving *something*—I slid out of the booth. I whipped my keys from my pocket and held the door open for September as we left the restaurant and hopped back into my car.

Usually, September and I had no problem with silence. She had a way of making it comfortable. This time, however, the ride back to her house was *painfully* silent. I didn't even say goodbye before she got out of the car and her door closed behind her. She jogged up the front steps and disappeared inside without looking back.

I didn't pull onto the road right away. I just sat for a few minutes, listening to the quiet pitter-patter of the rain, thinking. The realization that an *entire day* with September was gone hit me hard, like a punch to the stomach.

I only had thirty days with September left, and one had already slipped away.

2

mind the gap

"You're joking," Marcus said. He looked from Jack, to me, back to Jack, his glare burning holes into Jack's jacket. "Please, someone tell me he's joking."

"He's not joking," I mumbled, rubbing the sleep from my eyes. "He's insane."

"Oh, lighten up, you two," September said, shutting Charlotte's passenger door. "Live a little."

"My definition of living isn't getting up at dawn to go climb a mountain," Marcus complained, jumping onto a rock next to the sign indicating the trailhead. "My back is already hurting, and it's freezing."

"It's your fault for packing an entire three-course meal in your backpack," Jack said. "We're only going to be here for a few hours."

Marcus crossed his arms. "But it's *cold.*"

Jack strode past him. "And you're annoying."

"That's enough, you two," September insisted. It seemed that nothing could dampen her mood; despite the overcast sky and cold weather, she wore a bright smile and spoke with a shining enthusiasm. Her blinding neon yellow headband that sat atop her braided hair seemed to reflect her excitement.

Marcus dropped down from the rock, now using it as a chair rather than a platform to broadcast his complaints. "How far do we have to hike?"

"It's two and a half miles." Jack slapped Marcus's back as he passed before starting down the trail. He walked ahead of us, whistling a peppy tune.

"Is he whistling the Andy Griffith theme song?" I shut Charlotte's door, making sure to turn the lock before taking my place next to September. I blinked hard a couple of times, still trying to clear my groggy morning vision.

"I believe he is," she said, her grin growing. "I've never seen him in this good of a mood."

"He's one with *nature*," Marcus's mocking, irritated voice called as he pushed himself back up to his feet, "or whatever other crap that goes along with hiking."

A cold breeze blew around us and I shivered. I quickly zipped up the front of my jacket. We grew closer and closer to winter with every day. The leaves had already changed colors and fallen, and they crunched under our boots; a few defiant leaves hung onto the branches overhead, mixing pops of red and orange in with the dark green of the evergreens.

September tightened her backpack straps, motioning for Marcus and me to follow. "Come on. If we don't get going now, we'll never catch up to him." She pointed down the trail to Jack, who had almost made it around the bend. With a stretch of her arms, September took off down the path at a fast-paced jog.

"Oh, great," Marcus groaned. "I wasn't aware we were running a marathon today, too."

"Sorry, Mark. Guess you get to work off all of your breakfast."

"No worries. I'll just get it back when we stop to eat again."

Together, we took off down the path after September and Jack, catching up to them at a wooden bridge a little farther up the trail.

If you needed a good place to hike, Cascade Locks was your best bet. When Jack, Marcus and I were freshmen, we would always beg our parents to drive us out there to hike. As soon as Charlotte was road ready and I got my license, we went all the time. We'd memorize the maps and find shortcuts in the trails, veering off into the woods for new scenery every once in a while. Every trip had new sights to see, new adventures to experience. During the summer, we'd hang our hammocks at the top of the trails where we had a perfect view of the city.

When September came along in the late spring of junior year, we adopted her into our little group, and the first place we took her was Cascade Locks. We packed the summer full of hiking trips. She was more excited than we were, going as far as climbing one of the evergreen trees to get a better view. I've never seen anyone climb an evergreen tree like that, but sure enough, if someone could do it, it would be her. She didn't get far, but it beat anything I could've done.

Now in pursuit of crossing the hike off September's bucket list, we were back. Jack had called and woken us up at the crack of dawn so that we could have as much time as possible on the trails. The one he chose wasn't new; in fact, it was the first trail we ever explored with September. There were so many secrets that we'd discovered here that it would be a crime not to bring her back one last time.

"You two run like little girls," September teased as we caught up with them. I didn't know what she was talking about until I glanced over at Marcus who leaned with his hands pressed onto his knees, panting as if he hadn't breathed in hours.

"You guys… run fast," he huffed.

"You're on the basketball team, Marcus. This should be a piece of cake for you."

"The season's over, okay?" He straightened up, flipping his hair out of his face before tightening the straps on his backpack. "I think I'm okay."

"Good. We don't stop for lunch for an hour."

Marcus's jaw dropped. "You're joking."

Jack grinned. "You wish."

"Don't worry," September said, trying to make Marcus feel better. "I'll stay behind you so that you keep moving. Time will fly and we'll be eating before you know it."

"You talk to him like he's a kindergartener," I snorted.

"He *is* one."

"I can hear you guys!"

"We know," September and I said simultaneously.

Marcus scoffed, pushing past us and standing next to Jack. "I never thought I'd say this, but I think I'd rather walk with you than them."

I shrugged, exchanging a look with September and winking at her. "No complaints here."

"Slow your roll, Romeo," she said. "Save it. By the end of this hike, you won't have the energy to flirt."

I wiggled my eyebrows at her. "We'll see."

Jack and Marcus took the lead, starting up their own conversation about the high school cheer squad as they walked. I didn't hear much, but I did catch the words *big* and *curvy* before I tuned them out (I *didn't* want to hear anything else) and gave September my undivided attention.

"You know, it's been awhile since we've done something like this," she said, tilting her head back to look up at the evergreens growing above us. "When did we go on the last trip? Late summer?"

"Something like that." I watched her admire the scenery, a smile creeping onto my lips. I straightened up before she could notice.

"I miss this." She breathed in the cool, damp air and sighed. "I'm going to miss this trail."

"Who knows? Maybe it'll miss you, too."

She laughed to herself, turning her head to look at the tall rock walls that lined either side of the trail.

"Em, watch where you're—"

With her eyes trained on the surrounding stone, September rammed her shin straight into a rock. She lost her balance, almost falling until I caught her arm and jerked her upright.

"*Crap.*" Gritting her teeth, she pulled up her pants leg. The impact hadn't broken the skin, but she'd most likely have a bruise the next day.

I let go of her. "You okay?"

"Just clumsy. I'm fine." She peered down the trail. Jack and Marcus were gone. "Wow, they're fast."

"I don't think Marcus notices. Jack must have him in deep conversation."

She laughed. It was a good sound, her laugh—the sort that could make you smile even if you were having a terrible day. It could easily light up a dreary day like this one.

We continued down the trail.

"Will you come visit us?" I asked her.

"Of course," she said, holding her hands against her mouth to warm her fingers. "What kind of question is that?"

"I don't know. You might get really busy in England."

"And we're always busy here, too, but we make time for each other, don't we?" She offered me a reassuring smile.

I nodded, looking at the ground as we continued our hike. She slowed down as we reached a break in the rock wall.

"Want to take the shortcut?" She pointed towards the invisible trail. "It's been a while."

"Sure." I shrugged. She grinned, hopping over the crumbled rocks and into the woods. I followed suit.

It brought back memories, taking the shortcut. Climbing over the same rocks we always had, racing up and down the little slopes, jumping over the giant roots sticking out of the ground. The familiarity brought a settled comfort around us.

"Remember the time Jack almost got us lost?" she asked.

"Oh, please. He wasn't *actually* lost."

She frowned. "Um, yes he was. He *flipped out.*"

"He wanted you to *think* we were lost," I said, holding back a laugh. "You freaked out, too."

"No, I didn't!"

"You did. You tried to use the GPS on your phone to get us out."

"It was getting late," she defended. "I was afraid that we wouldn't be able to find our way out when it got dark."

"I used to think you weren't afraid of anything," I said, leaning up against a tree. "You seemed unstoppable when we first met."

She turned on her heel to face me. "Everyone's afraid of something, Reed. Your fears don't define you; it's how you respond when you're faced with them that counts."

"So you freaked out and tried to use a *GPS*?"

She tried to hit my shoulder, but I dodged her fist. I laughed. She tried to stifle a few giggles. When she stopped, she studied my face for a moment before continuing down the path.

"What are you afraid of, Reed?"

I shrugged. "Not much."

"Hmm." She narrowed her eyes. "You're lying."

How could she know that?

I frowned at her. "What?"

"Come on, Reed," she said. "We're behind. They're probably halfway there by now."

"I'm not lying!" I called after her. She ignored my protests, bounding through the forest and jumping over fallen logs as she went. I ran to keep up with her. Thankfully, my legs were longer than hers; I passed her within a minute or two.

"You may be tall, but I'm fast," she said between breaths. "I'm going to beat you there."

"You wish," I said. "Cross-country is my specialty. See you at the cascades!"

At full speed, I took off through the woods, dodging rocks and branches as I went. September yelled something after me. I kept running.

I only slowed down when I reached the edge of the tree line where the trees thinned and opened into a shallow chasm between rock walls. A small waterfall spouted at one end of the ridge, and a narrow rock bridge connected the two sides.

September yelled after me again, but I couldn't understand her.

"I beat you!" I yelled triumphantly, still trying to catch my breath. I dropped my backpack to the ground, spinning in a circle as I searched for September.

"Reed!" she called.

"I'm at the cascades!" I called back.

I didn't hear a response.

"Em?"

"Reed!" she yelled again. "Help!"

"September?"

My feet carried me back into the woods as fast as they possibly could, my ears straining to hear.

"Reed! Over here!"

I ran towards the sound of her voice, stopping when I came to the edge of another chasm-like groove in the rock. A narrow opening in the rocks dropped down into a deeper cave where her voice echoed up towards me.

"Reed!"

"I'm here, Em," I said, crouching. "Where are you?"

I caught a glimpse of September's eye in the opening. "I'm here!"

"What happened?" I asked. "Are you okay?"

"I landed on my ankle wrong," she said, her voice straining. "I ran after you, and I didn't watch where I stepped. I slipped and fell. I'm too short to pull myself up."

"Don't worry. We'll get you out of here."

"September? Reed?" Jack's familiar voice carried through the woods from the direction of the cascades.

"Jack! Over here!"

"Reed?" Marcus called. "Where are you guys?"

"Over here!" I yelled again. "September's trapped!"

Branches snapped as they ran through the woods in our direction.

"September, give me your hand," I said, extending my arm down into the gap. She caught hold, and I used every bit of my strength to tow her upwards.

"Holy crap," Jack said over my shoulder as they came upon us.

"Help," I breathed, huffing as I struggled to lift September with one arm. When her head and arms came above the rocks, I gripped her hand with both of my own, and Jack and Marcus hunched over and seized September's upper arms. The three of us managed to hoist her out in one piece.

As she landed on solid ground, I fell onto my back, closing my eyes and trying to catch my breath.

"You're a problem child, aren't you?" Marcus asked, huffing. "You never watch where you're going."

"I guess I need to work on that," she breathed out.

"You think?" Jack laid on the ground and reached his arm down into the hole as far as he could, his head disappearing into the dark for a split second before he sat back up with September's backpack. He handed it to her, then stood.

I opened my eyes, sitting up slowly and looking over at September. "Are you okay?"

"Besides my ankle," she said, "I'm fine."

I moved her ankle into my lap, rolling up her pant leg and examining it. "I think you're okay. Ice it tonight."

"Yes, sir," she joked. "Thank you, Dr. Reed."

I rolled my eyes. "I just saved your life. I don't deserve your sass."

"*We* saved her life," Marcus corrected, clearing his throat.

"Excuse me. *We* saved your life."

"It wasn't that big of a deal," she said. "I wasn't going to die down there."

I snorted. "Yeah, you would've just been stranded. I don't know; maybe we would've never found you. You might have starved down there."

Before she could argue, Marcus stood up next to Jack, stretching out his hands. "If she's okay, I'm going back to the cascades to eat. Are you sure we can leave you guys alone again?"

"Yeah," Jack said, looking at us skeptically. "Is she going to end up dead?"

"Oh, give it a rest," she said. "We're fine. Be there in a minute."

Jack didn't argue, turning and walking back towards the cascades with Marcus.

"Thank you," September told me as they left. "Again."

"Don't mention it."

"Really. I mean it."

"Me too. Don't worry about it."

She put her backpack on her shoulder, standing up and offering me a hand. I took it and stood up next to her. We began walking back towards the cascades together.

"You lied to me," she said. "You do have fears."

"Everyone has fears." I tossed her words back to her. "I just don't have big ones."

"Yes, you do. You don't think I noticed the look on your face when you found me?"

"I wasn't scared."

"Uh-huh." She sounded unconvinced. "You need to own up at some point, Reed."

"Own up to what?"

She opened her mouth to respond but changed her mind and shook her head. "Never mind."

The laziness won over my tongue, and I didn't press her about it. We didn't talk the entire way back to the cascades.

"Finally," Marcus said, catching sight of us as we came over the edge of the chasm. "I was about to eat your food."

"You better not." I snatched up my backpack as quickly as I could. "You brought plenty for yourself."

"He ate half of it on the way up here," Jack commented.

"You were right." September shook her head at Mark. "He *is* a bottomless pit."

"*I have a high metabolism!*"

"Oh, we know. You never gain any weight, no matter how much you eat."

He feigned pain in his voice. "It's a blessing and a curse."

I sat down on the edge of the rocks, my legs dangling over the edge. I pulled out my food—a sandwich and a bag of chips—and started eating. September sat down next to me, popping open a can of soda.

"September," Marcus called with a mouthful of food, "you need to cross hiking off the list."

She hummed in agreement, and her hand dove into her backpack, rummaging around before drawing out a neatly folded napkin and a pen. She unfolded the napkin and crossed out the word *hike.*

"What's next?" I asked.

"Making Midnight comes to town next weekend," she said with a grin. "Tickets go on sale on the sixth."

"Tuesday? I got it."

"You'll get the tickets?"

"Of course."

"Where is the concert?" Marcus interjected.

"Portland," Jack answered. "Couple hours from here."

Marcus nudged Jack's arm. "How much do you want to bet that half the cheerleading squad will be there?"

I rolled my eyes. "Oh, brother."

September threw her empty can at Marcus. "Don't objectify girls, Mark."

"Yes, ma'am. Wouldn't dream of it."

As Mark and Jack continued their conversation, September and I grew quiet. We looked out over the cascades in comfortable silence.

"I doubt England will have a place like this." I nudged her arm. "Not one that you'll be able to find, anyway."

"Maybe not," she said, "but I hear they have some really pretty places to explore."

I bit the inside of my lip. "Do you think you'll find any guys over there as cool as we are?"

She laughed, leaning back onto her hands. "You're asking me about boys?"

"Yes, I am."

"Let's stop right there. That's one conversation I really don't want to have with you."

"Oh, come on. You don't want to spill what your dream guy is like?" I teased.

"No, I don't because I know it would come back to bite me in the butt. You three don't let anything go."

"What about just me? Don't you trust me?"

"Depends on the day," she joked.

"Well," I said, shrugging, "I can't say I blame you."

She shook her head, her smile softening as she watched the water splash on the rocks below us. "You're something, Reed Davis."

"I could say the same about you, September Jones."

We sat in silence for a while, listening to the wind blow in the trees and the water rush down the cascade. Getting away from the buzz of the city felt good. The trails out here always provided a calm getaway. They weren't that far from town, but it seemed like miles and miles away. September pulled out Cora's Polaroid that Jack had brought her and snapped a few photos of the waterfall, the four of us, and the trees.

About half an hour passed before we packed up our stuff and head back down the trail. It didn't take as long to get back to Charlotte as it did going up the trail, and we were on the road within thirty minutes.

The ride back was quiet. Jack and Marcus both snored against the windows, each of them falling straight asleep as soon as we got in the car. September leaned against her door, looking out the window as we drove. We didn't turn on the radio; the comfortable silence complemented our exhaustion.

"Hey, Reed?" she said quietly after a while.

I glanced at her from the corner of my eye. "Yeah?"

She seemed to think for a moment before answering. "Thanks... You know, for being there for me."

I raised an eyebrow. "Of course, September."

"I mean it. I'm thankful I have you."

"I'm glad I have you, too," I said. "For a little while at least."

The corner of her lip twitched upward before she turned back to the window.

My hands gripped the steering wheel. I dreaded the time when I would no longer have September. One look at her, however, and my thoughts cleared.

Live in the moment, right?

3

don't drop the norwegian china

"Did you get the tickets?" September asked, rocking back and forth on her heels as I twisted the dial on my locker. I was tired—I'd stayed up until midnight to get the tickets as soon as they went on sale—but I managed a smile.

The things I do for this girl.

I swung open my locker, pulling out a folder of papers. She took it from me, flipping it open and gasping as her eyes traveled across the paper.

"You're the best, Reed!" she squealed, throwing her arms around my neck. "Thanks!"

I laughed, hugging her back. Her hair smelled like a mixture of something minty and something citrus. The scent was familiar. If I could buy it in a bottle to spray on everything I own, I would.

"No problem. You owe me, though." She let go, and I took the folder back from her, sliding it back into my locker and closing the door.

"What do you want?" She kept scrutinizing the blue, beat-up metal doors as if she could still see the tickets through them. "I'll give you anything."

"Anything?" A smirk crept across my lips. "That's a wide spectrum."

"Don't ask for anything stupid."

I gasped, pretending to be hurt. "Me? Ask for something stupid? Would I ever?"

"Yes," she said, "you would. What do you want?"

After taking a second to think about it, I raised my eyebrows.

"I know," I said with a triumphant grin. "It's not much, but it'll do."

She tapped her foot against the ground. "Well, what is it?"

Pointing to my cheek, I stooped down to her height. "Right there, missy."

She crossed her arms. "Are you serious? You get one wish, and that's what you ask for?"

"Shut up and kiss me already. My legs are cramping. You're too short."

She rolled her eyes and pressed her lips to my cheek. At the last second, I turned around and planted one on her other cheek.

"Hey!" she exclaimed. "Not fair!"

"Too bad." I turned on my heel as she swung at my arm. She narrowly missed my bicep and groaned in frustration. "See you around, September."

Her weak insults echoed down the hallway after me as I weaved through the people and headed towards the door. No way was I going to calculus today; I didn't have the energy or the desire to sit there and listen to the teacher drone on about radicals and lecture us on preparing for the ACT so that we could get into a good college.

Don't get me wrong—college is important. I know that. I already had my sights set on a college with a program for car restoration; I just didn't care much for the standardized testing, the pen-to-paper aspect of it. A test doesn't define how well I can fix a car. If you want to know that, take a look at Charlotte.

I hiked my backpack higher up on my shoulder, getting ready to leave. I would've asked September to come with me, but I knew better. She held the perfect student status, with near perfect attendance and perfect grades. All her teachers loved her. She had big plans for her future. She would attend the best college and not pay a dime to go there. No way she would leave school early if she could help it.

I would be lying if I said I wasn't jealous.

We are what we are, though, and we can't change that. I didn't need perfect grades to be a mechanic or to restore cars; I needed hands-on experience and knowledge you can't learn from books. That's one of the reasons I worked for Tom O'Brien at his car shop; he'd been doing it for years and had helped me out with Charlotte more times than I could count.

I pulled out my phone about to text Marcus but stopped when I remembered that I hadn't seen him all day. I shot him a quick text, asking why he wasn't at school. I watched as the read receipt popped up onto the screen, but he didn't reply. I almost texted again but thought better of it and decided to ask him about it later. I didn't want to get in his way if he was busy.

I pressed the button on the wall next to the double doors at the school's side exit, unlocking them and swinging them open. The sky was a monotonous shade of gray, and a brisk wind pushed rain and cold air against my body. The rain didn't surprise me; we had rain all the time in this part of the state.

I ran out into the parking lot and unlocked Charlotte as fast as I could before jumping inside to stay dry. I turned the key in the ignition, and soon I was on the road.

———

"How many days did you say she had left?" Tom rolled across the floor on the creeper. He worked under a 1974 Nova. I could hear his wrench turning as he tightened a few bolts.

"Twenty-six." I grimaced. It seemed like time was out to get me.

He paused. "Wait, you're actually keeping count?"

"You asked, I answered."

Tom pushed the crawler out from under the car, pointing the wrench at me where I sat on the rolling stool behind the car. "You need to get a move on."

For a twenty-five-year-old mechanic, Thomas O'Brien did well at his job. He brought in business and knew his trade better than most mechanics older than him, thanks to the extensive knowledge of cars passed down through his dad, his grandfather, and his great-grandfather. He made enough off of antique and show cars to live comfortably with his wife and to keep me paid well.

"She's not into me, Tom."

"Not that kind of move," he said. "You need to *move on.*"

"I wish it were that simple."

"Do you love her?"

"I don't know. Yes? Maybe... I don't know." I ran a hand through my hair, pulling it back down and rubbing my forehead. I wished things were simpler. I wished for the months back when she first moved to Greenville, back when she was just a friend and my feelings didn't make things complicated.

Of course, that phase didn't last long.

"Reed," he said, "do you know what love is?"

"Are you serious?" I frowned at him. "Are we going to have a conversation about love?"

"Answer the question, kid."

I looked away, feeling awkward. I studied the street signs and tools hanging on the walls as I spoke. "I don't know, man. I guess so?"

"What is it?"

"I'm *not* answering that."

"Man up, Reed. Answer the dang question."

"I can't 'man up' when you're trying to create a Hallmark moment. I don't do chick flicks, Tom."

"Would you for September?"

I turned back to him, narrowing my eyes. He grinned.

"You're *head over heels.*"

"No, I'm not," I barked, getting aggravated. "I just... I like her a lot."

"Obviously more than 'a lot.'" He slid back under the Nova, and the sounds of the wrench turning the bolt continued. "Have you told her how you feel?"

"Not completely," I admitted.

"*Not completely,*" he mocked. "Man, it's not a complicated question. The answer is yes or no."

"No, I haven't, and I don't plan on it anytime soon."

"Are you serious? You've just sat here and complained about how this girl is leaving in twenty something days and how much you like her and you aren't even going to tell her?"

"It could ruin everything," I snapped. "That's an entire month of awkward stares that I don't care to live through."

"Do you honestly think September would do that to you?" he asked. "I don't think she would."

"You've met her like, three times. You don't know what she'd do."

"I've heard enough about her to have an idea. I don't think she'd want to spend her last month here without her best friend. Speaking of which, do Jack or Marcus know how you feel?"

"Marcus is a bit in the dark, but I'm pretty sure he suspects something. Jack knows everything."

"So you told Jack but not Marcus?"

"Marcus wouldn't be able to handle it. He flirts with every breathing creature; it would upset his natural order."

"And you don't flirt with everyone?"

"No," I said matter-of-factly. "Why do you care?"

"I don't. Grab me that rag, would you?"

I groaned, rolling over to the workbench and grabbing the oil and dirt-covered cloth. I reached down and handed it to him. He took it from me with one hand. "Thanks."

"You're welcome." I sat back, looking around the shop. More cars than usual filled the floor, leaving just a few feet between each to walk. Almost every one of the twenty spots was taken, save for a little space on one end for the equipment. "Had a lot of business lately?"

"I actually wanted to talk to you about that. Can you start coming in on the weekends?"

"Depends on which weekends."

"We've been recommended by people that we've fixed up before," he explained. "I have two more cars coming in tomorrow that need some serious work. I can handle the ones here right now—they're nothing major—but tomorrow's cars are going to be a project. You're the best mechanic I have."

"I'm the only mechanic you have," I said, rolling my eyes. "Besides you."

"Exactly. I can't work on five cars at once."

"Maybe you should consider hiring."

"Bring me someone as talented as you and I'll consider it."

I shrugged, settling my eyes on a colorless 1968 Mustang. "I don't know about every Saturday, but I'll do what I can; once September's gone, I will for sure. I can't come in tomorrow, but I can come in Friday."

"Friday is great," he said. "You can take one and I'll take the other."

"Sure." I stood up, walking across the large garage to the Mustang. "Who brought you this beauty?"

He rolled out from under the car, sitting up to see what I meant. When he saw it, he nodded. "I thought you might like that." He pulled a rag from his pocket and wiped his hands. "It's mine."

"Yours? You're serious?"

"I am. Bought it from a new guy last week—he'd planned on getting rid of it. A steal if I ever saw one."

My hand ran along the sanded exterior. "What are you going to do with it?"

"Fix it up. Make it a show car. I haven't decided if I'll sell it yet."

My eyes traveled to the car sitting next to the Mustang, growing wider as I realized what it was.

"You're joking," I said, jogging around the Mustang. "Someone brought you an Impala?"

"Leo dragged it in," he said. "Who knows where he got it or for how much, but it's going to be a nice-looking car when it's finished."

Leo, Tom's older brother, popped into the garage now and then when he found a nice car, but otherwise, he had his heart set on being a lawyer. I'd only met him once or twice; I never spotted him in the garage working but saw him standing outside talking to Tom a few times.

"What year is it?"

"1967."

"Sweet." I opened the driver's side door, sitting down on the sleek leather. "The interior is nice."

"Had it done last week. Looks good as new, yeah?"

I nodded. "Yeah."

I was about to ask if I could take it for a test drive, but my phone buzzed in my pocket. I recognized September's caller I.D. pop up on the screen. I slid the lock across, holding the phone to my ear.

"Hello?"

"Hey," September's voice came across the receiver. "Are you busy?"

"Just finishing up at the shop. What's up?"

"Could you help me get some packing done? I need to get the fragile stuff put up and ready to ship, and some of it is *really* heavy."

"Sure," I said. "Be there in ten."

"Great."

The line went dead, and I pocketed my phone.

"That September?" Tom asked.

"Yeah. I've got to go help her pack."

"Superman to the rescue," he joked.

"Whatever. See you Friday, Tom."

He waved at me from under the car as I left. "Drive safe."

The drive to September's didn't take long. The rain had cleared up, but the sky still hung a dark gray color overhead. I turned up my radio.

I spotted September waiting in the open doorway when I coasted into the driveway. She had her hair tied up on the top of her head and wore sweatpants with a long sleeve t-shirt. She seemed strangely comfortable standing in the cold with bare feet.

"It's a little cold to be barefoot, isn't it?" I asked, slamming the car door.

"Maybe." She raised a hand to stop me before I came closer. "Before you come in, I need to warn you."

"About?"

"There's a lot of breakable stuff in here. I don't need my great-grandma's Norwegian china smashed to bits... Or glass in my feet, for that matter."

I frowned. "Norwegian china? You're serious?"

"Dead serious. If you break it, I might have to break you."

"Is that a threat?"

"No." She frowned, trying to appear menacing. "It's a promise."

I held up my hands in defense, playing along, though I wasn't all that afraid of her. "Alright. No breaking the Norwegian china."

She smiled. "Good." She stepped back for me to get past her. "Go on in. The boxes are stacked in the corner."

"Is the Leaning Tower of Never-Ending Boxes still intact?" I walked past her into the living room.

Immediately, I spotted the pile of boxes stacked ten tall to my right. "Never mind. I found it."

"Strong and still growing," she said, closing the front door behind her. "Do you want something to drink?"

"No, thanks. I'm good." I cracked my knuckles as I scanned the area. Boxes and random décor sat in clumps all over the floor. Most of the furniture was missing, but a few pieces were left half-disassembled and one or two pieces left unmoved. If she had a method to the madness, I couldn't figure it out. "Did your parents make their flight okay?"

"Yeah. They left early yesterday morning."

She moved past me, going into the kitchen and opening the cabinets at the top. I followed her in, my eyes widening as I surveyed the large collection.

"Hey, September?"

"Hmm?"

We both glanced up at the shelves bursting with stacks of china.

"Exactly how much did your parents leave for you to pack?"

"Anything loose," she said. "They took most of the furniture and sold a few pieces. Took most of the cookware and clothes. I'm mostly packing anything that wasn't essential."

"So," I gulped, "they left you all the china, huh?"

She nodded. "Every last bit."

I took a deep breath, scoping out the kitchen. "Well, we'd better get started." I pulled out my phone, finding my music and scrolling through my playlists. "Do you have a speaker?"

"You can hook it up to the kitchen radio." She pointed to the radio attached to the bottom of one of the cabinets. "There's a cord over there somewhere in that mess."

I did as she said, sifting through the piles of silverware and dishes on the counter below until I found the auxiliary cord. I plugged it into my phone, then the radio, and picked a playlist labeled *Charlotte's Soundtrack.* Soon the kitchen echoed with music.

"Have I ever told you that you have good taste in music?" she asked.

"Maybe once or twice." I chuckled. "Or five times."

"Oh. Well, you do."

I shrugged. "I try."

Her gaze traveled to the pile of empty boxes, foam, and bubble wrap by the windows. "I'll wrap if you pack."

I helped her slide the boxes into the middle of the floor. A small step stool rested against the front of the refrigerator; I used it to climb up to the top shelf where the china stood in tall stacks.

"You ready?" I asked.

She nodded. "Let's do this."

I rubbed my hands together, flexing my muscles for show. September snorted at me. Carefully, I reached for the bottom-most stack of plates, a motley array of colors painted in floral patterns.

I stepped down the ladder, setting the plates on the ground beside the boxes before going back up to grab the saucers, cups, and bowls. When the entire set made it safely to the ground, I sat down across from September, pulling a plate into my hand and layering bubble wrap over the top. I stacked another plate, repeating the process over and over again. She picked up the bowls and started doing the same.

"Thanks for helping me, Reed. I owe you a lot."

"You don't owe me anything."

"You do a lot for me. I owe you more than I can pay back."

"You don't owe me," I repeated. I flashed her a half-smile. She looked like she wanted to say something but changed her mind and settled instead for smiling back.

I finished wrapping the stack of plates and arranged them into the box in front of us, then moved onto the saucers. We took turns wrapping the cups and stacking the dishes into the box.

"One down," she said, stretching tape across the top. She frowned at the other stacks of china. "That many to go."

"I'll get the next stack." I picked up the newly sealed box, my arms straining as I moved it over to the window and set it down on the floor. Then, I climbed back up onto the stool and reached for the next set.

The music changed on my phone, playing an old song that I hadn't heard in a long time.

September perked up. "What is this?"

"I can't remember the name. I like it, though."

"I haven't heard it in months," she said through a wide grin. "I *love* this song."

As I set another stack of china on the ground, I caught sight of her bouncing her head back and forth to the music. Standing up straight, I offered my hand.

We danced around the kitchen like absolute idiots. We took turns twirling each other as the music built. I pulled her close, doing a wanna-be waltz, swinging our interlocked hands back and forth. She leaned back and forth as I swayed, laughing when she almost fell. I caught her in a dip, wiggling my eyebrows so that she laughed again, harder this time.

That laugh. I swear, I never got tired of hearing that laugh.

She rolled her eyes and escaped from my grip.

"You're quite the dancer," she joked, raising her arms and twirling me.

"Am I?" I asked, grinning widely. I turned over and over until she couldn't hold her arms up anymore. "I had no idea."

The close proximity to her sent my nerves into a frenzy. The feeling was exhilarating, addicting.

"Speaking of dancing," she said, raising an eyebrow suggestively, "you know that Homecoming is next week." I took her hands again and swung her around the kitchen.

"Is it?"

"Yeah. There's a dance and everything."

"Well, then," I said, pulling her to me and dodging the dishes on the floor, "I guess you need a date." I spun her once more, leaning her back and holding her in another dip.

I mocked her raised eyebrow with my own. "Do you want to go to Homecoming with me?"

She laughed, leaning her head back before I pulled her upright. "Sure, Reed."

"You have to be sure," I warned. "No takies backsies."

"What are you, a five-year-old?"

"Only in my heart."

She pursed her lips, but not the bad kind—more like a restraining-a-smile kind. "Yeah, I'll go with you."

"Great." I twirled her again as the song ended, giving her a cheesy bow. "Thanks for the dance."

"Don't mention it." She made a wobbly curtsy.

I looked back at the large stacks of dishes on the floor then at her. "We should probably get back to work."

She sat back down across from me. We both started wrapping dishes again.

This time, we finished without any interruptions—that is, unless you count singing at the top of our lungs and making the neighbor's dogs bark. Soon, we had six sealed boxes of china, neatly stacked by the window. One at a time, we loaded them into my car before locking up the house and driving out to the post office.

After dropping all of the boxes, we stopped for hot chocolate. We drank it in the car on the way back.

"Thanks again for helping me." I saw her look at me from the corner of her eye.

"No problem. Thanks for being my date to Homecoming."

She grinned. "No problem."

We were quiet for a moment, riding in comfortable silence until she decided to speak again.

"Hey, Reed?"

I glanced at her. "Yeah?"

"What are you afraid of?"

I turned back to the road. "This again, Em?"

"You ignored me last time I asked."

"I didn't ignore you; I just chose not to answer."

"Answer me now then. Please. I'm curious."

I didn't answer. She kept looking at me.

"Fine." I sighed. "I am afraid of a *few* things."

"Noted. And they are?"

"You want a list?" I joked, trying to lighten the mood.

"I guess not," she said. "What's your biggest fear?"

I waited a moment, swallowing hard. I couldn't bring myself to see her reaction to my next words when I finally spoke.

"Losing you," I said. "I'm terrified of losing you."

She paused for a moment, turning away from me and toward the window. I could hear her breathing slow.

"You won't lose me, Reed."

"You're moving across the world. I think we can agree it's a strong possibility."

"Reed, if your *biggest fear* is losing me, I think we need to talk."

"About what?" I asked, hurt. This time, I did look back at her. "Do you like me the way I like you?"

She didn't answer.

"I didn't think so," I said, facing the road again. "Please don't remind me of what I already know."

"I may have to if you keep this up," she said, her voice quiet. "You need to move on."

"I can't move on. It's not like there's an off switch for these things."

"Then maybe my moving will do you good. Being separated for a while will be a good thing."

"I don't want to be separated from you."

"You can't rely on me all the time, Reed. You need to take some responsibility. You need to find solutions on your own."

Agitated, I ran my hand through my hair and propped my elbow up on the door. "Let's change the subject."

"Reed—"

"I said, let's change the subject," I said more forcefully. "Please."

"Maybe you should find a new date to Homecoming."

I gaped at her. "You're joking."

"No, I'm not."

"I don't need a new date, September. I know my boundaries. I'm nothing for you to worry over." I turned into her subdivision, slowing down as we neared her house.

"I'll stop worrying when you stop giving me reasons to worry about you."

I laughed, a subtle anger residing in my chest. "Listen to us, arguing like an old married couple. It's a bit pathetic."

"Talking through your issues is *never* pathetic, Reed. You should be a bit more sensitive to feelings other than your own."

I swung into her driveway, pushing hard on the brakes so that the car jerked us forward in our seatbelts. I stared at her, waiting expectantly.

She sighed, wringing her hands. "Listen, Reed; I'm sorry. I just don't want you to be hurting when I'm gone, that's all."

"Then don't leave," I stated.

The corner of her mouth pulled upward in a pitiful smile—the kind you give a kid when they don't understand something. "I'm sorry."

"It's fine."

"No, it's not. I'm sorry that you're upset I'm leaving, but that's the way it is. We've still got a month, though, remember? Let's try to make the most of it."

I knew she was right. I sighed. "I'm sorry. That was a jerk thing to say."

"Apology accepted." She swung open her door and started out.

"And September?"

She turned back and raised an eyebrow.

"I'd still like to take you to Homecoming."

She smiled back. "I'd like that."

She leaned over, hugging me before stepping out into her driveway. I could see the FOR SALE sign in the yard behind her, a large red rectangle plastered across it with the word *SOLD* in bright white letters. My stomach ached.

"See you at school, Reed." She slammed the door shut and ran from the cold into the house.

I waved from the car, but I knew she was gone.

4

high expectations

"Here she is."

Tom, sipping a can of Red Bull as he walked, led me to a car in the corner of the shop. The car seemed a little too tall to be a car, from what I could tell, but Tom had the body covered with a dusty gray tarp.

"What is she?"

He pulled up the tarp. My jaw dropped.

The car had at least four inches of lift in the front. The color looked like it used to be a lime green but now appeared to be an ugly yellow, dirty, faded, and weathered. The corners were angled, the hood had multiple indents, and the front had a jagged zigzag pattern. The long body had a single metal line running down the side, the rims were rusted and falling apart, and the interior was in shreds.

"Meet Lucy. She's a 1970 Caprice," he said, standing back and crossing his arms over his chest. "Piece of work, isn't she?"

"You could say that," I said apprehensively, circling the car. It had to be the *ugliest* paint job I'd ever seen.

"Think you can work on her?"

Skeptically, I flicked my eyes to him and back to the monstrosity in front of me. "What're her issues?"

"A few things. She runs, but she needs new brakes and a new starter, not to mention A/C and heat. She needs a new transmission, too."

"What about the aesthetic work?"

He grimaced. "That's the part that's going to take up all our time. He wants fresh paint, new rims, and new interior—the lot. If it were mine, I'd be asking to lower the lift, too. It looks ridiculous." He leaned closer and lowered his voice, despite the fact we were the only two in the garage. "He says that he'll pay double, though; that's a big cut for you."

I nodded. "I'll get started."

"Good." He started to walk away, but I stopped him.

"Hey, Tom? When exactly does he need his car back?"

He thought for a moment. "He wants it show ready in... two weeks? Yeah, that sounds right. Two weeks."

I almost choked on my own spit. "You're joking. Two weeks?"

"Two weeks. Good luck, kid."

"Wait a second." I scanned the shop. "You said there were two cars. Which one are you working on?"

He nodded towards the tarp-covered shape in front of Lucy. I walked over, peeling the tarp away and dropping it to the floor.

"Meet Olivia," he said, a smirk playing on his lips. "She's a 1945 half-ton Chevy pickup."

"Glad to see you took first pick," I grumbled. "What are you doing to her?"

"New paint, rebuilding part of the engine, and doing some tune ups. She's due the first of December."

"Have fun with that."

"I will." He grinned, turning and walking towards the door with a wave over his shoulder. "I've got to clean up and meet my wife for dinner, so don't break anything while I'm gone. See ya next time."

"Bye. Be careful; roads are a bit slick today."

"Yeah, yeah, yeah." The door opened, then closed, and I stood alone.

I sighed, calculating the mountain of work that lay ahead of me as I once again faced the Caprice. It was *meant to be* a cool car, but the lime green was enough to make me nauseous. To meet the deadline, I would have to finish all the hood work in two days, at the max. I was *literally* seeing green.

"What have they done to you, babe?" I skimmed my hand over the rough hood. "You look like you've been through a war."

The green paint certainly didn't do it justice. Scratches marred every inch of it.

I shrugged my jacket off and rolled up my sleeves before dragging the creeper over to the car. Lucky for me, Tom already had the car jacked up so I could work on it. I pulled the toolbox over closer before lying on the creeper and sliding under the car to get to work.

Three hours later, I had the brakes, brake pads, and starter changed, and I got to work on the transmission. It was late—almost eleven—but I wasn't tired. Determined to get as much of the work done in one day as possible, I prepared to work well into the night; two Red Bull cans already laid empty on the ground near my feet.

My phone buzzed in my pocket; I ignored it. I had the transmission ready to go and had prepped to start installing it when my phone rang again.

"What?" I asked into the phone, annoyed. I hadn't seen Marcus in days, and now he was calling me at the most inopportune moment.

"Ouch," Marcus said. "What's up with you?"

"I'm working," I informed him. "What do you want?"

"My bad, man. I, uh... I just..." He trailed off. I could hear a loud crash followed by chaotic noises in the background.

I frowned. "Marcus?"

"Can you come get me?" he asked abruptly. His words kind of slurred together, like he didn't have the energy to pronounce them correctly.

"Come get you?"

"I can't drive. Heck, I can't even *see* straight."

My jaw tensed. "What happened, Mark?"

"I'm at a party," he admitted. "I drank a few. Then I got into a fight."

"You got into a *fight?*"

"He asked for it, Reed. He talked about September and you—bad stuff, man. What was I supposed to do?"

I really wanted to applaud him for defending her, but I couldn't ignore the fact that he fought for me, too. I wasn't worth getting beat up over.

"You ignore them, Mark. Whoever said it, they weren't worth it."

"We can argue over that later." He slurred worse with each word, and I couldn't tell if it was from the alcohol or whatever pain he was in. "Can you come get me or not? It's getting pretty wild over here. I don't want to be here if the cops show up."

"Yeah," I said, searching around for my keys and trying to remain calm. "Yeah, I'll be there in a minute."

"I'm at Louis Morrison's river house. They were having an early Homecoming party."

"Stay put, Mark. And don't take any more drinks."

"Don't worry." He groaned, evidently shifting position. "I won't."

The line went dead, and finally laying my hands on my keys, I darted from the garage, slamming the door behind me. Charlotte's ignition started up immediately, and I hit my speed dial as I pulled out of the parking lot.

"Hello?"

I didn't bother wasting time. "Marcus got into a fight."

"What?" Fear laced September's voice. "Is he okay?"

"I don't know. I'm on my way to him right now. He sounded pretty bad over the phone."

"Take him to the hospital," she said. "I don't care whether he's bleeding or if he just has a scratch on his cheek, take him to the hospital, anyway. I'll call Jack and meet you guys there."

"I will." I pushed the speed limit as I headed down the interstate towards the river. "Be careful."

"You, too."

I tossed my phone into the passenger seat, putting both hands on the steering wheel and gripping it until my knuckles turned white. I prayed that he wasn't too hurt. An unconscious Marcus meant dead weight to carry him back to the car. I didn't know if I could carry him far enough.

The road that led towards the river came up on my right, and I made a sharp turn onto it. Charlotte bounced on the rocks as I drove, jostling me in my seat.

I'd only ever been to Louis Morrison's house once, in the eighth grade for a birthday party, but I'd heard enough stories about the place to know it when I saw it. Teenagers swarmed all over the yard and in and out of the house. A bonfire burned out on the front lawn, casting odd shadows on and around the boys that surrounded it and making them look more disoriented than they already were. They swayed so much I was afraid they'd fall forward into it.

After cutting the engine and springing from the car, I shoved my hands into my pockets and started searching for Marcus. Everyone looked the same; the dark shadows made it almost impossible to tell who was who. The temperature had dropped pretty low. I wondered why Louis chose to have a party outside on a cold night like this, but then I realized that most likely none of them had noticed.

"Reed, my man," a rather drunk boy called as I passed, catching up to me and leaning over onto my shoulder. His weight made me stagger, and I almost fell over. "I didn't expect to see you here."

To my surprise, none other than Louis himself gripped my shirt, partying out on his front lawn. His breath smelled like alcohol mixed with something sour, and sweat rolled down his face, giving me the repulsive image of a pig. I grimaced, pushing his arm off my shoulder and taking a step back.

"Have you seen Marcus?" I dodged his arm as he tried to sling it back around my neck. He stumbled forward, spilling his drink out of his red Solo cup.

"Hey!" Frowning, he stared down at the half-empty cup, then showed it to me as if I could do something about the lack of liquid. "You made me spill it."

"You've had enough anyway. Where's Marcus?"

"How would I know?" he slurred. "I don't hang out with you *cool* kids."

In one swift motion, my hands gripped Louis's shirt, steering him over to the house and throwing his back against the wall. I held him there, watching the fear grow bigger in his eyes. His cup fell to the grass, and the ground soaked up the putrid liquid.

Thank goodness. One more sip and he'd pass out right here on the grass.

"You're wasting my time, *Lewis*," I sneered, mispronouncing his name on purpose.

"Let me go, man!"

"I'm sorry, where did you say he is?"

"*He's out back.*" His voice came out as an urgent, strangled whisper, his eyes so wide that I thought they might popped out of his head.

"Now, was that so hard?"

He shook his head, gulping as he stared back at me. "Um... could you let me go now?"

I dropped him, dodging his crumpled figure on the ground and jogging around the house to find Marcus.

"I'll get you back for that, Davis!" he yelled behind me. His voice came out weak at best.

The backyard hardly qualified as a yard; it had only a dock leading out onto the water, complete with string lights, tiki torches, blasting music, and more teenagers doing things they shouldn't be doing. I cringed as I made my way through the people, calling out for Marcus and avoiding the dock. Deep water in the dark was not something I wanted to go near.

"Reed," his familiar voice called. He'd propped himself up against the wall, huddled on the ground, and held his side with one arm. I couldn't see much through the shadows, but his face seemed bruised.

At least he's conscious.

"*Holy crap*, man." I crouched next to him. "What happened?"

"Just some juniors that needed to learn to keep their mouths shut." He winced as he sat up. "I won."

"I'm sure you did. How bad are you hurt?"

"They ganged up on me at first and got some good hits in before I ended it. I think I may have a few bruised ribs."

I took in the sight of his bleeding knuckles. "You really picked the worst people to fight, Marcus. Juniors? Really?"

"Give me a break. I couldn't let them get away with talking trash about my friends."

Honestly, I couldn't blame him. I'd have done the same thing.

"Let's get you to the car." I leaned over and wrapped an arm under his shoulders. He gripped my shoulder with his hand, using it to help stand. When we were on our feet, he put all his weight on me.

Around the house we went, dodging wild high school students and shoving away any cups offered to us. I sighed in relief when we finally made it back to Charlotte.

I helped Marcus into the back seat where he laid down with his hand clutching his side. I slammed the door and a minute later we were heading back onto the road headed towards the hospital.

When we got to the emergency room, September and Jack were waiting at the door. I swung into the drop off zone, cutting off the engine and running around to the other side. I felt them next to me as I opened the passenger door, and they helped me pull Marcus from the back seat.

"Why are we here?" he asked groggily. "Why are *they* here?"

"Because you're hurt and we care," September said, slinging his arm around her shoulders. She was wearing sweatpants and a sweatshirt that was two sizes too big for her. "Let's get you inside, yeah?"

He looked like he wanted to protest but didn't have the energy. He settled with a nod, hanging his head against his chest as the three of us all but carried him through the automatic glass doors. A nurse caught sight of us, hurrying to our side.

"What happened to him?" she asked, moving to help us set him down in a chair.

"He got into a fight," I said. "He's hurt pretty bad." Looking over at Marcus, I realized that he had fallen unconscious. I could see his face better in the fluorescent light of the ER. Yellow and purple spotted the side of his face and deep scarlet shaded his hands. The blood from his side had soaked into his t-shirt, dotting it up his left side.

"What's your name?"

"Reed Davis." I tore my eyes away from Mark. "This is September and Jack. We're close friends."

The nurse called over a couple of the male nurses bustling through the emergency room, and they lifted him into a wheelchair and pushed him back into a room. The three of us watched him disappear behind the curtain.

After about twenty minutes of shifting in the uncomfortable, plastic, waiting-room seats, a woman in a white coat approached us in the waiting room.

"Which one of you is Reed Davis?"

I exchanged looks with September and Jack and stood up. "I am," I said, raising a hand before shoving them both into my pockets. "How is Marcus?"

"He's fine," she consoled. "Nothing too serious. We're still running some tests, but he most likely just needs a little rest. I was wondering if you could give me the contact information for his parents."

As if on cue, Marcus's parents burst into the emergency room. His mother scanned the room with wide eyes as soon as she set foot in the door, searching for her son.

I leaned over and lowered my voice. "How did they know we were here?"

September looked back guiltily. "They deserved to know," she answered quietly. "What would they think if we brought him back home and he was covered in bruises and blood? Besides, the hospital would've called anyway. I just shortened the wait time."

"Where is Marcus?" Marcus's mom looked at us then to the doctor. "Is my son okay?"

His father came up behind her, putting his hands on her shoulders. "Calm down, Eleanor."

"I am calm!" she exclaimed, her voice breaking. She pulled away from his touch; he didn't react.

"Please," the doctor quieted her. "I'm Dr. Williams. Your son is fine. He should be getting dressed and getting ready to leave as we speak. He has a couple of bruised ribs and some cuts, but they'll heal up in a week or two. I'd really like to speak to you about the rest of this in private, though."

"What happened to him?" Marcus's mom asked, looking at me. "Did you see what happened?"

"I wasn't there," I admitted, shifting uncomfortably. "He called me and asked me to come pick him up from a party. Said he'd gotten into a fight and couldn't get up on his own."

"A fight?"

I nodded. "I brought him straight here."

Mrs. Holmes put her hand on my shoulder. "Thank you, Reed. And thank you for calling us, September."

"What's going on here?"

We all turned to see Marcus being rolled out in a wheelchair. He was clean, the blood gone from his hands and replaced with white bandages. The skin around his eye had turned a sickly purple, and several more bruises had settled in and decorated his jaw and arms.

"What are *they* doing here?"

"Marcus!" his mom said. "Are you okay?"

"I'm fine." He waved her off. His eyes set sights on Jack, September, and me, traveling back and forth before they landed on September. His stare was hard, his jaw clenched; he didn't blink until his parents disappeared into the hallway with the doctor. September shrank back, feeling the heat from ten feet away.

When he finally spoke, his hand balled into a fist so tight that his knuckles turned white. "You *called my parents?*"

September crossed her arms. "Well, what did you want me to do?"

"Leave it alone," he growled. "You didn't have to butt in."

"Well, excuse me for trying to help," she defended. "Remind me not to next time."

"Do me a favor and *don't.*"

"That's enough," Jack said, stepping between the two. "Marcus, the hospital would've called anyway. There's no reason to take out your anger on her."

"Thanks for that, *Dad,*" he barked.

On cue, Marcus's parents stepped back into the waiting room. His mother's expression was blank. His father was quite obviously aggravated.

"Marcus," his father warned, "get in the car."

Marcus rolled his eyes, pushing himself up from the wheelchair and storming from the emergency room with a limp. I could hear him muttering curses to himself as he passed.

"Well," September said, clearing her throat awkwardly, "that went well."

"I'm sorry about him," Mrs. Holmes said. "I don't know what's gotten into him."

"Me either," I admitted.

"We'll stop by to check on him soon," Jack said, "if that's all right."

"Please, do," said Mr. Holmes, "though I don't know if he'll want to see you for a while after this whole ordeal."

"He'll see us whether he likes it or not." September shifted her weight, nudging me with her arm. "We should get going. It's late."

"One in the morning already." Mrs. Holmes laughed nervously. "Be careful, you three. Thank you for taking care of Marcus. If your parents have an issue, don't hesitate to call." She hugged each of us before hurrying from the hospital, her husband trailing behind her. We waited until they had Marcus in safely in their little black Pontiac and had pulled out before we started towards our cars. The cold air nearly froze us that late at night—in all the excitement I hadn't noticed I wore a short sleeve until we'd got outside. September wrapped her arms around her sweatshirt to keep herself warm. Jack didn't look bothered.

"Look at us," Jack said. "We're a mess."

"You've got that right. We're two weeks into November, and September and Marcus have both almost died." I raised an eyebrow at Jack, a teasing smile sliding across my lips. "We picked some pretty clumsy friends."

September pushed my shoulder lazily, her breath turning into clouds in front of her as she exhaled. "You should go home, Reed. Get back to sleep."

"What makes you think I was home when he called?"

Her mouth fell open. "Have you been at the shop all this time?"

"Three or four hours." I shrugged. "There are new cars in."

"If that's not dedication, I don't know what is," Jack remarked. "Are we still on for the concert tomorrow?"

"I don't know," September said with a frown. "My guess is that Marcus will be grounded. Do we want to go without him?"

"I'll go ask him tomorrow," I offered. She nodded.

"Why did he get into a fight?" she asked. "You didn't say."

"He took on a group of juniors that were talking smack about us. He told me that he won."

"*Juniors?*" Jack asked. "And he walked away looking like that?"

I shrugged. "Just him against, like, five of them, Jack. I'm pretty sure he'd consumed quite a lot of alcohol before it happened, too. I'm willing to bet that didn't help his aim."

"He'd been drinking?" September asked. "You didn't tell us that."

"I didn't want to get him in more trouble than he's already in," I replied. "Besides, the doctors would've found it, and they'd have said something."

September shook her head. "That's disappointing."

"Maybe he had stuff on his mind," Jack said.

"That doesn't justify it," she said quietly. "I'm going home and going to bed. You two should do the same."

With that, September spun on her heel and strode towards her car, not bothering to say goodbye.

"Wow," Jack said. "Marcus really got to her."

"Think she'll be okay?" I asked.

"She'll be fine. She's tough."

"What about Marcus? I have a feeling he won't want to see any of us."

"If he will see someone, it's you." Jack shifted his weight. "I think September just crossed a line with calling

63

his mom and dad. I don't think he likes how she parents him sometimes."

"What about you?"

"I didn't do anything which is why he won't want to see me," he reasoned. "I just showed up. I didn't go with you to get him, and I didn't stop September from calling his parents. Frankly, I think she did the right thing."

I nodded. "Me too."

"Well, since we're both on the same page," he said, turning away to walk to his car, "I'm going home. Be careful out there, man. Don't let him get to you."

"I won't."

And then I was alone.

5

punching walls

"No," Marcus said adamantly. "No, I'm not going."

"Come on, man. It's September's last concert here."

"I don't care. I don't want to see her. I didn't even want to see *you*. Get out of my house."

I shifted my weight from one foot to the other, leaning on the back of the couch as I looked at him from across the living room. "Why are you so mad that she called your parents?"

"Why do you think?" he asked. "I'm basically under house arrest because they found out that I was drinking."

"I didn't tell them you were drinking."

"Does it matter? You took me to the hospital, she called them, they found out. Simple as that."

"They would've found out anyway. Besides, you shouldn't have been drinking in the first place, Mark."

"Whatever," he mumbled. "Would you get out of my house?"

"No. We have four tickets to Making Midnight in Portland tonight and *not one* of them is going to waste."

"Did you not hear me? I'm under house arrest. I'm not going anywhere. Even if I wanted to go, I couldn't." He shifted in his chair, his fingers pulling at the tightly wrapped white gauze on his knuckles.

I sighed, but shrugged my shoulders. "Let me know if you change your mind. Your friends are expecting you."

"But I—"

"Your parents also happen to *like* your friends."

He scoffed. "*What* friends?"

I grimaced. "I guess we don't know, then."

"Got that right. I need to go shopping for new ones that won't *sell me out.*"

"You're being serious right now? This is what you think? That we sold you out?"

"It's what I know," he spat.

"You think she called your parents because she wanted to get you into trouble? What's happening to you, man?"

"What do you mean? I'm fine!"

"You and I know that this is about a lot more than some alcohol at a stupid Homecoming party," I retorted. "What's happening, Mark? Why won't you tell me? We're like brothers, man. Does that mean anything to you?"

He didn't answer. His eyes didn't move from the ground.

"You go missing for days without a word and then show up wasted at some party. How do you think that felt? To find you half-conscious on the ground at 11 o'clock at night?"

No response.

"Is it us?" I asked. "Did we do something to you?"

"It's not you," he said quietly. "I'm fine."

"You're anything but fine, Mark. What's happening to you?"

"I said *I'm fine,*" he barked, glaring up at me with a new anger in his eyes. "Get out of my house, Reed, or I'll *make* you get out."

"I'm not leaving without answers." I planted my feet, held my ground by shoving my hands adamantly into my pockets. "You can hit me if you want; I won't fight back."

He got up from his chair, the limp still apparent as he gripped the wall to hold himself upright. Growling in frustration, he slid to the carpet, unable to stand. "If I wasn't hurt, you'd be on the floor right now."

"I'm sure I would be. It's your fault; you're hurt because you made a stupid decision."

"I'm hurt because I protected *you*. Sorry. I was under the impression that that's what friends do for each other."

"You're hurt because you decided to go to that party in the first place," I responded. "Besides, I was under the impression you had no friends."

He slumped against the wall, breathing heavily. I took a step towards him, crouching down to his level.

"Are you going to tell me what's wrong here? Or am I going to have to force it out of you?"

"How are you going to—?"

Not giving him any warning, I jabbed my hand into side. He cringed, writhing in pain.

"Now, are we doing this the easy way," I asked, holding up my hand, "or are we doing this the hard way?"

He eyeballed my hand warily, then pretended to inspect the floor.

"Yesterday, I didn't go to school," he said. "I didn't on Thursday, either."

"Yeah, I noticed."

He sighed, leaning his head back against the wall. "I was at the emergency room."

I shifted, sitting down on the wood floor across from him. "Do you want to talk about it?"

"Not really," he said, "but I will."

His fingers played with the bandage again, this time stretching it so roughly that he might've ripped it.

"There's something wrong with me, Reed," he said, leaning his head back against the wall and looking at the ceiling. "I don't feel right. I feel... *wrong*."

"Wrong?"

"I've been thinking things that are scaring me. I didn't know what to do."

"What are you talking about?"

He stared at me for a moment, absentmindedly tearing apart the bandages on his hands, one piece at a time, exposing the skin from his wrist to his fingers. I eyed the cuts that dotted his hands and wrists. The crumpled gauze fell to the wooden floor like snow.

"I didn't start a fight with those juniors," he said, twisting pieces of gauze between his fingers. "They were talking trash about you guys, so I told them to can it, but I didn't start the fight. They fought me and they won, obviously. I didn't do much fighting back. I couldn't really see straight."

"Why did you lie?"

"Would you like to admit that you got beaten up by some underclassmen? Besides… it wasn't that big of a deal."

"Obviously, it is." I nodded toward his hands. "If those aren't from fighting, what are they from?"

"I punched a wall," he said. "Twice. My room has some massive craters in the sheetrock."

"Do I want to know why?"

"Anger management issues," he said, twisting up the shredded gauze. "Or at least that's what the therapist told me. He told my parents he's worried about me hurting myself. I told them that I was with you guys last night just so they'd let me out of the house."

"What do you have to be angry at?"

"Life," he answered. "I don't have good grades. I'm hungry all the time. I can't keep a girlfriend. Did you know that every girl I've asked out in the past six months has ended it, like, two weeks in? My parents have issues, mostly related to me and my future. I had to quit my job. My teachers hate me. College is going to cost a fortune— and we're all going to go in different directions. September is leaving. She won't say it, but I know she's disappointed in me. I can see it in her face when she looks at me. I can hear it in her voice. Do you know how painful it is to watch someone—the person whose opinion matters most to you—be disappointed in what she sees when she looks at you?"

He pushed out a short breath as if it were supposed to be funny. "Our group is breaking up. You guys are the most important people in my life, and we're all going separate ways."

"We aren't going to stop being friends," I said. "We're going back to the way things were before September."

"Tell yourself that," he said. "I know you're more torn up about her leaving than any of us."

I didn't respond.

"I'm sorry."

Me too.

I cleared my throat, trying to somehow clear the now thick air. "You shouldn't be punching walls. You'll break your hands."

"I already broke this one." He held up his left hand. "That's why we were at the hospital in the first place. Minor break. Hairline fractures."

"Where's your cast?"

"Broke it. Hit it against the wall a few times. Barely convinced my parents that I could drive with one hand."

"You have to help yourself, Marcus. You won't get better if you keep this up."

"That's easier said than done." He rolled the leftover strip of gauze into a ball in his hands, throwing it at the trashcan in the corner. It bounced off the rim, falling back to the floor. "My life is a mess right now."

Aren't all of ours, though?

"Are you going to be okay?"

He shrugged. "I don't know. Maybe. Eventually."

I felt terrible that I didn't know about any of Marcus's issues before now. I wasn't the only one; unless he'd told Jack at some point, he'd kept all of it inside for who knows how long. The stress, the anger, the emotions, the pain—it probably festered in his head, bottled up inside for months.

That's no way to live.

"Come with us to the concert," I prompted. "It will take your mind off things."

"I'm fine here."

I wanted to protest but figured that I'd already bugged him enough for one day. I stood up, clapping his back before heading to the door.

"If you decide to come, we'll be at my house at 5:30," I said over my shoulder. "I'll even handle your parents for you."

"Hey, Reed?"

I turned.

"Tell September I forgive her," he said. "And I'm sorry."

I nodded. "I will. Don't punch any more walls, okay, Mark?"

The corner of his mouth turned up in a weak smile. "No promises."

———

"Are you sure?" Jack asked. We all stood outside of my house in the driveway, getting ready to make the drive to Portland.

"He'll be here," I said confidently, tossing a couple blankets into the back seat of Charlotte for the ride home. Jack leaned against the door and September leaned against the passenger seat with the door open. The sun wasn't covered by clouds for once, providing a little warmth to us. Still, the wind had a chill in it, and I wore a light sweater over a t-shirt.

"How do you know?"

"Because I know Marcus. He couldn't stay away if he tried."

"Did you talk to him this morning?" September wore jeans and a short sleeve shirt with a jacket thrown over her shoulders. She'd braided her hair down her back. Even braided like that, it reached her waist. "There's no way he's not grounded."

"We talked for a half hour and I left. He's grounded, for sure, but I called his dad and talked to him earlier. He's more open to it since Mark would be with us."

I stopped there. Contrary to Marcus's request, I didn't apologize to September or tell her that he'd forgiven her. I figured he'd be there to do it on his own.

That said, I also didn't tell Jack or September about his problems. He could tell them that on his own, too. He didn't need me to do it for him. He didn't lie without reason, and I wouldn't be the one to make him explain himself before he was ready.

"So, what's the plan?" September asked.

I checked my watch. "Well, if traffic isn't bad, it should take us about an hour and a half to get there. If we leave in the next twenty minutes, we should have enough time to grab food on the way. The concert starts at eight."

"Reed, I don't think Marcus is coming," Jack said. "Don't you think he'd call?"

"I don't know," I said, looking over his shoulder as a familiar black truck rolled down the street. "Why don't you ask him?"

Jack turned around, mouth dropping open in disbelief as Mr. Holmes rolled into the driveway and parked. Marcus hopped out of the car and limped towards us with his right hand shoved in his jeans pocket, knuckles wrapped in gauze, and his left, swollen and purple, held close to his chest. It was wrapped up to his wrist.

Mr. Holmes watched Marcus closely from the truck as he approached us. When I caught his eye, he nodded, offered me a weak smile and a wave, and then pulled back out of the driveway.

"Hey, guys," Mark said sheepishly, stopping in front of the passenger door. I couldn't see her face, but September didn't say anything. I leaned across the hood and propped up on my elbows from the driver's side.

"How are you feeling?" I asked. "Better?"

"I'm hopped up on pain meds," he said, flashing me a grin, "and I haven't decided if they're working yet. I'll let you know when I know."

His gaze shifted to September, then the ground, then back up to her face. Without warning, he stepped forward, engulfing her in a hug. She stood still for a minute, surprised before she hugged him back.

"I'm sorry, September," he said into her shoulder. "I was a jerk."

"It's okay. I should've thought about how you'd react."

"Don't apologize to me. Never apologize to me." He let go of her, turning and looking at Jack. "I'm sorry, man."

"You didn't do anything to me," Jack said. "You were just a jerk in general."

I scoffed. Jack cracked a smile.

"I thought over reasons to be mad at you," Marcus informed him, "but after a while I realized they were stupid and gave up."

"Good to know."

Marcus looked at me. "Thanks for waiting."

"No problem," I said.

His eyes narrowed, his expression growing nervous as he nodded towards Jack and September. "Do they—?"

"No," I cut him short.

He nodded. "I'll handle it, then. Thanks."

"Handle what?" September swung around to look at me.

"Nothing," I said. "Nothing to worry about right now, at least."

She stared at me for a moment. "Are you sure?"

"Don't worry. It's fine."

She turned back to Marcus. "I'm glad you're okay."

"Me too," he said. "Now, are we going to a concert or what?"

"Wait!" Em's hand dove into the back seat and produced Cora's Polaroid camera. "We have to get a picture first!"

Painstakingly, we all posed for a picture beside Charlotte. Jack pointed to his shirt in all of them, which had Making Midnight written in bold letters across it. When she had two or three shots, she ran the camera inside, saying that she didn't want to lose it at the concert.

"I'll take the back seat," September offered when she came back, moving from the front seat and jumping into the back. "I don't think it'll be very comfortable riding back here when you're feeling like that, Mark."

"Thanks." He offered her a smile. Jack and September settled into their seats as I helped Mark in before jogging around to the front.

Thanks to the unusually sparse traffic, we made short work of the drive. We made it to the Waffle House in Portland with an hour to spare. We took a booth by the window, settling into our usual spots—this restaurant was identical to the one in Greenville. Marcus handed Jack a five dollar bill as we settled in, telling him to find the Making Midnight album.

As Jack went to the jukebox to pick some music, September leaned forward on the table.

"Are you going to tell me what I'm not supposed to be worrying about?"

"You're nosy," I commented.

"I'm worried."

"Do you ever let things go?" Mark asked her.

She shook her head. "Nope. Spill."

"September, not right now."

"What are we talking about?" Jack scooted into the booth. "What's happening right now?"

"Nothing," Marcus said.

"Marcus, we're your friends," September said. "You know you can tell us anything."

"Don't pressure him, Em." I looked at September. "He's had a rough couple of days."

We all grew quiet. Marcus shifted in his seat.

"No," he said, "she's right."

"What's she right about?" Jack asked blankly.

I dropped my head into my hands and groaned.

"I didn't get into a fight," Marcus blurted.

"Right," Jack snorted. Marcus kept a blank stare. "Wait, you're serious?"

"A group of juniors started talking trash. I told them to shut up, and they ganged up on me," he explained, "but I didn't fight back. They'd had a little too much to drink and so had I."

"You're joking." September leaned forward onto her elbows. "You let them beat you up?"

"I deserved it. My life is screwed up right now, and it's all my fault."

"He *thinks* it's his fault, but he can't help it," I mumbled. "He has anger management issues."

"So, if you didn't fight," Jack said, "what happened to your hands?"

Marcus coughed, looking down at the fresh gauze on his hands. He moved his weakened left hand into his lap. "Anger management."

I coughed. "He punched a wall."

"You *what?*"

"Multiple times," I added.

"Marcus!"

"What?" he asked. "I can't help it!"

"How bad are your hands?" September demanded. "Let me see them."

"No." He glued his hands to his chest. "September, I'm fine. Leave it alone."

"I can't leave it alone when I know you've been hurting yourself."

"I'm fine," he insisted. "Give me a week or two to heal, and I'll be good as new."

We were all quiet for a moment as September stared at Marcus, eventually settling back in her seat and crossing her arms. Jack coughed awkwardly.

"Well, now that that's out of the way," he said, "how about we eat now?"

Thankfully, the waitress walked over to break the thick tension. We all ordered our food and ate in silence before piling back into the car.

The concert hall was packed when we arrived at the venue. We got in just in time, finding our seats and sitting down just as Making Midnight took the stage. Instantly, all of our uncomfortable feelings were gone, and we were on our feet to cheer on our favorite band.

Since we'd started listening to them, their following had grown. Now, instead of the few hundred that listened to them, they had a few thousand, and the fan base was growing fast.

Their music talked about life—real life—not any made up crap about how they wished their lives were. I guess that's what made them so appealing. We could all relate.

Standing in the music hall, screaming out the lyrics to my favorite songs next to my best friends, I felt something I hadn't felt in a long time. I felt complete. I felt comfortable. I felt happy, genuinely happy.

I looked over at September as she jumped up and down and screamed lyrics at Jack. They both started yelling the lyrics at Marcus who laughed and joined in, no longer looking stressed.

Good for him. He needed this.

September peered behind her, locking eyes with me. Her smile grew as she grabbed my arm and pulled me over, the four of us now screaming out lyrics at the top of our lungs as the music blared.

This is what I love. This is how things should be all the time.

The concert ended later than we expected. Making Midnight came back on for an encore that lasted for six songs. By the time we filed out of the concert hall with everyone else, the clock read 11:30.

"I'll drive," Marcus offered as we approached the car, obviously in a better mood.

"I don't know about that, man."

"Come on. I feel fine, I swear."

"It's an hour and a half back. Don't you want to sleep?"

"I'm not tired," he assured me. "You guys sleep. I'd like the time to think."

"Aren't you on pain meds?"

"They wore off a little bit ago. I'll take some Tylenol and I'll be fine." He seemed desperate, which startled me; I didn't think driving was a big deal. His eyes bore into me, silently pleading. *Please, Reed?*

I felt terrible. Marcus needed some normalcy, something to get his mind off of everything, but I wasn't sure about letting him get behind the wheel, even if his medication had worn off.

Reluctantly, I tossed him the keys and got into the passenger seat, making up my mind to stay awake until we got back to my house. I could keep an eye on him and be ready to take back over if needed.

After twenty minutes trying to get out of the parking lot, we finally made it back to the road. Traffic was thick with people driving home from the concert. Marcus drove effortlessly with one hand, holding his left in his lap.

"That was an amazing concert," September gushed. "Thanks for finding the tickets, Reed."

"Don't mention it."

"The view from our seats was great," Jack boasted. "They sounded better than ever."

"I'm sure their ticket prices will go up after this. Everyone's starting to listen to them now."

"They're going mainstream," Marcus added.

"I wouldn't say that." September leaned up onto the seat, her head resting on her arms. "I'm glad we all got to go together."

Marcus nodded. "Me too."

She smiled, leaning back and resting her head on the window.

The first one to fall asleep was Jack. His face pressed against the cold window as he snored. September came next, curled up with one of the blankets I'd thrown into the back.

We stopped at a gas station to get some caffeine. I held on longer than Jack and September, but the Red Bull could only do so much.

I don't know how much time passed while I slept, but I knew it wasn't long enough for us to be home.

The car jolted. My eyes snapped open to the bright lights of oncoming traffic, September screaming, and the sound of gut wrenching metal on metal.

6

narcoleptics don't need licenses

A piercing scream resonated in my ears as the impact of the truck jerked us all forward in our seats. My head hit the window next to me so hard that the already cracked glass shattered in the impact. Warm, sticky blood trickled down the side of my face, threatening to drip into my eyes. Charlotte creaked as she rolled across the opposite lane and into a ditch, leaning over to one side.

"Everyone hold on!" I yelled as she began to tip. Over we went, the metal roof crunching against the weight of the bottom, and our heads suspended a few mere inches above the ceiling. Another window shattered, sending glass flying at us. Shards cut my hands, neck, and face, stinging my skin. The cold wind blew through the broken windows, sending a shiver up my spine.

"Is everyone okay?" I cringed as my quivering hand yanked a shard out of my palm.

"I'm okay," called Jack, his usually confident voice now wavering. "September is unconscious."

Unconscious. She's unconscious. God, please let her be okay.

Stay calm, Reed. Stay calm.

"Marcus?" I tried to turn my head.

"I'm fine," his shaky voice answered. "Is September okay?"

"Her head is bleeding," Jack said. "Can any of you move?"

"I'm trying." I put one hand under my head, holding myself up as the other worked on the seatbelt. My fingers hurt as I tried to pull the metal piece from the clasp, but it wouldn't budge.

"Is everyone okay?" a man yelled into the car.

"We're okay," I said. "One of us is knocked out."

"I've called an ambulance," he said. "We're going to get you out of there. Nobody move."

"Thank you," Jack called back.

Marcus let out a strangled cry as he pushed against the ceiling with his already injured hand. He pulled it back to his chest. "I fell asleep," he breathed. His fists clenched as he tried to hold himself up. "I *fell asleep*."

"It's okay, Mark," I said, trying to calm him. "Accidents happen."

I was frustrated about Charlotte, but I was more worried about Marcus. We all needed to get out of the car in one piece; I could deal with the car damage later.

"This accident cost you Charlotte," he spat, pounding his fist against the crumpled ceiling. "And now September is unconscious."

"Mark," I warned. "Mark, you're going to hurt yourself. We need to focus on getting out of here."

"I totaled your car," he barked, kicking at the floor and trying to free himself. His hands found his seatbelt, unclasping it, and he fell on his back onto the ceiling. He worked on the door, kicking it as hard as he could and making the car shake.

Frantically, I pulled at my seatbelt, finally unclasping it and falling to my back next to him. "Marcus, stop it!" My mind went to September. The shaking car of the car could send more glass flying, and she couldn't shield herself. "Jack, pull Em away from the window!"

The shrill note of police sirens and the glare of flashing lights are what stopped Marcus. He froze in his seat, giving up and falling back.

"Everyone all right in there?" someone called, shining a flashlight into the car.

"One of us is unconscious," I called. "The rest of us are awake."

"How many of you are there?"

"Four."

"Hang tight, kids," he said. "We're going to get you out."

Several firemen came to Marcus's side of the car, working on his door until they had it free. He stumbled out of the car, pulling away from their grasp. They worked on mine next, the metal whining as they swung it open. They pulled me from the wreckage and laid me on the ground where paramedics leaned over me.

"What's your name, son?" a woman asked, shining a light in my eyes. "Honey, can you tell me your name?"

I looked up groggily, feeling dizzy. Their faces were blurry. I sat up, despite their protests, and my eyes found Marcus who paced in front of the car with his hands on his head. Several paramedics tried to get him to sit down so that they could check his vitals, but he didn't listen. I watched his hands fall to his side, clenching into fists as the anger built up inside him.

And then he punched the hood.

It was as if all pain had disappeared or at least was suppressed by the adrenaline. He appeared to have no notice of the coloring of his hand or the pain that should've been there or the people screaming around him. He didn't look like he'd stop any time soon.

Everything that followed happened in slow motion. The paramedic in the ambulance screamed as Mark took out his anger on the metal, his hand turning a deeper, horrible, sickening shade of purple. The firefighters who were working on getting September and Jack out looked alarmed, but they continued their work. A police officer tried yelling and grabbing him at the arms, but Marcus ripped himself away and continued his work. I sprang up from the ground, pushing past the medics, fighting the swaying ground, and stepping in front of Marcus. I had to use the car for support—my head spun at the sudden movement.

"Marcus, stop!" I yelled. "Give it a rest, man!"

"I ruin everything," he yelled, pushing me back against the car. "I ruin everything."

The police officer tried to pull Mark off of me, but I stopped him. "I'm fine!"

He grudgingly backed off, staying only a few feet out of reach of the both of us. I refocused on Marcus, struggling against the pressure, his arm held against my chest.

"You don't ruin everything. It was an accident. You made a mistake."

"I seem to make a lot of mistakes, don't I?"

"Dude, you wrecked the car. You fell asleep. Get over it."

"September is unconscious!"

That reminder sent my heart into my stomach.

Lie. Pretend you know she'll be okay. You've got to convince him to stop destroying himself.

I swallowed hard. "She'll wake up. Sit down and let them fix the hand that you just shattered."

He caught my bluff. "You don't even believe that." He glared at me, eyes blazing. "Move, Reed."

"If you're going to hit something, hit me," I said.

"*Move*, Reed," he warned again.

I stayed put.

The next thing I knew, the ground rushed up to meet me. My head hit the car behind me, and I ended up sprawled on the ground next to the wreckage. My fingers groped for my newly sore nose, and fresh blood streamed down my face. My vision went fuzzy, and I blacked out.

The smell of sterilized towels and the frigid air jolted me awake. The mattress below me was thin and firm and covered with a stiff, white blanket. The pillows behind my head felt like plastic. I scanned the area, finding myself in the emergency room in one of the patient stalls. A thin curtain hung on one side of the room, and a hard wall stood behind my bed. The clock on the wall read 4 a.m. I'd been out for a while.

Looking down, I noticed that my arms were wrapped in thick, white bandages. My hands were the same way, leaving only my fingers exposed. I twisted to look around the room and flinched as a sharp pain shot into my side. I lifted the dirty, bloodstained hem of my t-shirt to find my torso wrapped in more bandages.

I slowly sat up, sliding from the bed and pressing my bare feet to the cold tile. I had to hold onto the bed for a moment because my vision started spinning, but it cleared after a few seconds. A dull ache settled in my head as my hand pushed back the curtain that served as a door and I peered into the hallway.

At the end of the corridor, a female doctor spoke to my parents. Behind them, I could see Jack leaning against the wall. September stood next to him, her arms crossed over her chest and her head wrapped with gauze. Her expression was pulled into a subconscious frown, her eyebrows furrowed as she listened in on the conversation.

I couldn't take my eyes off her. Her shoulders slumped—tired, worn, and bruised—but she was still beautiful. Deep in my chest, a wave of relief rushed over me at the sight of her standing there living, breathing, and walking around. *She's awake.*

My friends are okay.

"Reed?"

I turned around, finding Marcus standing barefoot in the corridor behind me. They'd wrapped his left hand in a new hard cast. It looked terrible; the fingers peeking out of his cast were curled up, crooked, and an awful shade of indigo. He cradled it close to his side. Small pieces of tape held together cuts that littered his face. His right arm was wrapped from his wrist up to his elbow.

"Hey."

He nodded, looking me up and down. "How are you?"

"Fine. You?"

"I'll live." He glanced over my shoulder, locking eyes on September and Jack. "Are they okay?"

"I haven't checked, but they seem okay." I gestured to them, nodding. "We should go let them know we're awake."

Side by side, Marcus and I walked the hallway barefoot. I slowed down as I reached my parents, touching my mom's shoulder. She turned around, smiling as she saw me. Her arms came up over my shoulder and she hugged me tight.

"Mom," I groaned, "that hurts."

"Oh!" she said, pulling away. "I'm sorry."

I offered her a smile.

"How are you feeling?" my dad asked.

"Rough, but I'll be fine."

The doctor smiled at me. "You're very lucky, you know. A few more miles per hour, and you may have had injuries much worse than what you're walking away with."

"What did you have to treat me for?" I fingered the gauze on my hands.

"You have a fractured nose, a concussion, various cuts from the glass and bruising to your ribs. You're going to be feeling rough for a few weeks."

I nodded at Marcus, who talked to Jack against the wall, and lowered my voice. "What about him?"

Her eyes shifted to him, then back to me as she took a breath. "He's going to be under the weather for a few more weeks than you."

"How bad?"

"I'm sorry; that's confidential."

I narrowed my eyes. "I just survived what could've been a fatal wreck with three other teenagers, and my head is about to explode. My patience is wearing a bit thin, and we both know he'll tell me either way." I changed my tone before either of my parents could interrupt me. "Please, just tell me that he's going to be fine."

She pursed her lips, but relented, her eyes going soft. "He's shattered several bones in his left hand that already had hairline fractures. He'll most likely have some serious surgery to repair it. He also has a concussion and bruising, not to mention the bruises that haven't healed from his last visit." She stopped for a moment, looking over my shoulder at him once more. "He has several more issues in addition to these, but I've already told you more than I'm allowed."

I knew that there had to be something deeper, something related to his anger. "Where are his parents?"

"Reed," my mom said, laying a hand on my forearm, "let them handle it."

I pulled away. "Where are his parents?"

The doctor grimaced, nodding towards the end of the hallway, where Marcus's parents talked to each other in low voices by the door. Marcus stumbled their way and hugged them both.

I stepped away from my parents and the doctor but decided to let Marcus have a moment and instead moved to Jack and September.

"Hey, you," September said with a weak smile. "How are you feeling?"

I didn't answer. I wrapped my arms around her and hugged her tight. Relief flooded through my body, washing over every part of me at the feeling of her, standing here, in one piece, *awake*, in my arms. She hugged me back, rubbing my back with her hand.

"I'm okay," I answered, closing my eyes. "You?"

"I'm fine."

"What about me?" Jack asked sarcastically. "Don't I get a hug?"

I rolled my eyes, pulling away from September. "Be careful what you wish for," I said, launching at him and hugging him, messing up his hair with my hand. "How are you feeling, Jackaboy?"

He groaned. "Better, once you let go of me. I was joking about the hug."

I ignored Jack's comment, letting go of him. "What's your diagnosis?"

"Just bruising all over my body and a minor concussion. Nothing major." He nodded at September. "She got worse than me. She almost cracked her head open on that window."

I raised an eyebrow, assessing the cuts that decorated both of them on their hands, arms, and necks. September had a thin piece of tape on her cheek holding together a large cut and a long, red mark along her neck from where her seatbelt cut her skin.

I picked up one of her hands, turning it over in mine, examining the damage. She had a few large bruises on her wrist, black and blue.

She pulled her hand away, hiding it behind her back so I wouldn't reach for it again. "I'm fine." She offered a smile, trying to prove her point. I ignored the sting and changed the subject.

"So, what happened?" I questioned. "After I got punched in the face, I mean?"

Her eyebrows drew together. "You got punched in the face?"

"I got in Marcus's way. I figured better my nose get broken than his hand on the car, but I was too late. His hand is broken anyway."

"They sedated Marcus," Jack said. "Then they pried me and September out of the car and took us all to the hospital in the ambulances. They called all of our parents, too."

"Speak of the devil," September said, her phone buzzing in her pocket. "That's my parents. They're probably freaking out." She looked up, smiling apologetically. "Talk to you guys in a little bit?"

I nodded. "Talk to you later."

She nodded, walking past us and through the double doors out into the lobby to take her call.

"What a great last month so far, huh?" Jack asked. "This has to be the most stressful month since she moved here. Everything that could go wrong so far has happened."

"Probably," I agreed. "Now we're even. We've *all* almost died."

"Let's make a deal," Jack said. "Let's all try not to die this month. I think she'd go off the deep end if anything else happened."

"Deal." I shook his hand. "Nothing dangerous for a month… I think we can handle it."

"Why do I feel like this is going to be harder than it should be?"

I looked over to find Marcus pulling at the cast on his hand. He looked annoyed that he couldn't rip it apart, like he had the gauze they'd wrapped it in the day before. His parents were gone—most likely to join my parents in the lobby—and he leaned against a wall fiddling with the edges.

"Mark," I said, getting his attention. His head snapped up. "What're you doing?"

"It's uncomfortable," he said. "I don't like it."

Jack grinned. "Maybe you should avoid punching cars and walls in the future, Hulk."

Mark laughed darkly. "Right."

Jack cleared his throat. "What did the doc say?"

"Well, apparently I'm a hazard to myself, and I need to be medicated," he said. "Also, I have a jacked up hand."

"Lovely," Jack remarked.

"Are you going to be okay?" I asked.

He nodded. "I'll be fine. I really just want to go home and sleep in a real bed."

"I'm with you on that one." Jack stretched his arms back and stifled a yawn. "I need a couple of years of hibernation. Who knew car accidents were so tiring, right?"

Marcus smiled, but it faded after a few seconds. He looked to me.

"I'm sorry about Charlotte, Reed."

"Don't worry about it. I fixed her up once; I can fix her again."

Jack slapped his hands together, looking up and down the hallway. "My parents are out in the lobby, so I should probably go. I'll see you guys Monday?"

"Sure," I answered.

"Yeah," Mark said.

"Great. Bye, guys."

When he'd left, Marcus looked at me. "I'll see you soon, Reed." He held out his good—well, not broken—hand.

I gripped it, slapping his shoulder. "Be careful, Mark. I mean it. Call if you need anything."

He nodded, shaking my hand firmly. "I'll try."

He flashed me a smile—a weak remnant of his usual mischievous grin—then turned and opened the door into the lobby, leaving me in the hallway on my own without another word.

That was the last I saw of Marcus for a long time.

7

art club

I had Charlotte towed back to Tom's until I could figure out how to go about fixing her. While I waited on that, though, September agreed to give me rides to and from school.

She knocked on my door at 7 a.m. bright and early on Monday morning.

"You aren't even dressed?" She stepped inside, shivering in her coat as I shut the door behind her.

"Mom didn't wake me up," I said, rubbing my eyes. "She wants me to rest. She tried to stay home from work, but somehow I convinced her to go."

"Do you?"

"Do I what?"

"Do you need an extra day of rest?"

I scoffed. "Do *you?*"

She gave me that crooked half-smile. "Guess not."

"How are you feeling?" I asked, walking into the kitchen and sitting at the bar. "How's your head? Should you be driving?"

She shrugged. "I feel fine."

I stared at her. "You have a *concussion.*"

"So do you. Besides, it doesn't bother me," she shrugged. "Until it does, I'll keep doing what I do."

"And your parents are *totally fine* with you 'doing what you do'?"

"They called and told me to stay home, but I'm going to school anyway. I don't want to get behind. Besides, what they don't know won't hurt them."

I shook my head. "You may be one of the most stubborn people I've ever met in my life."

"It's a gift." Her eyes traveled around the kitchen, scanning the empty, white countertops. "Have you made breakfast yet?"

"Nope." I stifled a yawn. "I literally just woke up."

"Well," she said, looking down at her watch, "it's seven right now. If you hurry, we might have time to run to Waffle House for breakfast before school."

I perked up, jumping from the stool and jogging up the stairs to my bedroom. "Give me five minutes!" I yelled down the stairs. I could hear her laugh echo from the kitchen.

I got dressed with one hand on the back of my desk chair for support. It took longer than usual, but I got it done.

"You know, for a runner, you're slow," she said as I came back down the stairs.

"First of all, the cross-country season is over and track isn't until spring," I defended. "I can afford to be slow. Secondly, I'm injured. I'm sorry if putting on a t-shirt took a little longer than expected when every muscle in my body is sore or bruised and the ground spins when I stand up too fast."

"If you play it right, you can milk this injury thing for a long time," she said with a wink. "You almost had me convinced."

"Whatever," I said, rolling my eyes. "Let's go eat."

The drive to Waffle House was short. September seemed fine, but I kept a close eye on her, anyway.

The familiar buzz of the restaurant comforted me after such a stressful week. It felt weird sitting in our booth without Marcus or Jack, but the quieter air made it easy to relax. We ordered our food, said hi to Terra, and picked the music like we always did.

It felt nice to have a little routine.

"Do you think Mark is going to be okay?" she asked me. "Be honest."

I shrugged. "Mark's a tough guy."

"But?"

"He seemed pretty messed up." I sipped my coffee, letting the hot liquid warm me up against the freezing temperature not only outside but in the restaurant. It burned a trail down my throat. "I think things are going to be hard for him for a while."

She nodded, looking down at her hands resting on the table. "Do you think they're going to do anything for him?"

"What do you mean?"

"Like, doctors, hospitals, medication," she said. "Do you think that'll help?"

"I don't know. I can't see Marcus willingly being admitted into a hospital for something like his mental health."

"What if he needs it?" she asked.

"He doesn't."

"But what if he does?"

"I don't know, Em," I snapped, running my hand through my hair and exhaling. "Marcus will be fine; I promise."

She was quiet.

Guilt settled in my stomach. I felt nauseous. "I'm sorry."

"For what?"

"Well, your last month here hasn't exactly been the best so far."

"I didn't expect everything to go right. I mean, it's us. We always find some way to mess *something* up."

I exhaled sharply. "You got that right."

Terra brought us our food with a smile and an extra cup of coffee. We thanked her and began eating.

"How's Charlotte?" she asked.

I grimaced. "In pain."

"Did Tom assess the damage?"

"I stayed long enough last night to get her into Tom's garage, but I didn't stay long after that. He's supposedly seeing what can be salvaged."

"Supposedly?"

"He's got two new cars due at the end of the month. I don't know that he'll pay much attention to her."

"Maybe you should go yourself."

"I can barely see straight," I said. "I don't think putting tools in my hands is a good idea."

The corner of her mouth turned up. "Maybe not."

I looked at her, examining the scratch that ran across her cheek and the faded bruise on her forehead. "What else did your parents say when they called?"

"They were freaking out," she said, rubbing her hands down her face. "Mom insisted on coming home to take care of me."

"Is she going to?"

"No," she said. "I convinced her that it wasn't worth the money for the plane tickets."

"Well, you're not wrong."

"She called twice yesterday," she said. "She's afraid that I'm going to keel over or something."

"Tell her that my parents will keep an eye on you," I offered. "They've been watching me like hawks, too."

"I'll keep that in mind next time she calls," she answered. "We should probably go. The bell rings in ten."

I had trouble seeing straight the entire day. I didn't listen during class; instead, I put my head down on the desk and closed my eyes, trying to get rid of the queasiness in my stomach. I almost passed out standing up to leave first block and had to hold onto a desk for support. The sight of September at my locker brought some relief; I was ready to go home.

"Hey," she greeted weakly. Her face looked paler than usual. "How are you feeling?"

"Like crap," I said. "You?"

"Same here," she grimaced, "which will make what I have to say bad news."

I leaned on my shoulder against the locker. "What do you mean?"

"I forgot that I promised to help Hannah with the art club's show."

"And?"

"And I have to stay after today to set up the library and paint the banners," she said. "I'm sorry, Reed, but we'll be here for a while. Do you want to see if Jack can take you home?"

"Jack's parents wouldn't let him come today," I said. "They wouldn't let him drive with a concussion."

"I did."

"You shouldn't have."

"Whatever. The point is, I can't leave yet, and neither can you."

I slammed my locker shut, disappointed that I couldn't go home and sleep. I nodded down the hallway anyway. "Fine, let's go."

———

"You know," she said, dipping her paintbrush into a jar of bright green paint, "when I told you that we had to stay after school, I didn't expect you to take a nap on the couch in the art room."

Greenville High's art room was among one of the most comfortable places in the entire school. Long tables and chairs took the place of uncomfortable desks, and the walls were painted in patterns and covered with posters. Students in one class even took it upon themselves to paint the entire floor with bright colors and metallic paints. Blobs of paint that had dried littered every inch where people dropped paint and let it dry. Names scattered the walkways where seniors signed their way out before their graduation.

"My head hurts," I complained. I shifted from my back onto my side to watch her paint. The couch—old, paint-covered, stiff, and dusty—was brought in by a student a few years back. It was supposed to be an art project, I think, but it never got finished, so it sat against the wall. It served as more of a coat rack instead of an actual piece of furniture nowadays.

September turned the paper at an angle to continue her letters. "Mine does too, but you don't see me lying around like a lazy bum."

"I'm not part of the art club," I pointed out.

"Neither am I," she retaliated.

"Then why are we here?"

"Because I'm a good friend, unlike you."

"Acquaintance," I corrected. "You only talk to Hannah at school."

"And? *You* only talk to Hannah to ask for homework."

"I set her up with guys. I'm literally her personal wingman."

"So what? You could at least act like you care."

"I do care. I get A's in calculus because of her."

She rolled her eyes. "Not what I meant."

She pressed the brush against the large sheet of paper spread across the floor, dragging it downward, then up, then down again as she painted the letter W.

"What are you painting?" I asked.

"Welcome banners," she said. "To hang in the library."

"Why are you painting them? You aren't an artist."

"Excuse me?"

"You aren't in any of the art classes," I explained. "What makes you qualified to paint these? Why not an art student?"

"What makes you qualified to lie there and criticize my painting skills? You couldn't do any better."

"Sure, I could."

"Really, now?"

"Yeah."

"Fine," she challenged. "Get off your butt and come help me."

"Fine." I sat up, allowing myself a second for my vision to clear before walking over to her and crouching next to the paper. "Hand me that paintbrush."

She handed me an extra brush and a jar of green paint, moving to the side to give me room to work. "Good luck with that."

"Keep your luck. I don't need it." I dipped the brush in the paint, then dragged it across the paper next to the W to create a very neat E.

She blinked. "That's... better than I expected."

"And better than yours," I said. "You're jealous."

"Am not," she said. "You know why?"

"Enlighten me."

Her face broke into a satisfied grin. "Your letter is crooked."

I looked back at the paper, eyes wide. I relaxed as I looked at the bright green letters.

"I think you're wrong. *Your* letter is crooked, not mine."

She looked back at the paper, her mouth dropping open as she realized I was right.

I smirked. "Nice try, Em."

I stood up, about to lay back down on the couch when something wet hit the back of my neck. My hand ran across the skin before I held it up to find bright green paint smeared across my fingers. I turned back to her.

"Did you just throw paint at me?"

"No, it did it on its own," she scoffed, the paint still dripping from the brush onto the floor.

"I *liked* this shirt."

"You shouldn't have criticized my art skills."

"You gave me no choice. That letter sucks."

Her arm moved behind her and then brought it back around, slinging more paint at me. A wide strip of bright green landed onto the middle of my shirt, right over the logo of a Harley motorcycle.

"You destroyed the Harley!"

She giggled, her eyes glinting with something mischievous. "Green's a better color for it anyway."

I picked up the paintbrush I'd used, flicking it upwards and slinging paint into her face. She gasped, reaching up to wipe it away but only spreading it.

"I could do it again, considering you launched paint at me twice *and* ruined my favorite shirt," I warned, "but I'm a good person. Put down the paint brush and we'll call it even."

Her hand gripped the paint-covered handle tighter. "No way, Slick. You can't insult me and get away with it."

"You've already ruined my shirt!"

She rolled her eyes. "Don't be such a drama queen."

I clenched the paintbrush in my hand. "September, put down the brush."

"No."

I dipped the brush back into the paint. "Fine. You asked for it." I flung more at her, this time a large blob landing right in the middle of her white shirt.

She lurched forward with her paintbrush, no doubt about to get payback but stopped, falling on her knees to the floor and holding her head. The paintbrush fell onto the paper, bleeding green paint everywhere.

"Are you okay?" I crouched next to her.

"*No.* My head just started *pounding.*"

"Take a deep breath." I sat next to her, wrapping an arm around her shoulder. "It's the concussion."

She sat back, her eyes watering as she rubbed her temples. "It wasn't this bad this morning."

"It's all this moving around. You should be resting."

She chuckled weakly, looking at me from the corner of her eye. A tear escaped her eyelashes and rolled down her face. "I'm a mess, aren't I?"

The corner of my mouth pulled up into a half smile as I wiped it away, smearing paint across her cheek with my thumb as I did. "Join the club."

Taking a breath, she closed her eyes and sat in silence for a moment, trying to recover.

"I don't think I can drive," she said after a moment. "I think I may throw up."

"I can't drive, either. I'll call Dad. Hold on."

She nodded. "Do that."

I didn't want to call him—neither of my parents knew that I had gone to school against their advice—but I pulled my phone out of my pocket and dialed my dad's number, holding it to my ear as the dial tone sounded. It rang three times before he answered.

"Hello?"

"Dad," I said, looking warily at September, "can you come get us?"

"Get you? Get you where?"

"September and I are at school. Her head is hurting, and she can't drive us back."

"She shouldn't have gone in the first place," he said. "And I thought you were staying home today."

"Mom said I was staying home today," I answered. "I decided to come to school instead."

He sighed. "I'll be at the school in ten minutes."

"Thanks, Dad."

"You're welcome. Be ready for me at the door."

The line went dead, and I shoved my phone into my pocket. "Let's get you up, okay?"

She shook her head. "I can't."

I sighed, standing up slowly before reaching back down to her. "I'll help you."

She looked up at me, her eyes shifting to my hand before she hesitantly reached for it. I helped her stand up.

She instantly fell against my side, and I steadied her, throwing one of her arms around my shoulder and letting her use me as a crutch.

"This sucks," she moaned.

"I know."

We started walking towards the door to the art room, one step at a time. I silently thanked every art class for leaving paint all over the floors in previous years; our little mishap would be hard to see at first glance.

"How long do you think it will take for us to heal?" September's breathing sounded labored.

"Mine?" I asked. "Jack and I will probably heal faster than you. He says you hit your head pretty hard."

"I felt better than you this morning."

"That doesn't matter. These things take time, September; you can't rush them, or you'll hurt yourself. Sometimes you just have to sit back and go with the flow."

She looked at me without saying anything, like she was thinking about what I said. She helped me pull open the door, and soon we were headed down the hallway towards the front.

"Hey, Reed," she said suddenly, "what's the date?"

"The twelfth," I said. "Why?"

"Crap," she mumbled. "These concussions are going to lose us a ton of time. We're already a third of the way through the month."

Oh.

I'd almost forgotten that she was leaving.

I swallowed my grief. "Do you still have the list?"

"Yeah. It's in my car."

"You need to cross Making Midnight off the list. I don't think that updating the list was a priority while we were sitting in the ER getting stitches and pain meds."

She let out a short laugh. "Guess not."

We made it to the front doors. I smashed the button to unlock them, and we worked together to push them open. My arms were getting tired, and I started to get dizzy myself, but luckily we found a bench outside the lobby. We wrapped our jackets close to our bodies and sat as a cold chill blew against our faces.

Greenville grew colder by the day. It surprised me that it hadn't gotten colder sooner; we were notorious for getting early winter weather.

For some reason, the weather had me wondering about the towns that September had lived in before Greenville. Did she like them? Were they hot? Cold? Did she have a lot of friends?

"What was your life like before Greenville?" I asked abruptly.

She looked at me. "Why do you ask?"

"You never talk about it much. I'm just curious."

She breathed deeply as she looked away from me out at the parking lot, then at the tree line of evergreens. "There's nothing entertaining about the places I used to live. All of them were painfully average."

"Did you like any of them?"

"They were fine."

"How did you end up here?"

"My parents' jobs, but you knew that. Mom's a travel nurse. Dad teaches wherever we go. He likes variety, so he jumped at the opportunity to teach classes here. He hadn't taught at a community college until we moved to Greenville. He'd always taught at large universities, but he likes change."

"That explains taking the job halfway around the world."

The corner of her lip twitched. "He wanted a new atmosphere."

"I'd say that Europe constitutes as a new atmosphere. Or, you know, Portland would've worked, too."

A familiar hum echoed down the empty road in front of our high school as my dad's familiar gray Ford F-150 rolled up to the school. He cut the engine, got out, and jogged toward us. His eyebrows were furrowed over his concerned expression.

"What happened?" He crouched in front of the bench, still wearing his button-up shirt with his company logo printed on the side, once crisp but now wrinkled. He looked us up and down. "Why are you covered in paint?"

"Accident," I answered quickly. "She slipped."

"Is she hurt?"

"Just her head," I said. "Too much moving at too fast of a pace."

"What about you?"

"I'm fine for now," I answered, "but if I have to carry her again, I may end up on the ground."

"Hey," she said weakly, "I'm not that heavy."

I meant because of my dizziness, but I patted her arm anyway, taking the opportunity to try and crack a joke. "Keep telling yourself that."

My dad cleared his throat and flashed me a look. "You act like you have no manners," he said. *"Don't talk to a girl like that.* I taught you better."

"This is *September* I'm talking to, Dad."

"Does it matter?"

September looked over at me, a smug smile on her face. *"Does it matter,* Reed?"

I huffed, putting every ounce of fire I could into the glare I shot at September. She didn't seem fazed, but her smile grew even bigger. Before she could say anything, though, my dad had her on her feet and helped her down the sidewalk with an arm around her shoulders for support.

"Hurry up, Reed," he called over his shoulder, "or do you need my help walking, too?"

"I'm fine," I grumbled, standing up and following them to the truck.

"September," he said once we were all inside, "I called your parents on my way here. You're staying with us tonight."

"I'm *what?*"

"She's *what?*"

"I don't feel comfortable leaving you at your house by yourself with a head injury," he explained. "Not after this little incident. Miranda is going to look after you."

"No offense, Mr. Davis," September said, "but I can take care of myself. Tell Mrs. Davis thank you for offering, but I'm fine."

"It wasn't a question." He caught her eye in the mirror. "I'm sorry, but your parents and Miranda and I all agree that it's for the best until you seem well enough to be on your own."

"Reed, tell him that I'm well enough. I'm fine, right?"

"September, he's right."

Her jaw dropped in the rearview mirror. "You're kidding."

"Sorry, Em."

She sat back in her seat with a sigh, crossing her arms. "What about you?"

"Reed isn't going to school this week," my dad answered. "Neither are you, September."

At that, we both looked at my father with wide eyes. "What?"

"You both have concussions. You shouldn't be at school anyway."

"But I'll get behind!" September exclaimed.

"So will I!"

At that, September looked at me. I couldn't fool her; we both knew school wasn't on my list of priorities.

But September was.

"Which one of you could actually read the things written on the board today, hmm? Or could understand anything the teachers were saying?"

Both of us were quiet.

"Exactly," he said. "You're staying home for the week."

"But what about my car?" September asked, her voice growing louder. She gestured in its general direction.

"It'll be safe at the school until you're well enough to drive."

"And all my school books?" Her eyebrows raised, drawn together in worry. "Jack can't get them; he's staying home this week, too."

"Then I'll have Miranda call up there tomorrow morning. It'll be okay, September," he promised. "Breathe."

"Where is she going to sleep?" I asked curiously, looking back at the road.

"Your room."

A smile grew across my face as I raised an eyebrow and swung around to face September. "Looks like we're roomies, kid."

"Looks like you aren't, old sport," my dad said, reaching over to slap my back. His subtle, amused smile paired with his smug tone pounded my excitement into the floor. "You're staying in the living room on the couch."

September's previously shocked expression faded as she crossed her arms over her chest and looked back at me, fighting a smile. "Sorry, *old sport.*"

"Freaking five-year-old," I muttered under my breath.

My dad pulled into our driveway, cutting the engine and opening September's door for her. "How're you feeling? Any better?"

"Better than I was about twenty minutes ago, sprawled across the floor," she said, taking his arm and slowly getting out of the truck. When both feet were firmly planted on the ground, she let go of him. "I think I can walk now."

"Reed," my dad called, skeptically hovering around September, "can you walk?"

I opened my door, hopping out and trying to appear as energetic as possible. Blood rushed to my head and my vision got spotty, but I ignored it.

"Reed, your face is white," he said.

"I'm fine."

All of a sudden, my legs turned to jelly, and they buckled under my weight. I slumped against the truck. I blinked, trying to clear my vision, but the black spots didn't fade.

I focused on breathing for a moment before calling out to my dad. "I'm not fine."

"I'm fine," September said. "I can get in from here."

The sound of my dad's footsteps against the concrete driveway pounded against the inside of my head. He circled the truck and reached down to hook an arm under mine. Once I balanced on my feet, we staggered towards the door and into the living room where September sat on the floor against the couch. She'd leaned her head back against the cushion and closed her eyes.

"You two are a handful," my dad commented, huffing as he helped me to the ground. "Just sit tight." He dusted his hands off and disappeared into the kitchen. I heard him take the phone off the wall, and shortly after, the taps of his fingers against the buttons.

"This sucks," she mumbled.

"I know."

"You know what else sucks?"

Shrugging, I turned to look at her. "What?"

She opened an eye. "I have to be stuck here with you for an entire night, and then who knows how long."

"Hey, I'm not that bad!"

"Relax, Reed," she said, laughing. "I'm joking... sort of."

I narrowed my eyes at her. "Because you're such a bouquet of butterflies and rainbows."

"I am, actually. Didn't I tell you?"

She earned another nudge from me. This time, she sat up and pulled her knees to her chest. Her head rested against the top of her kneecaps.

"We're a mess, aren't we?"

"I thought we established this at school."

"Are we going to make it through high school?"

"Man, I hope so."

"How are we even still standing?"

"Technically, we're sitting."

She just looked at me. I wondered what she was thinking. Did she have the same fears I did? Would she miss moments like these?

Get ahold of yourself, Reed. She's turning you to mush.

My dad strolled back into the room, squatting in front of us. "I called Miranda, and she already called the school," Dad explained. "Hannah Stephens offered to bring you two your work."

"Great," I said, rubbing my hands together. "So, we're good here? Can I go?"

"Go where?" September asked. "You can't leave me here alone!"

"I'm just going to Tom's," I explained. "It's literally five minutes away."

"She's right, Reed," my dad said. "You can't leave her alone by herself, and you can't drive. You're staying here so you can keep an eye on each other."

Defeated, I exhaled rather loudly. "Fine."

"Fine. I have to go back to work, but Miranda will be here at four. Are you two okay?"

September nodded. "We're fine."

"Call me if you need anything."

When my dad left the room, and the lock turned on the front door, September hit my arm with as much force as she could muster.

I flinched, holding my hand over the already sore spot. "Ouch! What was that for?"

"You were going to *leave* me? I have a concussion!"

"So do I!" I defended. "You're also the one who decided to drive to school today!"

"That's no excuse! You were going to abandon me here!"

I rolled my eyes. "You act as if I was leaving you to die."

"I could've died by myself."

"You have a concussion, not a terminal illness."

Her arms crossed over her chest. "Whatever."

"Look, I'm sorry, but Charlotte's in pieces. I have to make sure Tom doesn't throw away something that can be salvaged."

"Then tell him not to touch her."

"He can't keep that garage space occupied forever. I need to get down there."

"We can go Wednesday," she offered. "We need to give ourselves a couple of days. If we're okay by then, I'll go with you. If Jack's feeling alright, he can drive. He said he didn't get it as bad as we did."

I wanted to protest, but I realized she was right. If either of us tried to go out on our own, we could end up in another wreck, and then we'd be back to square one. We didn't need any more injuries.

"Fine," I relented. "We'll go Wednesday."

She smiled. "Good."

Sitting up, I let out a yawn and stretched my arms. "So, what do you want to do?"

"I don't know. Do you have any movies?"

I scoffed. "Who do you think you're talking to?"

Minutes later, we sat on the couch while the opening credits of *The Breakfast Club* rolled onto the TV screen. I drummed my fingers against my leg to the beat of the familiar title music. September leaned against my shoulder, tucked up under a thick blanket.

"Hey, Reed?"

I shifted my gaze from the TV to her. "Yeah?"

She didn't look up at me. "Do you think we're going to be okay?"

"Yeah. The doctor said we'd be fine after a couple weeks."

"I don't mean like that," she said. "I mean when I leave. Do you think we're going to be okay?"

You or me?

After a moment, I looked away from her.

"I don't know, Em."

"Why not?"

My throat constricted. I cleared it before answering. "I just don't know. I think you'll be fine. I'm not sure about us, though."

"Us, as in…?"

"Us," I said. "Me and you."

"What about the boys?"

"It'll be hard for them, too. I don't think we'll exactly get over it."

"Why do you think I'll be able to?"

"You've moved a million times."

"I've never met a Reed," she said. "Or a Jack, or a Marcus."

"And?"

"The point is, I'm doubting my abilities to move on from this one."

I met her eyes, raising my eyebrows up at her. "You're joking."

"Why would I joke about this?"

"It's your dream to travel," I said. "Don't you want to go?"

"Of course I want to go, I just… I don't know if I'll survive it knowing that I left you three here, especially if you're hurting. You're the closest friends I've ever had."

Should I ask her to stay?

Could I do that to her? Ruin her plans by asking her to stay for me?

I could.

But will I?

I looked back at her.

No. Not this time.

"You'll be fine," I said. "Don't worry about it."

"What about you three?"

I forced the words out of my mouth. The lie tasted bitter on my tongue. "We'll survive, Em."

"But I—"

"September," I cut her off, "don't worry about us. We'll be okay."

Will we?

Will I?

8

when charlotte met lucy

Wednesday couldn't come fast enough. Doing homework and lying around got old real fast. Sure, I enjoyed being around September, but I itched to get back to the shop. Tom had called once to tell me that Charlotte looked rough to which I firmly instructed him to leave her alone until I could get there.

After hours of me bugging him on Tuesday afternoon, my dad grudgingly agreed to drop September and me at Tom's Automotive Repair and Restoration. I could see in his face that Tom was surprised to see me and even more surprised to see September at my side, but he pulled out chairs for us and offered each of us a Coke without a word about it.

"Thanks, Tom," September said, pulling back the tab on her Coke. It sputtered open and fizzed over the top of the opening.

"No problem."

I shifted in my seat, trying my best to ignore the headache rooted in my skull. My eyes scanned the shop until they landed on the pile of crumpled metal that once resembled Charlotte. The sight of her made me physically sick. She was in pieces.

Tom caught sight of me looking at what used to be my car and nodded towards her. "Do you want to take a closer look at her?"

"Yeah." Hesitantly, I rose to my feet and followed Tom around the cars to the back of the garage. I could hear September's quiet footsteps behind me as she came to see the damage.

"She's in a bit of pain," Tom said with a shrug, stopping in front of her.

"A bit?" I asked. "She's not even *intact.*"

Her top was missing—Scout 2's had removable hard tops—but I knew it had to have made it back to the shop with the rest of the car. I only took the top off of the car during the summer, so if Tom took it off himself, it had to be absolutely destroyed.

"She looks worse than she is." He moved around the car to the hood, which looked terrible, crinkled up like a potato chip. The metal squeaked and groaned as he pried the latch open and lifted it to reveal the motor. "See?"

Slowly, I stepped around the car so that I could peer further into the cavity. To my surprise, he was right; although the frame twisted up like a pretzel in the impact, the motor, along with almost everything else under the hood, remained merely scratched or dented in a few places.

"How is that possible?"

"Beats me." Tom shrugged. "Charlotte had a thick skin, though. Her frame must've been sturdy enough to protect everything except itself. A few things under the car are missing, too. Probably fell off in the wreck."

"Where's her top?"

"In the dumpster out back. It's bent up like an accordion."

"Will you help me fix her?"

He scoffed. When he realized I was serious, his eyes went wide. "Kid, it'll cost more to fix her than it will to buy a new car. The frame is in knots, the top is destroyed, the doors are in pieces, and most of the parts under the car are either missing or need to be replaced. Where are you going to come up with the money for that? Plus, I've got two cars to fix up, one due in a week and a half. "

He was right, and I knew it; it would cost every penny of the money I'd saved up from the past three summers to fix her frame and who knows how much more to replace the things I hadn't even found yet, but I was determined. I couldn't get rid of her. She held far too many memories.

"Anything can be fixed. Please, Tom—I can't trash Charlotte."

He crossed his arms over his chest, and he looked between September and me, no doubt deciding if she was worth his time. September didn't say anything. She only watched me.

"Fine," he relented. "But we still have to finish those show cars. Those come first, understand?"

My muscles loosened. I hadn't even realized I'd been holding them tight. "Thank you."

"Don't mention it. Now, I've got to make a dent in the workload on these new cars since I'm down a man. Make yourself useful and roll the toolbox over to Lucy."

"Yes, sir."

While Tom worked on opening the hoods of Lucy and Olivia, September and I ventured around the cars to the far wall where a tall, faded yellow toolbox stood on a set of wheels. She took one side and I took the other, and together we wheeled it carefully around the cars and back to where Tom worked.

"Lucy?" September asked.

I frowned. "What?"

She looked at Tom. "Who's Lucy?"

I couldn't suppress the laugh that bubbled up in my chest. "Lucy's a *car*, Em. She's a beautiful, old car with a terrible, *terrible* paint job."

"I'm sure it's not *that* bad."

"Oh, it's bad."

We pushed the toolbox over to Tom, who thanked us. He had a tarp across Lucy and Olivia, both pulled back just far enough for him to lift the hood.

I motioned to September. "Come here."

I walked her to the passenger side of the car and threw up the tarp far enough for her to see the door.

"How's that for a bad paint job?"

Her mouth formed a wide 'O' shape. "This is a joke. Is this a joke?"

I shook my head. "Someone really painted their car neon green."

"Who does this?" she asked, gesturing to it. "Please tell me the owner asked you to fix it."

"He did," Tom piped up. "When we're finished, Lucy here will be a lovely midnight blue."

September gave her approval with a slight nod. "What about Charlotte?"

I frowned. "What about her?"

"What color will Charlotte be when she's done?"

I shrugged my shoulders, shifting my weight. "I like her color."

"Her color is almost nonexistent," she commented. "It's all been scratched off."

"*If* I repaint her, she'll be red."

"She's already red—er, what's left is red."

"And?"

She shrugged. "You don't want to change it up a little?"

I thought for a moment, then shook my head. "Nope."

"Not even a little?"

"Not even a little. Red suits Charlotte. Some things are best left unchanged."

I caught her glance at me from the corner of her eye, but her gaze darted away. "Change can be a good thing, you know."

For some reason, her comment tugged on a nerve. *A good thing? You're joking, right?*

"You mean like moving across the world?" Sarcasm dripped from my tone. It came out with more force than I meant for it to, but I couldn't stop myself. "Yeah, that's a *great* thing. I'll keep that in mind when the time comes to paint her. Maybe I'll go with neon green like Lucy here."

She cocked her head, dropping her mouth slightly open and narrowing her eyes. "There's no need to get sharp with me. I was just saying."

"You were just reminding me of something I already know."

"Chill out, Reed. There's no need to make a big deal out of it."

I wanted to come back with something that would make her angry or maybe even hurt her feelings, but I resisted. I shook my head, trying to clear it of the nasty thoughts that had taken up residence there. They seemed to only trigger whenever someone brought up September's departure, and I almost couldn't control them.

Instead of replying, I stayed quiet. I could tell she was waiting for me to answer by the way her shoulders tensed, but after watching me for a few seconds, she relaxed and moved on.

"Wow," Tom remarked. "Talk about tense. Do I need to leave the room?"

"We're fine."

"You two bicker like an old married couple."

"Far from it," I snapped.

"Mhm," he hummed. "Hand me that wrench."

I did as he said. September leaned back against Lucy and sipped her Coke, watching Tom carefully.

"Who named the car?" she asked after a moment.

"The original owner apparently had a thing for *I Love Lucy*," Tom remarked from behind the hood. "It's carved into the passenger side door."

I remembered watching reruns of *I Love Lucy* as a kid. At first, I'd only watched it because my mom wouldn't let me change the channel. After a while, though, it grew on me. For a little while, when I was 8 or 9, I would quote Lucy to my parents all the time.

September shared my excitement, apparently. "You're joking! *Really?*"

Tom nodded at the car. "See for yourself."

She stood up and pulled the door open, slid into the cracked leather seat and pulled it slightly closed so that she could inspect it. "Wow. You weren't kidding."

I stepped around the door to peer inside. True to Tom's description, the words *I Love Lucy* were neatly carved into the wooden panel under the window.

"That's dedication," I commented.

She laughed. "Why didn't you carve *Charlotte* into Charlotte's door?"

"Because I *respect* my car."

"You could put *my* name in your car."

"Sure. I'd totally do that."

"Yeah, Reed," Tom called. "That's the way to treat your girl."

"I'm not his girl," September called, eyes still on the carving.

He seemed amused. "How long are you two going to pretend to be friends?"

"We don't pretend, Tom. We *are* friends."

"How many single guys and girls do you know that are friends and stay friends?"

"More than you," I retorted. "Don't you have any friends that are girls, Tom?"

"Of course I do," he said, "because I'm *married*. You know what went on between my wife and me before we dated? We were *just friends*." He made quotation marks with his fingers over the hood when he said the words *just friends*.

"Give it a rest, Tom," September said playfully. "We're just really good friends and have been for a long time."

Oh, how I wish it were more.

"Alright," he relented, "but you know I'm right."

September just shook her head and laughed. "When did you become a relationship expert?"

"When I took in a teenager as a mechanic working on cars worth more than both of us combined," Tom muttered.

I crossed my arms across my chest. "*This teenager* has brought in more business than you ever have by yourself, Tom. People love the cars I churn out."

"Not true. Anyway, I never said I was ungrateful."

I rolled my eyes, shifting my weight and glancing back over at Charlotte again.

September caught me. "I guess it'll be awhile before you can drive Charlotte again, huh?"

"I guess so."

"What're you going to drive between now and then? You can get rides from me, but I'll have to put my car up for sale before I leave. Besides, I know you won't want to ride with me everywhere you go."

"I don't know what I'll drive. I guess I can ask my dad if I can drive his truck."

"You can borrow one of my cars if you need one that bad," Tom piped in. "If you wreck it, though, you're paying for it."

"You're joking. You'd loan me a car?"

"Borrow," he corrected. "You'll need one for Homecoming on Friday, won't you?"

Homecoming. I almost forgot.

September slapped her forehead. "Crap, I don't even have a dress for that."

I shifted uncomfortably. "I probably need a tux, don't I?"

Her head dropped into her hands. "There's no way we can go at this rate."

"Don't be so dramatic," chided Tom. "Reed, I have a tux that will probably fit you. September, just go get your dress tomorrow."

"Why do you own a tux?"

113

"Because it's what you wear to a wedding," he remarked sarcastically. "Honestly, boy, I thought you were smart."

"What I find interesting is how you knew when Homecoming was and we didn't," she pointed out.

"I keep up with the school now and then. Gotta know when to expect trouble."

I scoffed. "What's that supposed to mean?"

He leaned up from Lucy, wiping his hands on a rag as he stepped around to her side and leaned against her. "Nothing. Say, how's Marcus doing?"

My arms instinctively crossed over my chest. Talking about Marcus made me uncomfortable. So far, everyone talked about him as if he were sick. He wasn't sick; he was… dealing with some issues.

"I don't know," I answered, shifting my weight again. "I haven't spoken to him since the emergency room."

"September? Have you?"

To my surprise, she nodded. "I called him yesterday. He's… well, he's dealing with stuff. He has surgery on his hand on Thursday."

"Did he sound okay?"

"Honestly, no. But, like you said, I think he will be. He's tough. I know that he'll find a way to manage everything. I told him to call me if he needed anything."

Tom bobbed his head slightly, looking at the concrete floor. "Good. I like that kid. Keep me updated, okay? And next time he picks up the phone, offer him a job here. I'll teach him whatever he needs to know; I just want him to have something stable."

"I will. Thanks, Tom."

"Don't mention it."

My phone dinged. After retrieving it from my pocket, I read the text from my dad.

"Dad's on his way," I told September. "We'll see you later, Tom. Take care of Charlotte for me."

He waved at us, ducking behind the hood of the blinding lime-green Caprice. "Will do. Careful out there."

We waited in silence outside the shop for my dad. The guilt of snapping at September had been eating at me since I did it, and I finally gave in to it.

"I'm sorry." I shifted uncomfortably on my feet and crossed my arms. "I'm an idiot."

"You're right," she agreed quietly. "You are."

"Can you forgive me?"

"Of course I can. I know the move is kind of a touchy subject for you."

"That's no excuse. I was a total jerk to you in front of Tom."

She shrugged her shoulders, shaking her head and meeting my eyes. "Reed, it's fine. I appreciate the apology, but I don't hold grudges. Besides, if we didn't fight every once in a while, I don't think we'd be as close as we are. Just don't worry about it, okay?"

Grudgingly, I left the subject alone. Something about September was just so... calming. Her eyes were so genuine, so real. There were few people I knew that were genuine through and through, and September outranked everyone on that list.

She had a sort of fire in her heart and light in her eyes that couldn't be extinguished, no matter how many things went wrong. Time after time I teased her, I hurt her, and I made life hard for her, yet she still stuck around. She had hope in me when no one else did. She had hope in all of us. I couldn't help but wonder if she was stupid or just a really, really good person.

The rest of that day we spent lying around the house, slowly conquering my large collection of movies and playing card games. We bet candy on who would win each game. By the time my parents got home and had supper cooked, our appetites were spoiled, September's more than mine. September had the best hand at Go Fish I'd ever seen. She beat me six times in a row without breaking a sweat. I demanded that we play something cooler, like poker, but she refused and insisted that I was just embarrassed that she beat me.

She wasn't wrong.

That night as I settled onto the couch with a quilt and a full stomach, I got a text from Jack.

Still going to Homecoming? he asked.

Yeah, I replied. *You?*

Planning on it.

Got a date?

Nope. Do I need one?

Guess not. Need a ride?

And third wheel you and Em? No thanks.

I laughed to myself, fingers poised and ready to reply. He beat me to the punch.

Do you have a tux?

Borrowing from Tom. You?

Got it. Wanna hang tomorrow?

I thought for a moment about my plans, remembering that September still needed a dress.

Have to take September to find her HC dress.

Let Cora take her. She's coming in for the weekend tomorrow morning.

He didn't give me any time to respond. *You have no choice. My sister will murder one of us if you say no, and I'm willing to bet it's going to be you rather than me. Besides, we can hang out tomorrow. I've been isolated for too long.*

Fine. What time?

Ten? Cora will drive her car and I'll drive mine.

You can't drive, Jack.

September did.

You can't use that as an excuse.

Whatever. I'll be at your house at ten.

Dude, I am not riding with you. That's suicide.

He didn't respond.

I'm serious.

No answer.

116

I gave it up, putting my phone on the floor next to the couch and closing my eyes. I prayed that Jack didn't show up driving himself because the last thing we needed was another car wreck.

———

Jack had a slightly different taste in cars than I did. While I loved old, historic, vintage cars, his vehicle of choice was a sleek black 2009 Audi A4. He'd saved up for two years to get that car, working at the only fancy restaurant Greenville had from four to ten every day. Used, but it still cost way more than he could afford. He carried loads of scalding hot dishes across the kitchen of that restaurant until his arms almost fell off, but he never complained. Not to me, at least.

He took good care of his car, always keeping it in pristine condition in case he decided to take someone out. That didn't make sense to me; he'd told me on multiple occasions that he had no interest in the girls who went to our school. If I were being honest, though, I'd say he'd probably keep it clean whether he took a girl out or not. He didn't like feeling confined or trapped by loads of junk.

My doorbell rang at 9:50 a.m. It kept ringing until 9:53 when September bounded down the stairs to answer it after I ignored the annoying sounds and buried my face into a pillow.

"Cora?" The surprise in her voice was prominent. "Jack?"

"Em! It's good to see you!"

It sounded like she stumbled because I heard a thud on the wall. Cora must've sprung a hug on her.

I could hear several pairs of footsteps grow louder as they moved from the front of the house towards the living room. I heard a rustling sound, and then a pillow came down hard on my head.

"Ouch!" I sprang up into a sitting position.

"Dude, you were supposed to tell September we'd be here at ten." Jack threw the pillow to the opposite side of the couch.

"You didn't tell me to tell her," I groaned, falling back onto the pillow I'd slept on and closing my eyes.

"It was kind of implied," he scoffed. "Get up."

Being the drowsy, delirious, complete idiot I am, I replied with, "Make me."

The weight of Jack's body crushing my stomach pushed every ounce of air out of my lungs. The soreness in my abdomen and the sting of the cuts from the wreck came back strong. My eyes snapped open, and I gasped for breath, doing my best to push him off me. When I finally had him on the floor, I shot up onto my feet and socked a punch with as much force as I could right on his left bicep.

"Come on, man! Grow up!" My lungs heaved in my chest. I angrily straightened out my t-shirt, clenching my fists at my sides.

He gripped his arm in pain. No doubt that would leave a bruise. His angry glare took me by surprise. "Dude, chill out. Go get dressed; we're leaving in fifteen minutes."

September shifted her gaze between Jack and me a few times, her eyes wide. Cora put a hand on her shoulder and steered her from the room, taking her back upstairs and away from us. The tension between us was thick and awkward.

"Quit staring at me like I murdered your dog or something," he snapped. "*You* punched *me*, not the other way around. I'm going to wait in the car."

He turned on his heel and did just that, making sure to slam the front door behind him.

Fuming, I stared after him, eyes narrowed and knuckles turning white, until I came to my senses and realized how stupid I was. I mean, he *sat on* me. That's not exactly the best reason to start a fight.

Great way to start off the day.

Jack and I always just got along. We'd never had any big arguments, and we'd definitely never started beating on each other. Jack put up with me, and I put up with him, and we just went with the flow.

I'm just stressed out. He probably understands.

I shook my head, clearing my mind. I decided to move along and get dressed. He didn't have much more patience, and neither did I.

A few minutes later, September bounded down the stairs wearing a gray knit beanie over her dark auburn hair and a loose sweater over her dark jeans. Cora followed at her heels.

"We're going dress shopping," she said awkwardly, lingering at the base of the stairs. "I guess I'll see you later?"

"Guess so."

She hesitantly stepped forward, like she wanted to hug me but changed her mind and took a step back. I tried my best to look indifferent, but the pit in my stomach told me otherwise.

"Try not to kill Jack," she commented.

"No promises."

I ignored Cora's skeptical glance as they left. Contrasting Jack's efforts of closing the door as loud as possible, the door closed almost silently behind Cora and September.

I bent down and picked up my phone from the floor. There were five missed calls from Jack starting at 9:30 a.m. I deleted all of them.

September and Cora had already pulled out when I closed the front door behind me. Jack was the only one in the driveway since both of my parents had gone to work. I opened the passenger side door and slid into the seat, not bothering to say a word as he backed up out of the driveway and onto the road.

We rode in silence for a few minutes before I spoke.

"Where are we going?" I asked.

"There's a new skate park on the far side of town that I want to check out," he said, his voice level.

"You're joking. *Skateboarding?* Since when?"

"I picked it up back at the beginning of the month. I was going to see if you wanted to learn with me, but you were a bit preoccupied."

He didn't have to say it out loud for me to know what he meant. He wasn't wrong, either; I'd spent most of the past few weeks with September, savoring every last moment because the day she would leave was closing in fast. Jack and I hadn't hung out like we used to, which didn't bother me. I knew things would go back to normal once all the drama of September's move was over.

"I don't have a skateboard, and I don't know how to skate," I pointed out.

"I've got you a board. I borrowed it from Marcus."

I furrowed my eyebrows and turned to look at him. "You've seen Marcus?"

"I've visited him four times since the wreck."

"And you didn't think to tell me?"

"You were busy."

I rolled my eyes. "You didn't think I'd want to see him, too?"

"I don't know. I think if you really wanted to, you'd have been to see him by now. It's been almost a week."

"A week. That's not that long."

"That's longer than you've ever been without seeing him."

"What's your problem, man? Why are you all of a sudden so fed up?"

He shrugged. "I'm fine. I'm just answering your questions honestly."

I exhaled, turning to the window and crossing my arms. "Why did Marcus have a skateboard?"

"He's been learning to ride with me. Or, at least he was, before the wreck."

"Should we be riding skateboards with concussions?"

"Eh, probably not. What's the worst that could happen, though?"

"We could suffer serious brain damage," I said. "Which reminds me—you shouldn't even be driving right now. Can you even see straight?"

"I didn't get it as bad as you and September did. I'm fine. Take a breath."

I was suddenly very aware of my lack of a seatbelt. I reached over my shoulder and pulled it on.

Jack didn't have much else to say during the ride to the skate park, and neither did I. It still irked me that he'd been to see Marcus and hadn't told me.

You could've gone yourself, said my conscience.

Shut up.

This silence was awkward and foreign to me. We always had something to talk about, and if we didn't, we were comfortable in the silence. Not just with Jack, either; September and Marcus were the same way. I couldn't think of anything to say, so I scrolled through notifications on my phone until we got there.

We pulled into the skate park about fifteen minutes later, safe and sound. I was relieved that we made it in one piece.

Jack turned off the car and hopped out, walking around to the back. He popped the trunk and pulled out a black helmet and two skateboards, one blue and one black. He slammed the top down and handed me a board and the helmet.

"Put on the helmet, since you're so afraid of hurting yourself."

"I'm not sure about this," I said, rubbing the back of my neck.

"Come on, Reed. It's not that hard."

"Why skateboarding, man? Why didn't we just play video games? It's cold out today, too."

"Because I don't feel like staying in your room all day long. Besides, you need some space and some air. Being cooped up is making you extra irritating."

I chose to ignore that comment.

Jack led me out to the half-pipe where several skaters were already riding their boards up and down the concrete. A guy in a blue snap-back cap flipped his board under his feet. Another in a gray hoodie skidded across a handrail.

"It's not as hard as it looks," he repeated.

"Yeah, I believe that," I replied sarcastically.

This time, he ignored me. He dropped his board to the pavement and hopped onto it, using his right foot to propel it forward. When he pulled his leg up and secured both feet onto his board, he stood on the edge of the half-pipe. He wasn't fazed at all by the drop as the board rolled down the steep decline. By his stature and confident expression, he'd had loads of practice. Loads more than me, at least.

Jack rode his board around the half-pipe several times. He didn't do anything fancy. He just rode. After a few turns, he made his way back to me and hopped back off his board.

"See?" he asked. "Easy."

"For you," I muttered.

"Start small. Put your board on the ground and just try to balance on it for a second."

I did as he said, easily standing up straight on the board. "Standing on it isn't *riding* it, Jack."

"You're right," he responded. "You should be riding it."

"Well... Are you going to teach me how?"

"Sure."

I stood awkwardly, waiting for instruction. Instead of tips, however, I got a hard push against my back. The board started moving without my permission, and my body lurched forward, trying to regain balance.

"I really hate you right now!"

"Shut up and focus on staying on the board. And steer clear of the half-pipe!"

I looked down at my feet, doing my best to move them into a position that would give me balance. Unfortunately, looking down kept me from looking ahead, and my stomach plummeted as the board rolled down the half-pipe. The steep incline threw me off the board and onto the ground. I rolled over my shoulders and hit my helmet against the ground. Grateful that I wasn't passed out on the concrete from another head injury, I stumbled to my feet, dodging the skaters who zipped past me. None of them stopped to help me or even flinched; they all continued doing what they were doing as if they'd seen it a million times.

"You alright? I told you to stay away from the half-pipe."

I looked up the slope at Jack, who held his board against his side.

"Fine," I said through gritted teeth. "Can we leave now?"

"Seriously? You're going to give up?"

"I'm not in the mood, *Evans*," I spat.

"You haven't been in the mood for weeks, *Davis*."

"Whatever. This is a waste of my time."

"I'm a waste of your time now, huh?" He slid down the concrete incline and stood in front of me. "This is the first time we've hung out in a long time, Reed."

"I've been busy."

"We've all been busy. You still seem to find time for September, though."

"She's leaving."

"And?"

"What, are you jealous?"

"Of September? No. She has to put up with your bitter attitude all the time. Luckily, I haven't seen it most of this month. Heck, I haven't seen *you* most of this month."

My fists clenched at my sides. "What's your point?"

"Just because September's leaving doesn't mean you can forget Marcus and me. Honestly, I thought you'd be clinging to Marcus, but he told me that you haven't even called him."

"I haven't had the time."

"There you go with the excuses again, man. Just hear me out."

"I'm hearing you. I just don't like what I'm hearing."

"You don't like a lot of things you've heard. Get over it."

"Jack, I hung out with you and Mark. We went hiking, and we went to a concert together."

"With September," he reminded me. "You haven't done anything with just me or just Marcus in a long time."

"There's nothing wrong with September."

"Of course there isn't anything wrong with September. I love her, I really do, but even she's told me that you need some guy time."

"*She* told you that?"

"She did. Ask her yourself."

I looked away from him, trying to contain the bubbling anger in my chest. I couldn't figure out what made me feel so defensive; I felt like throwing punches.

"I'm leaving," I said. "I'll see you tomorrow."

"You don't have a ride."

"I'll call Tom. I don't want to be in the same car with you right now, anyway."

The helmet clanged against the ground. I didn't bother going back for the board. As I passed him, I could see his fists clench and even shake a little. A few seconds later, he let them loose again.

I trudged past him, purposely jostling his shoulder as I climbed the ramp and stormed off to his car. I leaned against the trunk while I dialed Tom's number.

He didn't ask any questions when he showed up in the unfinished Impala. He simply said, "Get in." The rest of the ride was silent. When he pulled into my driveway, I hopped out, muttered a simple, "Thanks," and then headed inside. Immediately, I ran up the stairs, changed into shorts, and left again with earbuds in my ears and music turned all the way up. Concussion or no concussion, I was going running. It always helped me clear my head.

I took off down the street at a faster pace than usual. There was so much aggression inside of me, and I had no outlet. All I could do was run.

I was out of breath at about thirty minutes of more-or-less sprinting. I stopped, sat down in the grass on the side of the road, and breathed heavily to rejuvenate my lungs. My head was killing me. The road started wobbling back and forth.

Suddenly, Cora's familiar silver car rolled past me, honking as it went. I knew it was time to start back, so I pushed through my burning lungs and jogged on the street behind her car all the way back down the neighborhood and to our house. I still felt aggravated, but I didn't feel like hitting anything anymore. I was too tired.

"Hey, Reed," September said, emerging from Cora's car in the driveway with a white garment bag in hand. "How was skateboarding?"

I didn't answer. I didn't even acknowledge that she was there. I walked right past her and into the house, going straight to the bathroom to shower. I didn't have anything nice to say to anyone, so I wasn't going to waste my breath on trying to speak civilly.

Storm clouds rolled in that evening. The outside light coming in through the windows shone pale gray. I sat on the couch in my favorite pair of sweatpants and relaxed back into the cushions to watch a movie. I could hear September pad down the stairs, but I didn't turn my head to look at her.

I could feel her presence behind me, but I didn't say anything or acknowledge that she was in the room. I kept my eyes trained on the screen. The air tensed; I figured she had something she wanted to say to me. Instead, her footsteps traveled away from me and back up the stairs one by one until I was left alone in the living room.

Just me, myself, and my thoughts.

9

baby, you're a firework—no, i mean literally

I fidgeted with my collar. With every pull against the stiff fabric, it seemed to close tighter around my neck. Trying to punish me for acting like a jerk all week, I guess. I deserved it.

I jammed my thumb against the doorbell. The sooner September got out here, the sooner we could get to Homecoming, then the sooner we could leave and I could get out of this monkey suit Tom had called a tux. I caught my reflection in the window at the top of the door. I'd fought a war with my usual messy hair; no matter what I tried, I couldn't get it to stay put on my head. My bowtie kept turning sideways, too, so I set to work on straightening it before September could get to the door.

As I tousled with the little piece of fabric, the door opened to reveal Jack, dressed similarly to me.

"Cora's finishing up the final touches," he told me solemnly. He didn't give me much more than a sideways glance before pushing past me and stepping out onto the driveway to lean against his car. I wasn't surprised. I didn't expect much out of Jack. We still hadn't talked since I blew up at him (several times) the day before.

I awkwardly shifted my weight and looked down at my watch. A quarter to seven. I raised my hand to mash the doorbell again but stopped when the door swung open once more.

"She's ready." A satisfied smirk played on Cora's lips as she stood right in the middle of the doorway, blocking my view into the house.

"Great." I tried to peer around her. "Where is she?"

"I'm here."

As September stepped around Cora, my jaw dropped. I hoped I wasn't drooling.

September was unlike anything I'd ever seen. She wasn't just beautiful. I had no word to describe what she looked like, but it beat "pretty." She positively *glowed.*

It wasn't the makeup, or the hair, or the dress. Her makeup looked so natural it took me a moment to realize she was actually wearing any. I never noticed that she had freckles until then. They dotted her nose and faded onto her cheeks.

Her dark hair curled and draped around her shoulders. The dress she wore was simple, the color of storm clouds with tight lacy sleeves. It flowed down and brushed the ground just slightly. There was nothing special about it, besides the fact that September wore it. No, September didn't need those things to be beautiful. The most striking part of the whole ensemble was just... her.

She was breathtaking.

Her smile was radiant and infectious. I couldn't stop looking at her.

"Are you done staring?" she asked. "You're kind of making me feel uncomfortable."

I cleared my throat and shook my head, still unable to break my gaze from her. I offered her a hand, which she promptly refused, hopping down the porch steps one at a time.

"How girls manage to jump in heels is beyond me," I muttered, following her down the stairs.

"Who on *earth* said I was wearing heels?" Her hands grabbed at her dress and lifted it several inches to show me her worn-in gray Vans. The laces were a bright white, totally untarnished and bold against the scuffed and faded gray canvas of her shoes.

"Why am I not surprised?" I nudged her shoulder. "Are those new laces?"

"Brand new, special for the occasion. Cora was totally against me wearing sneakers, so we had to compromise. I wasn't about to buy new shoes, so we settled for laces."

"I see that."

She winked at me before turning around and spotting Jack at his car. "Jack, where's your date?"

"I'm going to pick her up," he said nonchalantly. "I just wanted to make sure I got to see you before I left."

"If you're late to her house, I hope she doesn't come outside," September teased, hopping down the steps on both feet. "You see me all the time."

"I don't see you dressed up like this all the time. You look great."

"You're not so bad yourself, skater boy." She stood on her toes to hug him around the neck.

I did my best to push aside the aggravation that bubbled up in my chest. Jealousy apparently had become an issue in my own mind, and I still hadn't figured out a way to put it to rest.

"Alright, Davis," September said, stepping back from Jack, "where's your car?"

I looked down at my watch. "According to my calculations, it's not here yet."

She swatted at my arm. "Very funny, smart aleck. How did you get here?"

"I rode with Jack."

She raised an eyebrow at me. Obviously, she knew Jack and I were on rough terms. She didn't press the issue, and I silently thanked her; I didn't want to relive the painfully awkward car ride that I endured to be there.

Thankfully, the sound of a roaring car engine broke the awkward lull in the conversation.

"Is that... Charlotte?" September asked, looking towards the road.

"No," I said loudly, "this is Charlotte's substitute. Meet Drama Queen."

Tom rolled onto Jack's street in a sleek, black, 1974 Nova. He honked the horn a few times, just to show off.

"Drama Queen?" she asked. "Is she named after you?"

Jack snickered over by his car, crossing his arms and shifting his weight. I shot him a look, which only made his smirk grow.

Tom parked the car next to Jack's, stepping out and tossing me the keys. "Don't scratch her, Reed. Her owner needs her back Sunday, and he only wanted a tune up under the hood. Don't make me take a new paint job out of your paycheck."

"Yes, sir."

Tom slapped me on the back and nodded at September.

"Need a ride back to the shop, Tom?" Jack piped up. "It's on my way."

"Are you sure?" he asked. "I can walk. It's only a couple blocks."

"Get in."

Cora brought out the Polaroid camera just as Jack pulled out of the driveway. "You left this inside, Em."

September accepted it. "Thanks. Can you snap one of me and Reed real quick?"

Cora did as she asked, and the pictures actually turned out good. I almost took one but decided against it.

I walked around the car and opened the passenger side door for her. "After you."

She thanked me before taking the camera back from Cora and sliding into the seat. I made sure not to catch her dress before shutting the door behind her and retreating to the driver's side.

Once we were both safely in the car and on the road, things grew quiet between us. It wasn't uncomfortable to me; the only uncomfortable thing about it was the amount of thoughts running through my head. *Should we have called Marcus? Should we have begged him to come to Homecoming with us? Should Jack and I have pushed aside our arguing to focus on him? Should I have let it go?*

"Are you okay?"

I snapped out of my trance, blinking a couple times and shaking my head to clear it. I glanced quickly at her before fixing my eyes back on the road.

"Yeah, I'm fine."

She kept her eyes on me. "You don't look fine. What're you thinking about?"

I swallowed hard. "Nothing."

"Come on, Reed. I know you better than that."

I didn't answer, tightening my grip on the steering wheel. She didn't push me. She waited patiently until I got up the nerve to speak again.

"I feel guilty about Marcus," I confessed quietly. "I feel like I should've asked him to come."

"Why didn't you?" she asked.

Again, I didn't answer. Not because I didn't want Marcus to be there but because I just didn't have an answer. Why hadn't I asked him?

Why hadn't I called him at all?

Why did I let him get behind the wheel that night? If I hadn't, we could've avoided all this.

"He misses us, Reed," she said.

"I suppose he told you that?"

"I've talked to him every day since the concert. He has a lot going on."

"Why hasn't he called me?"

"Everyone isn't going to do things your way, Reed."

"And *him* calling *me* is my way?"

"Yes, actually, it is. You've got to come down off your pedestal sometime and realize that you've got to do some things yourself. Marcus needs you. I'm sorry that you're afraid to call him, but you need to man up."

"Who said I was afraid to call him?"

She shifted her body to face me. "Is there some other reason you haven't picked up the phone or driven yourself to see him, then?"

I didn't have an answer for that, either.

"He's afraid too, Reed. He's afraid that we won't accept him for the decisions he's made. He's afraid you won't accept him."

"Why me?"

"Why do you think? Reed, both Jack and I have at least talked to him since he retreated from the outside world. You're the only one who hasn't made an appearance."

I turned into the school lot and parked farthest away from the doors in the empty portion of the lot. Once we'd parked, I rested my forehead against the steering wheel.

"I don't hate him," I muttered.

I felt her prod at my arm. When I looked up, she was holding my cellphone out to me.

"Then tell him that."

Hesitantly, I took my phone from her and dialed Marcus's number. It seemed like forever before I finally pressed the call button.

The phone rang once. Twice. Three times.

Voicemail.

I found myself slightly relieved. I wanted to speak to Marcus, but I didn't want to have to pour my heart out in front of September. The pressure of eyes watching and ears listening in weighed on my shoulders.

The robotic voice told me to leave a message.

"Hey, Mark, it's me…" I began. "It's Reed. It's been a while, man. Call me when you get the chance."

I ended the call. September looked satisfied.

"That's a start," she said. "At least now you can think through what you're going to say."

I nodded in agreement, but I knew that I wouldn't get very far in planning out my apology. Even if I did, I'd forget everything as soon as I answered the phone.

Inhaling deeply, I shook all the confusing feelings out and tried to focus on September. I reached into the backseat and produced a small, clear box containing a corsage.

Thanks, Tom.

"You can't have a proper Homecoming without a corsage," I said, opening the box.

She laughed, shaking her head at me. "This isn't Prom, Reed."

"I won't get to take you to Prom. This is the next best thing."

She held out her wrist for me, her genuine smile radiant. I slid the band over her hand, careful not to ruin the flowers.

She admired the mini bouquet on her wrist. "Thanks, Reed. That's really sweet."

"Don't act so surprised. Sweet is my middle name."

I got an eye-roll for that one.

I turned off the car and moved around the front to open her door for her. As we walked across the asphalt of the large parking lot, September laced her fingers through mine. Her hands were soft. I didn't say anything about it. Neither did she.

I shouldn't have thought anything of it. She'd held my hand before. It wasn't like this was something new. We were a close group of friends. She could hold my hand if she wanted to.

This felt different, though. New. Like it meant something more.

I pushed the thought away. It wasn't something I needed to bring up until later.

I squeezed her hand as we walked through the front doors of the school. She gently squeezed back.

The gym was already bursting with people when we got there. The lights were low, and string lights hung from the walls and ceiling. A DJ had set up on the small stage at the far end of the gym, and he had his own intricate lighting system that strobed green and blue lights to the beat of the music. Food sat on tables against one of the walls, and a photo booth in the corner had a line that wrapped around the gym.

The people who weren't in line to get a photo danced in the center of the room to upbeat music. Instantly, I recognized Jack, who danced with someone I couldn't see. When he moved to the side, I recognized none other than Hannah Stephens with her short blonde hair bouncing to the music.

"Did you know that Jack was taking Hannah to Homecoming?" I asked September.

She hesitated. "Yeah, I did."

I turned to look at her. "Why didn't you tell me?"

"For the same reason *he* didn't tell you. You haven't exactly been the easiest person to talk to lately, Reed. You've developed a bit of a temper."

"I don't have a temper!"

She looked at me, raising her eyebrow as I proved her point. "Really?"

I shut my mouth. I couldn't think of anything to say.

September rolled her eyes, tugging at my hand. "Come on, Drama Queen. No need for you and Jack to get in each other's way tonight. You asked me to Homecoming, so let's *be at Homecoming.*"

I knew she was right. I was going to make the most of tonight, make this memory last. After all, it wasn't every day you got to take September Jones to a formal.

"You're right. Where are my manners?"

"I've been wondering that for the past year."

I swatted at her arm, but she pulled away and spun out of reach, laughing at me as she went. She stepped backwards on her dress and started to fall. I shot my arm forward and caught her before she hit the floor.

"Nice catch," she said, breathless and still laughing.

"Thanks." I flashed her a smile.

She used me as support to stand up straight.

"So much for the sneakers, huh?" I asked. "You still tripped over them."

She shrugged. "Yeah, I guess you're right." She reached down under her dress and pulled the laces on her Vans, sliding them off her feet and tossing them against the wall. They bounced off the painted cement blocks and landed a few feet away on the floor. "There. That's better."

She took my hand again and pulled me towards the center of the floor. The music changed as we got there, moving from a pop song to a more mellow, upbeat song called "Back to You."

"I *love* this song," she commented, twirling under my arm. "It's probably my favorite one on the album."

"Really? Mine, too."

"Come on, now, Reed; don't go copying my song choices. Those are sacred."

I held up my other hand in defense. "Honest, it is. I listen to it on repeat all the time."

She grinned, taking my free hand in hers. "Don't make me do all the work, Davis. Dance with me."

I shook my head. "I don't dance."

"I know you can."

"Not a chance. And we aren't stealing song lyrics here, Jones. *High School Musical* isn't my style."

Her laugh brought a smile to my face. "Come on, Reed. You can't go to the Homecoming dance and not dance. It's unnatural."

"You know what else is unnatural?" I asked. "Me. On a dance floor."

"Don't be like that. We both know you're just afraid I'll out-dance you. Besides, didn't you say this was your replacement Prom or something?"

I knew she was right. After all, when would I get another chance to dance with September Jones at Homecoming?

I took control of the dance after that, spinning September under my arm. The music changed again to an upbeat indie song, so we started doing some sort of swing dance we'd seen other people around us do a couple times. Turns out, it's harder than it looks, so we just made up the moves on our own. September would go under my arm, then I would follow under hers, and we would keep going until we ended up in an arm pretzel. Then she'd laugh, and we'd start over because it beat the boring step-touch-step-touch dance that the rest of the students did.

When the dance ended, we were both out of breath and slightly dizzy. September swayed and grabbed onto my shoulders for support.

Jack pulled Hannah by the hand towards the refreshments and spotted us. He stopped to look us both up and down. "September, I didn't think you were the slow dancing type."

I hadn't realized that the music had changed. Now, it was a slow, ambient song.

"I'm not," she said, out of breath. "Don't be fooled. We're just holding onto each other so we don't pass out."

He chuckled. "Concussions suck, don't they?"

"Speaking of which," I said, "why aren't you dizzy or anything? You've been dancing longer than we have."

Jack looked at me for a moment with uncertainty before he shrugged. "Healed fast, I guess. My concussion was minor to begin with. I stopped having symptoms a few days ago."

"Fantastic," I muttered.

Hannah tugged on Jack's arm. "Excuse us, guys. We were just going to get some drinks. You can come with us if you like."

September started to answer, but I cut her off. "No, thanks. We were just about to leave."

Hannah shrugged. "Suit yourselves. We'll see you later."

As Hannah steered Jack by the elbow towards the refreshments, he cast a long, suspicious look at us. Finally, he turned around and disappeared with her into the crowd of teenagers.

"Excuse me." September tapped my shoulder. "Since when are we leaving? We got here, like, an hour ago."

"Since now," I said, tearing my gaze away from the direction the pair had gone in. "This is lame, anyway."

She crossed her arms. "I'm not arguing, but who said that we were going to treat this like Prom?"

"Prom is lame, too. Come on; I've got a better idea. It doesn't involve passing out on a gym floor."

A smile blossomed on her lips and she rocked on her heels. "I like the sound of that. Where are we going?"

"It's a surprise. Get your shoes."

"Are we there yet?"

"Em," I replied in exasperation, "that's literally the tenth time you've asked that."

"You can't pull me away from my Homecoming but not tell me where we're going, Davis."

"Too bad. I did."

I dodged her fist, catching it with my hand and moving my fingers so that they laced with hers. I flashed her a satisfied smile.

Her hand tugged away from mine, and she turned back to the front of the car. "Okay, I won't ask anymore. That was punishment enough."

"Oh, I'm so hurt."

"Good."

She leaned forward to turn on the radio then settled back in her seat to look out the window. Neither of us spoke, but I didn't mind.

Soon, the road turned to gravel, and then to dirt, and then it disappeared altogether. Gone was the city; in its place laid a huge, wide open field.

"What're we doing here?" she asked, turning her head to look at me as I cut off the engine but left on the radio. "There's nothing here."

"We're here," I said, winking at her.

As her smile grew wider, I pushed open my door and pulled off my tux jacket and bowtie. I threw them onto the seat before I slammed the door. The tall grass brushed my knees as I rolled up my sleeves and rounded the Nova, unlocked the back hatch with the key, shoved it open and reached into the space for the quilt and the bag I'd stashed there earlier. After opening up the quilt and spreading it across the hard floor of the back, I dove into the bag and produced a flashlight.

September appeared at the side of the car, her shoes in one hand and a fistful of her dress in the other. She'd pulled her hair up on her head so that it would stay out of her face.

"Did you drag me out to the middle of nowhere to murder me?" she asked, shifting her weight and leaning against the side of the car.

"Totally. The Homecoming dress is just for the aesthetic." I beamed the flashlight at her dress before using it to illuminate the sharp edges of the hatch so that I could avoid them.

She cracked a smile, peering over into the hatch. "What's the blanket for?"

"Stargazing."

"Wow, how romantic. Who's your date?"

I fought back a grin. "I'm looking at her."

Her head turned back and forth as she searched the area around her. "Funny, I don't see anyone. I guess I'll have to fill in, like the good Samaritan I am."

I rolled my eyes and scoffed. "Oh, how kind of you."

Her lips relented and curved into a wide, smug smile. "I know."

I hopped backwards into the car, leaning back on my elbows and getting comfortable. September watched me, an unrecognizable expression on her face.

"Come on, Em." I patted the spot next to me. "You know you want to."

She rolled her eyes at me. I wondered if she did that all the time or if it was just to me.

Her shoes landed next to my head as she tossed them in and then hiked her skirt up to her knees so that she could climb in. I offered her a hand, and she took it to help her slide next to me. When she finally leaned back next to me, the flowing fabric of her skirt draped over her legs and then over the edge of the car, barely grazing the grass.

Together, we lifted our gazes to the sky, inspecting the vast array of glittering spots that filled the darkness. The night was peaceful, much more peaceful than the blaring music in the gym and the flashing lights. Here, it was calm.

"You know," September began, "you're not as bad as some people make you out to be."

I laughed. "Wow, I'm flattered."

"I mean it. I mean, sometimes you really can be a jerk, and insensitive, and an idiot, and oblivious—"

"I get it!"

"My point is," she said, shifting on her elbows and glancing at me in the corner of her eye, "you really are much more than that, and I appreciate how hard you try to be a good friend to me."

Because I've been such a great *friend lately.*

"It's no big deal," I said.

"But it is. People like you are what makes it hard to move from city to city. I know this one's going to be hard to move on from."

I shifted my weight onto one arm, turning my body to face her. "Then don't."

She didn't look at me when she answered. "You know I can't do that."

"But you *can*. You'll be eighteen soon. You won't have to live with your parents. You could stay here."

"Reed, this is a big opportunity for me. Traveling is what I've dreamed of. If I give it up now, I'm afraid that I won't have another chance."

"You will," I told her. "I'll take you traveling."

Finally, her eyes met mine. "What?"

"You heard me. I'll take you traveling. We'll go together."

She sighed, laying all the way back and looking up at the ceiling of the Nova. "Reed, you and I both know that's not going to happen."

"But—"

"Reed, I'm serious. Let's move on. Talk about something else."

She sounds like me.

Hearing that felt like two tons pressing down on my chest. Like ice water being poured down my back. Like someone had ripped my heart from my chest and stepped on it in front of me.

But she didn't know that.

Will she ever?

I didn't know why it was so hard for me to figure out what I wanted. Tell her, don't tell her. Would confessing how I felt be worth the risk of ruining a friendship? Would she feel the same way?

Why couldn't she just *stay*?

The once light air now felt heavy and tense. I was suddenly very uncomfortable where I sat. Desperate to change the subject, I picked up the bag from the floor again and handed it to September. She raised an eyebrow at me, silently asking, *What is this?* But she sat up and reached in anyway. I shone the flashlight at it so that she could see. A few seconds later, she pulled out a handful of sparklers. She peered down to the bottom of the bag.

"You brought fireworks?"

"Yep."

She looked at me. "Please don't tell me you just *happen* to carry fireworks with you everywhere you go."

"Oh, please. I'm reckless, but I'm not *that* reckless."

Her bright giggle brought about an end to the suffocating and awkward air. "So, have you been planning all this time to kidnap me from Homecoming and to come shoot fireworks?"

"Pretty much."

Her hand ventured into the bag again, this time producing five rockets and a box of matches. She spread them out on the floor. "If we get arrested for this, I'm blaming you."

"We won't get arrested. Besides, I think the experience is worth it, don't you?"

She just smiled and picked up a rocket to inspect it. I took it as a *yes.*

I hopped out of Drama Queen—the car, not me—and offered September a hand which she accepted. When both of us had our feet on the ground, we advanced further out into the field and picked a spot a little ways from the car. She helped me pull up some grass to plant the first rocket, and after striking the match, we both sprinted back to the car and waited for the explosives to detonate.

With a sound like a whistle, a bright pink trail of sparks flew into the air, exploding into bright colors of blue and purple as it traveled farther into the sky. Immediately, two more sparks in hues of green and red followed and made a loud *boom* as they rained colorful sparks back down.

September clapped her hands and laughed. "That was perfect!" She reached over the seat and grabbed the Polaroid camera, prepping for the next one. "I need a picture of this."

I tossed her another rocket. "How about another go?"

Again, we raced out into the field and planted a rocket before sprinting back for cover behind the Nova. This time, yellow and orange sparks swirled in the sky, lighting up our faces with bright colors and putting dashes of light into our eyes.

The next hour consisted of running back and forth in the field, watching the sparks of the fireworks blend with the stars in the background, and making shapes in the air with sparklers. The music had cut off long ago, so we filled the void with our own terrible singing and echoing laughs.

She was the light in the stars, the spark in the fireworks. Her laugh illuminated her entire face and rebuilt the feelings in my chest with each giggle. She grabbed my hand and pulled me along behind her towards the car, going to grab another rocket. Here, with no other distractions, I saw her more clearly than I had ever before.

I couldn't figure out why it took me so long to realize it. Sure, I'd found September pretty before, but this?

She was much, much more.

This was simply... September. Pure, stunning, radiant, beautiful September. It was as if our previous conversation had never happened. She was kind, and loving, and forgiving. She was everything I wanted. She was everything I needed.

It was in that moment that I realized how deeply and truly in love I was with September Jones. Not a crush, more than a desire. No, it was more than that—I loved her.

I *loved* her.

And I wasn't sure I'd have the strength to let her go.

The past eight months of getting to know her and creating this close-knit friendship felt like nothing compared to the emotions that were spinning around in my head. I'd spent all that time trying to make her like me, trying to get her to take down the confident façade and melt like every other girl had. I'd enjoyed the chase. I'd grown impatient in the absence of a reaction. I had been in love with the idea of her, with the idea of being in love with her. Infatuated. Mesmerized. I'd cared for her, sure, but not like this.

I didn't want to stop looking at her. Her smile, her laugh, the way she turned her head to look me—I loved all of it.

My mood skyrocketed. For the first time in a long time, I didn't worry about the coming weeks or even the coming days. I was in the moment. I *was* the moment. I enjoyed every second and savored it. I reveled in it. I *lived*.

When we finally ran out of sparklers, we were out of breath and our stomachs hurt from laughing so much. We went back to the Nova, lying on the quilt under the hatch and gazing at the stars like we had earlier as we recovered. I kept on saying stupid things to make her laugh, and she kept laughing until tears sprang to her eyes. It grew quiet once again, but this time, I didn't mind. It was usually very easy to sit in silence with September. She knew how to avoid awkwardness. I just wasn't as great at it as she was.

The silence covered us like a blanket. I closed my eyes for a split second, listening to the sounds of our breathing and the crickets in the grass. I wondered how I could make the night last longer because I knew that once we drove back into the sea of other people, I'd miss this night more than any other.

10

confrontation

When I woke, September was sleeping silently beside me, curled into a ball with her back to me. Her long skirt, dirty from running through the grass, covered her like a blanket. The moon still dimly lit the sky. I shivered; the grass already sported a thin layer of frost.

As quietly as I could, I slid out of the back of the car, doing my best not to move or jostle it so that she wouldn't wake up. Once I got to the driver's side, I reached in and found my phone. I had three texts, a few missed calls, and one voicemail. I ignored them and checked the time.

1:17 a.m. *No wonder people are wondering where we are.*

I tossed my phone back into the seat and moved back towards September but not before opening the passenger side door. She hadn't moved an inch. As smoothly as possible, I supported her head and slid my arm under her knees so that I could carry her to the front. She stirred, but she didn't wake.

I put her on the bench seat and strapped her in before shutting the hatch, jogging back to the driver's side, and starting the car.

The loud roar of the engine made her open her eyes. She didn't say anything. She just leaned over in the seat and rested her head in the middle of the bench. Before I put the car into drive, I lifted her head and slid my jacket underneath her to use as a pillow. Her long, wavy hair spread across it and ran down the edge of the seat.

I left the radio off as I turned back onto the road, enjoying the peaceful silence. I'd always loved the later hours of the night. The cool and quiet atmosphere appealed to me. The low hum of the car once it warmed up, mixed with the sounds of our quiet breathing, was comforting, familiar. I could've listened to it for hours.

Tiny water droplets gathered on the windshield, mixing with the dew and streaming down the glass. It surprised me—not because it was raining (rain was expected in our part of the state)—but because it had been so long since the last time it had rained. It had been sunny for a few weeks which was strange; November was one of our rainiest months. I'd like to blame the lack of precipitation on September, like I did with everything irregular that happened around us, but I knew that wasn't true. She loved rain. I guess that's why Greenville became such a great fit for her. If she had her way, six days of the week would be quiet and rainy. Not that I'd have a problem with that; rain was another one of those little things I'd grown to appreciate since September moved here.

I relaxed a little in my seat, glad the roads were empty. Nothing would disturb the peace.

My gaze flickered over to Em, still curled up asleep. She was beautiful, no doubt. Her makeup had run a little under her eyes and the bottom of her skirt had turned brown, but somehow that just added to what I already saw. She didn't need any of the formalities to be beautiful.

I guess that was one of the reasons I loved her.

Oh, that's right. I love her.

Remembering my revelation from hours before picked up my energy. I wasn't sleepy anymore—just happy.

Disappointment crept in and ruined my mood as I pulled into my driveway and shut off the car. My peaceful ride had ended.

Back to reality.

Again, I nudged her shoulder. "Em."

"Hmm?" She curled into a tighter ball.

"Em, we're home."

She raised her head, sighing as she rubbed the sleep out of her eyes. "Already?"

"It's after one in the morning."

She raised her eyebrows but didn't say anything. Then she just laid back down on the seat and curled back into a ball.

I shook my head and gave a short, low little laugh. The keys were pulled from the ignition, and I jogged to the front door and unlocked it, leaving it open. Then I went back for September who wrapped her arms around my neck and went back to sleep when I picked her up to carry her inside. I bumped the door closed with my hip.

I took the stairs one by one, balancing September's weight (which wasn't much at all) with my own on the incline. My foot prodded the door to my bedroom open, and I flicked on the light.

The light finally seemed to pull September out of her groggy slumber. She tapped my shoulder so that I'd put her down. When she was on her feet, she picked up the clothes bundled on the desk chair and headed back into the hallway. After grabbing some pajamas, I followed her until she closed the bathroom door behind her, murmuring a low, "Wait here."

She appeared dressed in a plain t-shirt and shorts a moment later. She tilted her chin to look at me.

"Thank you," she said softly. "It was fun."

The corner of my mouth twitched upwards. "It was fun?"

This time, she smiled lazily. "Yeah. It was fun."

Unexpectedly, she lifted herself onto her tiptoes and planted a soft kiss on my cheek. Before I could react, she'd said goodnight and closed my bedroom door behind her.

If my mind was awake before, it *buzzed* now. Thoughts of asking her to stay flooded through my head as I descended the stairs. I imagined what it would be like to date September. Not as a joke, or a dare, or just because she seemed like a good time, but to spend time with her. To learn more about her than I already knew. To fall deeper in love with her, and hopefully, for her to return the feelings. To one day propose to her. To wake up to her every morning.

Every one of those thoughts was naïve, and I knew it. But I didn't care.

When I got back to the living room, I could see the light from the kitchen shining onto the floor. I raked my hands through my hair and tossed my pajamas onto the couch as I made my way through the living room and stepped onto the tile.

My dad stood at the fridge in his long plaid PJ pants and a rumpled white t-shirt. It wasn't strange for my dad to be here at this time of night; he was one of the few people I knew who actually got up for midnight snacks.

He saw me out of the corner of his eye as the fridge door swung closed. He held a package of cheese in his hands. His eyebrow raised.

"Homecoming fun?" he asked, putting the cheese on the counter. He reached into a cabinet for the box of crackers.

"Yeah." I moved towards the plate cabinet and pulled one down for him. He took it and nodded. "We went stargazing afterwards."

I chose not to tell him about the fireworks. He honestly probably wouldn't have minded, but if he told Mom, she'd freak out.

"Sounds fun. Did she have a good time?" With the knife in his hand, he pointed to the ceiling where September was staying in my room.

"I think so. She seemed like she enjoyed it."

He smiled, turning back to his plate and slicing up the cheese into squares. "Good. You two needed a break."

"A break? We had an entire week off from school."

"With concussions," he pointed out. "I wouldn't call that a break. Speaking of which, how do you feel?"

"Chipper. Well, both of us got dizzy at the dance, but I haven't considered throwing up in the past couple days, so I guess that's an improvement."

"That's good. What about Jack? How's he holding up?"

Sighing, I sat down at the kitchen table. "Jack said something about how his symptoms were already gone. Minor concussion, I guess."

Dad picked up his plate, grabbed a soda from the fridge, and joined me at the table.

"Is something wrong with you two?"

I frowned. "Why would you say that?"

He gave me a look that said *seriously?* before popping a cracker in his mouth, chewing, and swallowing. "Reed, I helped raise you. I've heard you talk about Jack many times, and I've never heard you say his name like you're choking on something. I haven't seen him around here in a while. What's bothering you?"

I settled back in my seat. "We just have... a misunderstanding."

"About?"

I sneaked one of his crackers before he could poison it with Tabasco. He frowned but didn't say anything. "September."

"Oh no, " he said. "Please don't tell me you two are fighting over a girl."

"We aren't. Not over her, at least. We just have different opinions on her situation."

"Yours being?"

I shrugged, popping the cheese cracker into my mouth.

"You don't know? Son, how can you have an argument over something that you don't even have an opinion on?"

"I have an opinion," I answered once I'd swallowed. "It just keeps changing."

"Well, do you want to talk about it?"

"Not really, no."

"Am I allowed to offer advice?"

I let out a short laugh and shrugged my shoulders. "Yeah, I guess."

"Alright then; I'm going to go out on a limb here and assume that you've got some urge to ask September to stay here or make some compromise."

I started to interrupt, to ask how he could possibly know that, but he held up a hand to stop me. "Interrupting proves that I'm right. Anyway, knowing Jack, he probably just wants you to leave the subject alone, correct?"

Reluctantly, I nodded.

"Here's the advice; are you listening?" He cleared his throat. "You've got two friends here, right? You've been friends with Jack since you were kids, and you've been friends with September for a year. Are both friendships worth saving?"

Again, I nodded.

"Then you need to find a way to make it work because if it's important enough to you, you'll think of a way. You're a smart kid. Is there a reason that you feel the need to make September stay?"

I swallowed hard, looking down at my hands in my lap. "I think I love her."

"Have you ever heard that if you love something, you've got to let it go?"

I met his eyes again. *Let her go?*

In my mind, those words translated to *give up*.

That wasn't happening anytime soon.

149

Abruptly, I stood up from the table. "Thanks, Dad, but I think I'm going to go to bed now." My voice came out more forceful than I intended.

"I was just trying to help, Reed."

I shrugged. "I know."

I turned on my heel and headed back to the living room, snatched up my clothes, and changed in the hallway bathroom. I crashed on the couch and turned so that I faced the cushions. When my dad walked through and turned out the lights, I ignored him and pretended to be asleep.

I couldn't figure out why the conversation had suddenly made me so irritable. Giving up on September seemed like a joke. Who could ask me to do that?

I realized how tired I was when my thoughts finally settled down. My eyes fell closed.

I slept hard until about 8 a.m. when my ringtone woke me. Tom's name scrolled across the top of my screen.

"Hello?" I asked groggily.

"Reed, when are you bringing the car back?"

"Well, good morning to you, too."

"I'm serious. The owner will be back for it in an hour, man. *One hour.* I have to wash it from top to bottom so that I don't get skinned for letting you take it."

I bolted from the couch and grabbed the keys from the coffee table, slipping on my tennis shoes that were on the floor next to the door. I hopped into the car in my slept-in t-shirt and gym shorts and got it running.

"I'm on my way," I said before I hung up.

I drove like a demon to the garage, hopping out as soon as I pulled in and shoving all the remains of our fireworks and the quilt into the bag I'd left in the back. As I slammed the hatch closed, Tom rolled out from under a car.

"I called you like three minutes ago. How the crap are you here?"

I shrugged, walking over to him and tossing the keys to him. "I'm here. Does it matter?"

He raised an eyebrow. "Guess not. Since you're here, you can get back to work on Lucy while I scrub DQ down. You know Lucy is due in less than a week? The owner is out of town and won't be back until Thursday. You got lucky." He stood up and wiped his hands on an oily rag. "Are you free all day today? And are you healed enough to work?"

"Yeah, I think so," I said groggily. "I planned on catching up on sleep, but forget that."

"What time did you get in last night?"

What time did I go to sleep? "About two."

He waved his hand at me, dismissing my comment. "That's six hours of sleep. You're fine."

"How many hours do you get, Tom?"

"Usually? About five. Now come on, let's get to work."

Luckily, Lucy was in better shape than when I last worked on her. Tom had fixed the transmission instead of replacing it, which probably saved him some good money. The seats were also gone, meaning he'd probably already dropped them off to be upholstered. All that was left for me was the A/C, the paint, and the rims, which I figured were probably in the cardboard box leaning against the car.

I knew nothing about cars when I first decided to fix up Charlotte. She was a mess when I found her parked on the edge of the road with a For Sale sign in the window. Every time I passed her with my parents in the car, I told them that she would be mine. I would be the one to fix her up.

When I turned sixteen, my parents surprised me when I found her sitting in the driveway on a trailer. I loved everything about her—the way her doors creaked, how worn in her seats were, how she smelled of old cigars.

My dad hooked me up with Tom, knowing I wanted to get into cars. Tom's father and mine had apparently been friends, and he called in a favor. Tom was more than willing to take in an apprentice. He told me he started fixing cars at sixteen, too, with his dad and his grandfather. He was only twenty-three then—young for someone to be fixing up cars like that, but he had the talent.

Piece by piece, we put Charlotte back together. Almost everything had to be replaced; it was like someone just put a shell of a car on the road and wanted someone to drive it away. He showed me how to make different repairs to an engine and then how to put it into the car; he showed me how to fix a transmission and put that in, too. A/C, heat, radio, brakes, starter—you name it, he taught me how to fix it or replace it.

The only thing we didn't do to her is paint her. Tom offered, but I refused; I loved her worn in, rusty red paint.

"It's a disaster," he told me.

I shrugged at him. "I like it. It gives her character."

When we finally finished her about six months later, I drove her to school, ready to show off what I'd accomplished. Marcus and Jack were immediately impressed; they decided I would be the designated driver of us all.

We had trouble naming her for a few months. We had a running list of names written on a napkin in the glove box. Every couple of days, one of us would jump into the car after school and suggest a name. We'd all think on it a bit, and the next day we'd decide it wasn't right and cross it off the list.

Marcus suggested something hardcore, like Rex or Bone Crusher. Jack shot that down, saying that she wasn't going to be named Rex and that a Scout II hardly qualified as a bone-crushing car. I agreed with him.

Jack suggested something meaningful, like Hope or Liberty. We all decided that wasn't right, either.

One day, I started looking online for names. It drove me crazy that we couldn't find something to call her. I stumbled across Charlotte on some website that listed the meaning of names. The definition listed was *free man.*

Free man. Huh.

We were free men, right? Well, maybe not men—we were still sixteen—but we had new freedom that came with driving around a car that belonged to me. It made sense in my head at the time; looking back on it, it was a stupid way to pick a name. Charlotte suited her, though, so I kept on it. I also just thought the name was cool. But that wasn't as cool of an explanation. So the next day, when the car doors slammed shut behind Jack and Marcus, the first thing I said was, "Her name is Charlotte." I left no room for argument, and they didn't argue.

Now, two years later, I used all the knowledge Tom had passed along to me on the cars in his shop. Everything came naturally now. I rarely had to ask him to show me how to do something anymore. I just did it. And he trusted me to do the job.

I got to work with the A/C and heating system. Luckily, Tom had ordered new parts to fit the original system. All I had to do was replace and put together. Still, I worked on the A/C for a few hours on my own before Tom came over to help.

Around 1 p.m., Tom left to go grab us some food. While I had a bit of a break, I remembered the missed messages and calls I'd had from early this morning.

One call and three texts from Jack from last night.

Where are you?

Man, answer your phone.

Seriously?

These texts I ignored. I didn't want to talk to him; things still felt tense and awkward.

One text from September, fairly recent.

Where are you?

I quickly responded.

At Tom's. Won't be back until this evening.

I had a missed call from my dad from late last night. I figured he didn't need me to call him back.

The last missed call made my stomach drop. Marcus's name appeared at the top of the screen with a voicemail from him.

I wasn't sure what I'd hear on that voicemail. Did he even want to see me? Would he be angry?

I swallowed hard and pressed play on the message.

"Hey, Reed." His voice came out quietly. "I got your message. Um, thanks for calling. Call me back... you know, whenever."

The line went dead. I breathed a sigh of relief. He didn't sound angry. He just sounded... off. I could hear something different in his voice. He didn't sound confident, or even remotely happy. He sounded weak.

I decided I'd call him back later when I had time to sit and talk for a while. Or better yet, I could find a time to go see him.

Tom came back into the garage, his shirt spotted with rain. He handed me my lunch, and we ate quickly before getting back to work on Lucy.

Around five, Tom told me I could go home. We'd accomplished a lot on Lucy, and the owner of the Nova had picked her up. Before I left, he handed me a couple of hundred dollar bills.

"You'll get more once Lucy is finished," he explained, "but this is for a couple of days' labor. You've worked hard. Thanks."

With a nod, I headed to the door and stepped outside. The rain had thinned out, and what had been a downpour faded to a light drizzle. I looked down at my phone to call my dad to pick me up until a horn honked at me. I looked up.

Jack sat staring at me behind the wheel of his Audi. One hand drummed on the steering wheel. The passenger window rolled down.

"Need a ride?" he yelled.

My skeptical expression didn't faze him. Slowly I nodded before approaching the car and sliding into the passenger seat.

"Thanks," I mumbled, buckling my seatbelt. "How'd you know I was here?"

"I called September," he answered, eyes trained on the road as he pulled out of the parking lot.

"Is there something you need?"

"Yeah, you could say that. We need to talk."

"What about?"

Actually, I knew exactly what he wanted to talk about. I just didn't want to talk about it. Not now.

He didn't answer me. We approached the turn onto my street, and he kept driving.

"You missed the turn," I said.

"We're not going to your house. We're going to mine."

"What for?"

He gripped the steering wheel so hard that his knuckles turned white. "I told you. We need to talk."

"Fine, we're talking. If you want to say something, say it. Don't be shy."

"Cut the attitude, Reed. Where did you take September?"

I blinked. "Is this what you're mad about?"

"Answer the question, Reed. You were out all night."

"And? You aren't my dad, Jack."

"Did you...?" he trailed off.

"Did I what?"

I waited for a response, but I didn't get one. After a moment, I understood what he meant.

"Are you serious?" I asked. "You think I'm that kind of guy?"

"I don't know what kind of guy you are anymore, Reed."

"No! No, of course not! How could you—no!"

"Fine. Sue me. I honestly thought you'd be willing to do anything to get her to stay. So yes, it crossed my mind that you could've taken advantage of her."

"I can't believe this."

"Well, I couldn't believe that you were acting like such a four-year-old about September's future, but here we are."

"I *love* her, Jack."

"Come to that conclusion, have you?" He turned into his driveway. The rain had stopped. "Reed, last I checked, you were obsessed with her, not in love with her. Those are two different things."

"I know they're different. You don't have to lecture me."

"Someone has to."

"I don't need a lecture. I need you to stay out of my business."

"This is *our* business. You just don't get it, do you?" He swung open the car door and started walking towards the house, his fists clenched at his sides.

"What am I supposed to get?" I hopped out of the car and stormed after him. "It *hurts*, Jack. How do you expect me to deal with it? Just let her go without even trying to change her mind?"

It was like he purposely wanted to call me out, to tell me I was wrong. The anger grew stronger in my chest and my head burned hot.

"Don't you think I know it hurts?" he spat, turning back to me. "She's one of my best friends too, Reed. She's *leaving the country.* I *know* it hurts."

"You don't understand anything," I mumbled, turning around and heading towards the road. "I'm walking home."

His hand grabbed at the back of my neck, pulling me to the ground. Water from this morning's rain splashed up from the grass and soaked the back of my shirt. With the wind now gone from my lungs, I looked up at him. His eyes were fiery with an anger I'd never seen before.

"*I don't understand*, do I?" he snarled. "No, *you* don't understand, Reed. We're supposed to be here for her. We're supposed to support each other. Tell me, how can we do that if she's packing her house up on her own and you're *moping* like a child?"

I narrowed my eyes at him, still struggling to breathe.

"Get a grip on yourself, Reed. I don't think you understand what it means to be a friend anymore because you've lost all the ones you had. First Marcus, now me, and soon enough, September will be gone, too. You're pushing everyone away like you're the only one whose emotions matter. Marcus needed you, man. September needed your support; you know she can't do this on her own, no matter how hard she tries to make everyone else believe she can. And me?" He laughed a disgusted laugh. "I don't even know who you *are* anymore. How hard would it have been to grin and bear it for a month, man? To at least pretend you were okay until she left? Because the Reed I used to know wouldn't have a problem doing that."

He shook his head at me. The disappointment in his eyes made my blood boil. "Get off my lawn. I've tried talking to you, but you just won't listen. Clean up your attitude because I'm done taking care of your *crap*."

He turned away, walking back towards his house. I scrambled to my feet, unable to control my emotions. With every word, every berating sentence, I could feel the emotions rising up my throat. I needed them gone. I needed them gone *now*.

And I had the perfect outlet right in front of me.

"*Jack!*" I called after him. My hands balled into fists so tight that I couldn't feel them anymore.

"What do you want?" he yelled over his shoulder.

Turn around. Come on, turn around.

Lucky for me, he did exactly that. He faced me with his eyebrows drawn together in a frustrated stare.

"I said, *get off my lawn*," he repeated, his teeth grinding together.

Without warning, I reared back, moving all my momentum into my fist. My knuckles popped as they met Jack's jaw.

Before I could catch my breath from the exhilaration, Jack's foot swung full force at my abdomen, pushing me back onto the ground a second time. As I struggled to regain my breath, he took a step forward and leered over me.

"Are you serious?" he asked. "This is your solution? You're going to take out all your frustration on me?"

If I thought Jack was angry before, he was livid now. I barely recognized the person in front of me. Still, I didn't back down. I had a lot of frustration just waiting to be unleashed, and in my mind, Jack made the perfect punching bag. My head ached and the ground had started to wobble, but I was determined.

I looked up at him before spitting in his face. "*Screw you*, Evans."

His jaw tensed. His voice came out strained and through gritted teeth. "Fine. If this is how you want to play, I'll play along."

His hand came down to yank me up by the collar, cutting off my air supply. When he finally released me, I stumbled onto my knees, writhing for oxygen. I had no time to recover, though, before he swung at my face, nailing me hard in my left eye. The cold air only made my skin sting worse. Now, only able to see half of what I could before, I swung blindly, grimacing when I heard a sickening *crack*. I hoped his nose—not my hand—had made that sound.

My prayers were answered when he yelled out in pain, swinging at my chin in response. He narrowly missed me, staggering a few steps forward and throwing himself off balance.

"What's going on out here?" someone yelled from the house. "*What are you doing?*"

"Go back inside, Cora," Jack yelled. "Now!"

Crap. Cora's still home.

I caught a glimpse of Cora on the front porch. She tensed when Jack yelled her name. She seemed to want to protest, but when his head whipped in her direction, she backed up into the house. I wasn't surprised; I doubted she'd ever seen Jack that angry, either.

"Way to boss her around," I taunted. "I'm sure she *loves* having a brother two years younger than her telling her what to do."

"Leave Cora out of this," he barked at me. "This is about you and your pitiful attitude, Reed. Take some responsibility for once."

I kicked at Jack's knees, causing one to buckle and sending him to the ground. I grabbed onto his shoulder and kneed him in the stomach on the way down. He dropped onto his back and gasped for air.

Before I could get another blow in, Jack's arm swiped my legs out from under me. Now, we fought to beat each other to our feet.

Jack's fist made contact with my face again, hitting my mouth with enough force to make me groan. I tasted the hot, sticky blood at my lips. I gritted my teeth and stood up to swing at him. As I reared back, though, a car on the street honked loudly at us before pulling into the driveway.

While I was distracted trying to make out who the driver was, Jack took the opportunity to knee me once again in the stomach. Angrily, I swung at his face, missing the first swing and grazing his ear with the second. Once he was in my sight, I got in two or three good, hard punches, landing them on his face and jaw. I was ruthless. I had nothing to hold me back.

"Stop it!" A car door slammed shut, and I heard the soles of someone's shoes hitting the pavement and then stop when they hit the grass. "Break it up!"

A pair of small hands grabbed at my arm. I jerked away, launching my hands at Jack's neck.

"Reed Davis," September screamed, "get ahold of yourself! Jack, stop!"

Jack dodged my hands, swinging at my face again. We were both dizzy, and I'm sure he noticed, too; our attacks were getting sloppier.

September managed to pry me away from Jack, shoving her way between us before pushing against my chest to make me step back. The front door swung open, and Cora burst out, pulling at her brother's arms and doing her best to pin them behind his back.

I glared down at September, some of the anger shifting towards a new target. What made her think she could step in?

Before I realized what was happening, September's hand came up and slapped me hard across the face.

My cheek stung where there were already bruises forming from Jack's brutal attacks. I grabbed at her arms, making it impossible for her to reach at me again.

"Get ahold of yourself," she spat. "You're better than this. *Both* of you. Stop acting like *children*."

"Better than what?" I tightened my grip on her wrists. "I'm not better. *I'm not.* This is what I am."

"You are, and you know it. Now, move it. Get in the car."

"Don't tell me what to do," I growled. "You aren't even supposed to be driving."

"Neither are you," she said. "Get in the car. And let go of my arms; you're hurting me."

I held on to her tighter, staring her down.

"Reed, stop. *Let go of me.*"

I purposely squeezed tighter to make her flinch. Then I dropped her hands and stormed towards the car, scuffing my sneakers against the concrete as I went. I turned around and leaned against the car when I got there, looking towards Jack. He had a deadly fire in his eyes as he stared down at September.

"Let go of me, Cora," he warned in a low voice. Cora shrunk back, but September marched right up to him and slapped him across the face just like she did me. Instead of getting angrier, like I had, he simply closed his eyes and took a breath. When he opened them, he quit straining against Cora and looked at September, visibly calmer.

"That's enough, Jack," she said firmly. "You're better than this. It's over."

He didn't answer. He shot one more look my way then turned to Cora and gently pulled his arm from her grasp. He trudged past both of them to the front porch and went straight into the house.

Cora turned to September, her cheeks red and swollen from crying. September pulled her into a hug, but didn't say anything.

"Thank you," Cora said shakily. "I didn't know how else to break them up."

"It's fine," September assured. "I'll call you later. Just stay out of his way for a little bit, okay?"

She nodded, gripping Em tight before letting her go. Her wary glance at me lasted long enough for me to notice. I turned away, her gaze tugging at something in my chest. The guilt settled in.

Once Cora disappeared into the house, September sighed, running a hand over her face and hair before turning back towards me and trudging to the car.

"*I told you* to get in the car," she said over her shoulder.

"And I told you not to boss me around."

"Are you drunk?"

"I wish."

She rolled her eyes. "Do you have to make everything hard?"

Taking my own sweet time, I walked around the front of the car and opened the passenger door. I stopped there and looked at her.

"Why are you here?"

"Why do you think I'm here?" she asked, her tone tired but threatening. "I came to break you two idiots away from each other. Cora called me because she thought you two were seriously going to hurt each other. She was *scared* of you two. How does that sound to you, *hmm*? Do you *enjoy* scaring people?"

"We didn't need your help," I growled.

She scoffed. "Right. If I hadn't shown up, you two would've beaten each other into the ground until one—or both—of you was unconscious or in the hospital."

She swung the car door open, jumped into the driver's seat and slammed the door. Reluctantly, I got into the car, too. As soon as I was in, she started speeding out of Jack's neighborhood.

"How did you get your car back?" I asked.

"Your dad got it for me today," she answered.

She passed my road, just like Jack had.

Great.

"Where are you going?" I asked.

"My house. Do you think your parents are going to be okay with you walking into the house looking like that? Your mom will have a heart attack. Besides, I haven't been there in a week. I need to get more packing done."

"Take me home," I said. "They've seen worse."

"Do them a favor. I'm not taking you home. Your mom will be afraid you've made your concussion worse."

"Great."

When we got to her house, she cut off the engine, but she didn't get out. We just sat in our seats, staring out the front window.

"What was it about?" she finally asked. "Why'd you punch him?"

"How do you know I punched him first?"

"Because Jack is more mature than you in many ways. He knows when it's worth it. I don't think whatever you fought about was worth it."

"He fought back, you know."

"You deserved it. You've been a real jerk to everyone lately, not just him. It's about time someone did something about it."

"I deserved it, did I? Who was it that spent all night with me? If I deserved it, why did you bother coming with me to Homecoming?"

"Because you're my friend and I love you. But we aren't talking about me; we're talking about you."

"So this is all my fault, then?" I asked. "You're just going to blame it all on me? You don't even know what happened and you're siding with him!"

"Yes, I'm going to blame you because I know you started it. And I don't need to know what happened. The two of you argued, you fought, and now he's sitting in his house with a broken nose, and you're covered from head to toe in bruises. I think that says enough about the situation for me. There's a reason he didn't re-break your nose like you broke his; he was holding back. Face it, Reed; you have issues."

"No, I don't," I defended. "*Marcus* has issues. I just don't enjoy being lectured like a child. And what do you mean, he was holding back?"

She didn't answer.

"Go on, lecture me again," I dared. "Tell me I'm a child, that I have issues, that—"

"Reed," she cut me off, "shut up."

"No. Come on—enlighten me with all of my flaws."

"I'm not going to tell you any of those things because you obviously already know them," she snapped. "Why would I repeat them for you?"

I opened my mouth to say something, but closed it again. *What?*

"If you would just stop and listen to people every once in a while, things might make more sense to you," she said. "You could avoid all of this anger and stress. It wouldn't kill you to at least *listen* to advice."

"All this anger and stress generates from you," I pointed out. "If you weren't leaving, none of this would be happening. I'd still have my friends, and you wouldn't have to be telling me what I'm doing wrong in life."

"We've been over this so many times, Reed. I can't help my parents' decision, and quite frankly, I think it will be a good experience." She sighed and shifted in her seat. "You know, Reed, sometimes, I think I need to distance myself from you. Sometimes, you can just be so... *destructive.*"

The word made my blood run cold. "Destructive?"

"You know what I mean. You have the hardest time seeing the good that I see in things. I didn't want to spend my last month in Greenville having to divide my time between friends. I didn't want to get a call saying I needed to come break you away from a fight."

"Well, I'm sorry to disappoint."

"Me too."

We fell silent. I rubbed a hand over my face but that hurt, so I ended up folding my hands into my lap.

"Come on." She nudged my shoulder and unbuckled her seatbelt.

"What're you doing?"

"We're going to clean you up so that you don't look like you walked out of a war zone. Then we're going to pack."

I didn't argue this time. I got out of the car and followed her to the front porch.

"Why didn't you just take me home and leave me there?" I asked. "Aren't you mad at me?"

"I'm not mad. I'm aggravated, but I'm not mad."

"Why not?"

Her key slid into the door lock, and she pushed it open and flipped on the lights. "I can't get mad at you, Reed. You should know this by now."

"But what if you did?"

"I won't."

"But *what if you did?*"

She bit her lip. "I don't know."

"Oh, come on," I prompted, halting to look at her. She stopped in the middle of taking her jacket off, holding eye contact with me.

"I'd get over it, I suppose." She shrugged. "Unless you did something terrible, like murder my family or something, then it'd all work out, eventually."

"What if I did something to hurt you?"

"You wouldn't mean it," she answered quietly, taking a step back from me.

I stepped forward, my voice suddenly low and solemn. "What if I *did* mean it?"

I'd already hurt her so many times; there was no doubt that I would do it again. Whether or not I would realize it was a different question. Would I care? Would I do it on purpose? I held so much resentment for her decision to leave. I knew it wasn't her fault for leaving. I knew it couldn't be helped. But did I care?

At the moment, no. No, I didn't.

I inched another step closer to her, cupping my hand to her cheek. She swallowed, glancing behind her. The wall was at her back, and she had nowhere else to run. For a moment, I could've sworn she leaned closer, but she stood up straight and looked up at me.

"That's enough, Casanova." Her voice came out hoarse. She cleared her throat, putting a hand on my chest and pushing me back. "Let's get you cleaned up."

September darted around me, throwing her jacket on the couch and going towards the kitchen. I stood there, staring at the wall. Another moment wasted, another moment gone.

Man up, my conscience screamed at me. *Pull yourself together.*

"Reed?" she called.

"Coming." I balled my hand into a fist but released it before I entered the kitchen. She stood at the counter with a large Tupperware box full of medications and bandages. She gestured to the counter.

"Sit," she commanded. I followed her orders, wincing at the soreness of my muscles when I pulled myself up onto the counter. She turned the water on at the sink, wetting a washcloth before returning to me and pressing it lightly to my face.

The warm water stung the cut on my lip and under my eye but felt soothing after a moment. The washcloth glided smoothly across my face, and with each stroke, I could see the blood staining the once white cloth a pale red color.

"Does it hurt?" she asked.

I reached my hand up to touch the cuts and bruises then hissed at the sting. Funny—they hurt worse now than when they happened in the fight.

"I'll take that as a yes." She reached into the box and produced an ointment and a roll of bandages. "Some of that adrenaline must've worn off."

I winced again as the cloth ran over my eye. "Must have."

She laughed a humorless laugh. "Remember when you wrapped my leg up after I hurt myself on our hike? I guess we're even now."

"Guess so."

The room remained quiet while she cleaned the blood from my face, moving up and down and picking up my hands one at a time to clean the cuts on my knuckles.

"Honestly, Reed." Shaking her head, she assessed the damage. "Is it *that hard* just to walk away?"

"You weren't there. You didn't hear what he said."

"Ignore him," she snapped.

"He asked for it," I muttered bitterly.

"*You* asked for it."

She used a gauze pad to spread the ointment on the cuts across my face. It stung at first but gradually faded into a cool sensation. Next, she carefully placed small, thin bandages across my cuts to hold them together.

She clasped my hands in hers as she wrapped each one carefully with gauze. "You didn't hold back, did you?"

"No. I was mad."

"Well, I can see that. I just don't understand how you could willingly beat up your best friend."

"I'm telling you, he was asking for it. He provoked me."

"Somehow, I still don't think he did," she said. "I know you two."

She tore off a piece of medical tape, securing the gauze on each hand. "You know, when we first became friends, I didn't know that the contract required me to clean you up when you get into fights."

I cracked a smile. "Sorry."

She sighed, pretending to be inconvenienced. "I'll contact my lawyer." After cutting off the excess gauze, she picked up the scraps and moved across the kitchen to throw them away. I hopped off the counter, walking to her fridge.

"Wait just a second, Davis," she said, closing the door in front of me. "I didn't invite you over here to eat my food."

"Then why am I here?" I asked, opening it again.

"So that I could make you look like less of a murderer. Your face was covered in blood. Jack got you good."

I rolled my eyes. "Right."

"Besides, I'm your designated driver. You don't have Charlotte, and you can't call your parents. You need me to take you home. And since you're here, you can help me pack."

"Fine," I muttered.

"Great." She clapped her hands. "What should we do first? Furniture or closets?"

11
regret

Sunday and Monday passed, and Jack and I still hadn't spoken. That was fine by me because I didn't know what I'd have said to him if we had had the chance to have a conversation.

Sorry I punched you in the face. We cool?

Hardly an apology.

I wasn't even really sure that I wanted to apologize. Admitting that I was wrong was a big step, especially when I thought my reasons for hashing it out with him were pretty valid.

September stayed out of it altogether. "Work it out yourself," she'd said, irritated. "You guys aren't five."

Even if I had actually wanted to apologize, I didn't have an opportunity. Jack did his absolute best to avoid me, and I did the same. It wasn't hard for us to keep up with each other; September always hung out with one of us. She ended up dividing her time between the two of us for those days. It drove her absolutely insane. She lectured me several times in the car over how dramatic I was being, and I'm almost positive she'd had it rehearsed to repeat to Jack.

All of us went back to school that Monday. That is, all of us but Marcus.

This time, though, I didn't fall over unconscious. Both September and I made it through the entire day with only mild headaches. Mine wasn't as much from my concussion as it was from all the questions I got about the bruises and cuts that littered my face and arms.

Jack seemed fine, apart from the blue and purple splotches on his jaw and nose. It still bothered me how much quicker he had recovered from the accident. I had to keep reminding myself that he had less impact than the rest of us, but it still set my teeth on edge and made me jealous that he didn't have to put up with it like I did. It made me look weak.

The sky wore a sad shade of gray. It seemed to be swelling with tears, but it didn't rain. I wished that it would let go and put me out of my misery—I ached for some sunshine—but as the days drawled on, the sky stayed the same numbing color, and nothing fell from the clouds.

Hannah and Jack walked to all their classes together. When they had different classes, he dropped her off at hers and barely made it to his. I envied that, too; he looked so happy. I wondered why he never told me about her.

Because you make a big deal of everything, my conscience told me.

Do not, I responded.

Do too. That's why September is growing tired of you.

Growing tired of me? Am I really that bad?

A chill went up my spine. I shook it off and tried to focus on calculus.

A sharp vibration against my leg made me jump in my seat. The people in the seats around me glanced out of the corner of their eyes before refocusing on their work. My hand slid into my pocket, and I retrieved my phone, making a mental note to take the vibration setting off later.

I quickly unlocked the screen and pulled up my messages. I found a text from Marcus.

Are you doing anything today?

I made sure the teacher wasn't looking before responding.

No. Can I come over?

Yeah. After school?

I was thankful that he texted. I wasn't going to waste a second in apologizing to him. I'd already screwed up my friendship with Jack, and my relationship with September was unstable; I wasn't about to lose the last person I cared about. *No. I'll come now.*

Gathering my things and pocketing my phone, I abruptly stood up from my desk and made it out the classroom door in a few strides. The teacher didn't even seem fazed, probably because leaving calculus was pretty normal for me. There was no telling how many times I'd not shown up for that class or left early. At some point, she gave up trying to send me to the office.

It had been a week and a half since I had last seen Marcus. I wondered if he would look any different. Could he really change all that much in just eleven days?

Thankfully, Dad lent me his truck for the week; I didn't have to ask anyone for rides. I turned up the radio as loud as it would go to drown out my thoughts on the way to Marcus' house. Thinking had proved dangerous for me lately.

I pulled into his driveway with a pit in my stomach and a determination to make things right. I forced myself up the front steps, raised my hand to the door, and knocked.

I was wrong. He did look different.

He looked skinnier. Thinner. Paler. He was dressed in a pair of sweatpants and a long-sleeved shirt a size too big for him. His left hand was still wrapped in a cast though it was a different color than the one he got after the wreck. His fingers weren't as purple, but they still looked terrible. Despite all this, though, he still managed to smile at me. His smile convinced me that he was still Marcus.

"Hey, Reed. How's it going?"

I raised an eyebrow, still shocked at his appearance and happy to see him again. I let out a short laugh. "I'm alright, man. How are you?"

I hugged him, patting his back. He laughed. "Actually, I'm doing better. Come on in."

I lingered awkwardly in the hallway as he shut the door. He led me back to his bedroom where I could see the paused image of a movie on the screen. He turned off the television and leaned against the bed frame.

Marcus's room was simple. I'd been here a billion times over the years, seen it evolve as we grew up. When we were in elementary school, the walls bore posters of trains and the floor was littered with little train sets that he'd gotten for his birthday. Now, as seniors in high school, the walls stood almost bare. He had only a desk and chair, a bed, a bookshelf, and a TV mounted to the wall.

"What's been going on, man?" he asked, leaning against the bed frame. "Take a seat. Catch up. Let's start with why your face is covered in a lovely shade of purple."

I pulled the desk chair out and straddled it backwards, leaning on the top of it with both arms. "Nothing much here, man. Just bruises from the car shop; I guess that concussion is making me clumsier. Tom and I are rebuilding Charlotte. I took Em to Homecoming, too."

"Oh, yeah. I heard about that."

"What'd you hear?"

"Just that you two were out all night." He grinned. "Nothing bad. September told me that she had a lot of fun."

"Really? Has she been here?"

"Yeah." He shifted his weight awkwardly. Her name seemed to brighten his mood, though, and he offered a small smile. "Yeah, Em has been here a few times. She came after my surgery and hung out on Sunday afternoon. We play video games whenever she's over. She brings me food and never lets me pay her back."

Typical September.

171

"How did your surgery go?" I asked, nodding to his hand. I felt guilty for not calling and checking on him.

"Fine. I have to have a cast for a while, but my hand should heal back to normal. September said she's going to come over before she leaves and make it look like part of an Iron Man suit." He grinned widely. "A little ambitious, don't you think?"

"Sounds like her," I agreed.

"She mentioned something about you and Jack when she left on Sunday. Is everything okay?"

I nodded, then shrugged, then sighed. "I don't know. No, I guess not."

"Did you really get those bruises from the car shop?"

I shook my head, pausing for a moment before speaking. "Courtesy of Jack."

"You're serious? What did you two have to fight over?"

The mattress sunk beneath me as I plopped down onto it. "September."

"What about her?"

"He thinks I'm moping too much over her."

"Are you?"

"What? No—I love her."

His eyes went wide. "*Oh...* Wow. Good for you."

"What's that supposed to mean?"

"Nothing, just... Are you sure you love her? Are you sure you aren't just, I don't know... obsessed?"

"I'm not obsessed—at least, not anymore."

He held his hands up. "Sorry, man. Just had to be sure. There is a difference, you know."

"I know, Mark," I snapped. "Jack already covered it."

His eyebrows drew together. "Whoa, man."

"What *now*?"

"What's up with you? I think I see what Jack was talking about now. Are you sure you've even considered what he's been saying?"

172

"Of course I've considered it," I barked, "but none of it is true."

"Are you sure?"

"Of course I'm sure!"

"Reed, stop yelling at me and shut up for a second. I want you to think really hard. What have you done that's made Jack angry?"

"I—"

"Think harder. What did he tell you that you did?"

Grudgingly, I closed my mouth and did my best to think back. What did he yell at me for? Moping? Getting angry?

Yeah, that sounded about right.

"I told you. He thinks I'm moping."

"And?"

"I don't know—maybe I get angry too easily?"

"And?"

This time, the reason I gave was not something that Jack had gotten onto me for doing. "I've kind of neglected him. And you."

"Do you see why he's angry?"

I shrugged my shoulders. "I guess so."

"You've got to get out of your head," he told me. "You're so focused on your emotions that you're not seeing anything else around you. You've turned into a completely different person; the Reed I knew never fought with any of us, and he *sure* didn't yell at September. You're hurting Jack. You're hurting Em." He cracked his joints on his right hand and paced a little. "I'd say you're hurting me, too, but I kind of did this to myself."

I took a long look at Marcus. He looked sunken, more hollow than the last time I saw him, which scared me; it wasn't that long ago that we were in that car accident. His knuckles were taped, and on his other hand, the new cast was plastered and wrapped in a dark gray color. My eyes wandered to his wall, and I found several large circles in a slightly lighter shade than the rest of the wall where holes were patched up.

He'd broken another cast.

Despite all the problems Marcus had, he seemed different to me now. For once, he was consoling me, giving me direction—not the other way around.

Well, he has had plenty of time to think.

The mattress sank and made a small creak as he sat down, bringing me back to reality.

"Listen, Reed," he said, his gaze locked on the patchy wall. "September isn't dying."

I wanted to protest, but for once, I shut my mouth and kept it closed.

"She's not dying. She's moving to a different country. Sure, it's far, but it's not forever away. If you love her, save up your money. Buy a plane ticket. Go see her.

"You know what she told me? She's *excited* to go. She's always wanted to go to England, and now she gets to go to college there if she wants to. She'll miss us. Believe me, I know she will. We're going to miss her, too, but it isn't the last time we'll see her, okay?"

I nodded.

He finally looked at me. "I'm not mad at you. I'm not trying to give you a hard time, either, but you've *got* to give her a break. It wasn't her decision, but she's happy with it anyway. Don't make this any harder for her—or Jack—than you have to, okay?"

My response came out weak. "Okay."

"Good. Now, do you want to mope around, or do you want to play some video games?"

I laughed, shifting the chair around to help him set up his gaming system. Once he'd turned it on and inserted "Call of Duty" into the console, we sat on the floor and started playing.

"So." I kept my eyes trained on the screen. "How are you?"

"Me?"

"Yeah, you. You haven't been at school in over a week."

"Oh," he said. "That."

"Yeah, that."

He sighed, but kept playing the game. "I'm on medication now. I was totally against it, but I haven't hit the wall in a couple days, so maybe it's working."

"It is?"

"I guess so. I don't feel like destroying anything right now. I don't know; it's weird. I have good days and bad days. I kind of feel like I'm in a bubble."

"Do you feel… okay?"

He shrugged. "I'm just glad that I'm not itching to break my hand again, okay? Being angry is exhausting. They told me it had something to do with stress and something in my brain that I didn't understand."

"How long do you have to take the medicine?"

"Something like six months. Sort of a test trial. You know, to see how well I respond to it."

"Dude, that's like, half a year."

"Wow, thanks, Sherlock. I'm gonna be fine, Reed; I feel better already. Honest."

I shifted in my spot, glancing at him in the corner of my eye. "Alright man. I'm glad you're okay."

He smirked. "Me too."

"I'm sorry I wasn't here."

"Forget it. I'm tired of dwelling on the past. And dude, I'm literally playing one-handed. If you shoot me one more time in this game, so help me, I'm taking that controller away from you."

———

Later that day, after spending a few hours with Marcus and catching up, I changed into work clothes and went back to the shop. When I got there, Tom was standing next to Lucy, who now showed off a glossy midnight blue.

"How much more work does she need?" I asked as I walked in.

"She's almost done," he answered, not looking up. "I started painting her after you left Saturday. I got the rims and seats back in today and the finish on it this morning. I'm going to let her cure until Wednesday, and then the owner should be here to pick her up."

"She looks great," I praised.

"She'll drive pretty nice, too." He turned around to look at me but did a double take when he saw me. "Dude, what happened to your face?"

"That's a real self-esteem booster," I said, throwing my sweatshirt onto the workbench.

"Cry me a river. Why is half of your face blue and purple?"

"I got punched."

"By who?"

I exhaled. "Do you want to work on the car, or do you want to keep playing twenty questions?"

"Is it that hard just to answer a question?" he asked, his tone taking a sharp edge. "Who punched you and why?"

"Jack punched me," I snapped. "He's just a jerk."

"Him being a jerk isn't a reason to punch you. What did you do?"

I threw my hands up. "Why does everyone assume that I did something?"

He rolled his eyes at me. "Because we've met you. What did you do?"

"He thinks I've been neglecting him. He's just being a toddler."

"Or maybe you really have been neglecting him. He used to come here with you all the time, and now I rarely see him anymore."

"I got busy."

"You've always been busy."

"Okay, okay, I got it. I heard it already from Marcus earlier."

"Then why are you still arguing with me? Next time you see Jack, you need to apologize to him. Good? Great. Let's get to work."

I bit my lip to keep from arguing. Instead, I pointed over to the half-ton Chevy pickup. "How's Olivia?"

"She's almost done, too. I've got another week on her."

I scanned the garage, hunting for something to occupy my attention. "So is there anything for me to do here?"

"Yeah, actually." He moved around the Caprice and waved for me to follow him across the garage to a tarp-covered car. He pulled the tarp off, revealing Charlotte, still damaged. "Today is Charlotte's day."

Last time I saw her, wasn't the frame twisted up?

"Charlotte's day? Are you serious?"

"I've got extra time," he said with a shrug. "I used the machine and straightened the frame earlier today with my brother. Thank me later. Push that toolbox over here and let's get started."

I pushed the toolbox over to Tom, but instead of getting under the car, I moved to the driver's side where the door was already taken off and leaning up against the body. I sat in the driver's seat and found the key—which hadn't been taken out of the ignition since the wreck—and turned it. Charlotte stalled a couple of times, but eventually, she started up.

"Wow," I said, astounded. "She runs."

"Doesn't mean that she's road ready." Tom put a hand on the top and leaned against it. "But yeah, she'll start."

I turned her off and left the key in the ignition. "I can't wait to get her back on the road."

"We have a lot of work ahead," he commented. "Where do you want to start?"

"First, I'm going to go get the top out of dumpster," I said, moving to the back door.

"That thing is trash."

"That thing is Charlotte's," I corrected. "And anything can be fixed. I'll work on hammering it out. You can work on whatever you want."

I could hear him muttering the words *stupid* and *crazy* under his breath as I went out back to get Charlotte's top. I laughed. Charlotte was getting fixed up; nothing could sour my mood.

Right?

12

what happens at the drive-in stays at the drive-in

"Are you busy tonight?" I asked September as we walked out to the school parking lot together.

"I don't think so. Why?"

"We're going back to the drive-in. We've got another item to cross off your bucket list."

That familiar, bright smile blossomed across her lips. "Sounds great. Have you told Marcus and Jack yet?"

I shook my head. "I haven't told Marcus yet."

"Jack?"

I shrugged. "I wasn't going to ask him."

"I will, then," she said.

I looked at her.

"What? Just because you aren't talking to him doesn't mean I'm not. I want all my friends in one place. Sue me."

I shook my head but didn't say anything. We got to our cars and hugged goodbye.

"The movie is at 7:30," I told her.

"I'll be at my house packing."

"I'll pick you up at seven then."

She nodded before getting in her car and driving away.

I sat in the front seat of the truck and dialed Marcus's number. He picked up on the second ring.

"Hey, man."

"Hey," I said. "We're going to the drive-in tonight. Do you want to come?"

"Sounds fun, but I can't. I'm sorry."

"Why not?"

"I'm meeting my tutors tonight. My parents invited them over for dinner. They decided to have me at least finish this semester at home. They want me to decompress or something like that."

I blinked. "Wow."

"Yeah, I feel fine so far, but they want to give me space. I'm not particularly sad about not going back to GHS yet anyway. It's not like it's forever."

"Well, I hope it works out."

"Thanks. Sorry I can't come with you."

"Maybe next time. We'll all hang out before September leaves."

"Sounds great. I'll talk to you later."

"Bye."

The line went dead, and I settled back into my seat, exhaling before starting up the car. I was still worried about Marcus, but at the moment, he seemed fine.

Seven o'clock snuck up on me before I realized what time it was. At ten till seven, I hopped out the door with one shoe on, two coats, and a huge quilt under my arm. I threw everything into the cab and jumped into the truck, rushing to pick up September. I ended up pulling into her driveway with a minute to spare.

I quickly put on my other shoe and turned off the truck. My sneakers made a thud against the pavement as I jumped out and made my way up to her front door, pressing the doorbell once I got there.

September swung open the door, and immediately her eyes went up to my hair. She grinned.

"Did you not have enough time to look in a mirror?" she asked.

"What do you mean?"

She pulled her phone out of the back pocket of her jeans and took a picture of me then turned the screen around to show me. The bruises on my face were still there but had faded to a more yellowish color. I looked past my confused expression up to my hair, which stuck straight up on my head. I quickly pressed my hands to the top of my head, trying to calm the mess.

"Here." She reached up onto her toes and scraped her hands through my hair. "There. That's better."

She adjusted her big, gray sweater on her shoulders and reached behind her to close the door. "Holy crap, it's cold today."

"I know. I wish it would just snow already. I put a blanket and a couple coats in the car, so maybe we won't freeze. Oh, and Marcus isn't coming. He's got tutor stuff."

She nodded, walking down the steps next to me. "Jack isn't coming tonight, either."

"Didn't want to see me?" I asked.

"He has a date," she said. "With Hannah Stephens."

I raised my eyebrows. "Wow. Are they serious?"

"I think so. He told me that he really likes her."

"Hmm."

She nudged my arm. "What is it?"

"Nothing," I said, smiling at her. "Hey, do you want to go on a date tonight?"

She laughed. "With who?"

"With me, of course," I teased. "Come on. I'm a great date."

"On a Tuesday night?" She rolled her eyes. "Sure, Reed."

I smirked. "Great. How about the movies?"

"We're going there, anyway."

"Exactly. I'll buy."

She shook her head at me and laughed as she got into the car. I ramped up the heat and turned on the radio before pulling out of her driveway.

"What movie is playing tonight?" she asked.

"I think they're playing a rerun of an older movie," I said. "I want to say it's a Disney movie."

"Yes!" she exclaimed. "I love Disney movies."

"You would."

"Don't pretend that you don't like them. I caught you watching *WallE* the other night. You fell asleep with the TV on."

"That doesn't count. *WallE* is a classic."

"Is not. *Up* is way better."

I scoffed. "Please. You were crying in the first fifteen minutes."

"It's sad!"

"And that makes it better than *WallE*? Not a chance."

Her playful glare made me grin as I pulled into the drive-in parking lot. Once I had paid the man at the ticket window, I found a spot to park and turned off the car but left the radio on. I tossed her a jacket and put one on myself before spreading out the quilt over our legs.

She pulled her feet up into the seat and tuned the radio to the station projected on the screen. It started playing the audio to match the ads on the screen. I turned it low so that we could talk until the movie started.

"I saw Marcus yesterday," I said, breaking the silence between us.

"Did you?" She turned in her seat and gave me a wide smile. "How is he?"

"Better than I expected." I traced the steering wheel with my thumb. "He has a new cast on his hand."

"Oh, yeah. He broke the last one a few days after he got home from the hospital."

I shook my head. "I can't believe that he was so angry. It was like it all of a sudden became a part of him."

"Not even a part of him. It was more like a parasite. It took him over bit by bit until he couldn't hide it from us anymore." I looked at her, confused. She shrugged. "His words, not mine."

"Well, he seemed better when I was there. He's on medication."

"Yeah, he told me."

I almost told September about Marcus's advice for me, but I decided against it. I didn't want to make a big deal out of anything. I was just going to keep my mouth shut and do my best to stop showing September whenever I was angry. It stressed her out, and she already had enough on her plate. Maybe by holding back, I could take myself off her list of things to worry about.

The opening credits of the movie played, so I turned up the radio. The sun was already setting on the horizon and darkening the sky. We watched as the title screen for *Up* appeared on the screen.

"Told you it was the best," she whispered, though no one else was around to hear us.

"You're still wrong," I whispered back.

She bit her lip to keep from laughing. "You're still an idiot."

As expected, fifteen minutes into the movie, September's eyes were glistening. I'd stopped paying attention to the screen a few minutes before, and now I just watched her.

"Em," I whispered. "Em, are you crying?"

"It's sad." She sniffed. "Yeah, I'm crying."

"This is why *WallE* is better."

She reached over, and without warning popped me on the shoulder. "Shut up and watch the movie, Reed."

I smiled, settling back into my seat to watch the movie. The beginning actually was pretty sad. I didn't admit it to September, though.

"Hey, Reed?"

"Hey, Em?"

"It's kind of cold in here."

"Yeah," I agreed, opening my mouth to exhale. My breath turned to white fog. "It's pretty cold."

"Can we turn the car on?"

I shook my head, giving her an apologetic smile. "I can't leave it running through the entire movie." I raised an eyebrow at her, teasing her with my expression. "You can scoot closer, if you want."

"Not a chance, Davis."

"Come on. You said you were cold."

She thought about it for a moment, then groaned. "Fine."

She scooted to the middle of the bench seat and wrapped the excess quilt around her body. She leaned into me for some warmth.

"You're freezing," I noted as her cold cheek came into contact with my arm. "Holy crap."

"I told you."

I leaned my head down and rested it on hers. "You'll warm up in a minute."

"Thanks, Reed."

The rest of the movie played on, occasionally interrupted by comments we made to each other. Everything I said was aimed to make September laugh, and I succeeded more than once. I loved the way it sounded. She even pulled out the Polaroid camera to snap a picture of the movie through the windshield. We both warmed up quickly sitting next to each other.

When the closing credits played, we stayed in the same position. I wondered for a moment if she'd fallen asleep, but she spoke quietly to me after a few minutes of silence.

"Thanks for the date, Reed."

"Don't mention it. I had fun."

"Me too. I had a lot of fun."

Cars started pulling out of the parking lot around us. I expected her to move back to her side of car, but she didn't. She stayed put.

I looked down at her. Her cheeks were slightly pink with the cold and her eyes were closed, just enjoying the peace.

Man, I love her.

"You're so beautiful," I whispered.

She smiled but didn't open her eyes. "You're funny."

"I'm not joking. You're perfect."

That made her sit up straight and look at me. Her eyes were guarded, her voice nervous. "What brought this on?"

I shrugged, looking back out at the screen to avoid her gaze. She wasn't having it, though, and she turned my chin back towards her.

"I don't know."

"Yeah, you do. Come on. What's on your mind?"

I met her dark eyes. They were so sincere; it was hard to lie to them. I opened my mouth and closed it again before mustering the courage to speak.

"I'm in love," I said, looking back at her.

Her eyes went wide and her eyebrows raised, but she didn't falter. "With who?"

I swallowed hard before letting the next words tumble off my lips, my knee bouncing up and down without my permission. "With you."

Her lips parted, and I could hear her breath hitch. "You love... me?"

I could feel my pulse in my ears as I waited for her response, but I didn't get one. She just kept looking at me, speechless in the dead quiet of the car. In a moment of bold confidence, I raised a hand up to her cheek. To my relief, she leaned into it, closing her eyes for a forever long second before opening them again.

I swallowed hard. "Can I kiss you?"

She didn't speak, but she nodded. That was enough for me.

My lips met hers in a moment of rushing emotion. My eyes were closed, just feeling the moment, feeling the softness of her cheek and her lips. It was a wave of relief. Month after month of just wanting the perks of calling her mine held no competition to the few days I spent in love with September Jones. It seemed like the wait had been five years long. A fire shot up my spine, making my muscles tense.

She pulled away. I opened my eyes but saw that hers were still closed.

I ran my thumb against her cheek, almost afraid to speak. "Okay?"

Her eyes opened, and I could see that she was crying.

"Em?"

"I'm fine," she whispered. "I'm sorry."

"Don't apologize. You did nothing wrong."

"I'm so sorry," she repeated. "I can't do this."

My heart came to an abrupt halt in my chest. "Do what?"

"This." She gestured between us. "I'm sorry, Reed. I can't."

I could feel the anger fighting with my conscience, struggling to come out through my words. I forced it down and kept my tone soft. "Why not?"

"It's not you. I can't have a relationship with you, not now. I'm moving around the world in less than two weeks."

"We could make it work," I offered quietly.

"No." She shook her head and dried her eyes with her sleeve. "We couldn't. I'm sorry, Reed. I can't do this. Especially not now."

I remembered her holding my hand, kissing my cheek, dancing with me. I remembered how she laid her head on my shoulder. Now she was telling me that we couldn't do this?

"You've sort of paved the way for this," I said. "You can't do things like hold my hand and not expect me to feel something."

"I know, I—"

"Why?"

She blinked, wiping a tear from her cheek. "What do you mean?"

My eyes studied her eyes, her expression, her lips. I turned back to the front of the car, looking forward but not focusing on anything.

"Why did you do this to me?"

She couldn't have been quiet for more than a few seconds, but it felt like an eternity. When she did answer, her voice came out soft and broken.

"Because—because I thought... I thought maybe..."

"Maybe what?"

"I thought we *could* make it work, okay?" she admitted. "I felt something for you that I didn't mean to feel. I thought we could make it work, but I was wrong. I was treading into dangerous territory, and I realized it too late. That's why I have to end it here, Reed. We can't do this— not when I'm about to move 5,000 miles away."

I didn't answer. It angered me that she did this, that she led me on, even if she didn't mean to do it. I felt used.

Is this how she feels when she's with me?

"I'm sorry," she repeated.

I shook my head. "It's okay. I understand."

Do I? Of course I do.

Do I agree with it? Not one bit.

Am I going to give her a hard time? Make things worse than I already have?

I looked back at her. I could feel the anger rising, banging on the bars of its cage deep in my chest. The emotions threatened to override my brain.

No.

Not this time.

I offered her a weak smile. "Let's go home, yeah?"

She looked at me and nodded, drying her tears. "Yeah."

Once again, I expected her to move back to her seat, but she didn't. She lifted her head and gave me a little more space, but she stayed put next to me as I turned the car on and pulled back onto the road.

September switched on the radio to fill the silence. It was quiet, but loud enough for us to hear in the empty air of the car. The cab warmed up as the heating system got going.

The good thing about living in Oregon was that no matter where you drove, you could find a scenic route somewhere. Greenville was the perfect example. Since it was situated so close to Cascade Locks, it wasn't unusual to see a stream, a creek, or part of the Columbia River when you drove. Evergreen trees were everywhere, too; since we lived in such a small town, there were plenty of roads just surrounded by evergreens on both sides.

Instead of going straight home, I took one of the scenic routes. It was only a few minutes longer, and I knew it would cheer up September. It was one long road surrounded by evergreen trees, usually empty. I expected it to rain—it had been cloudy all day—but the sky held in its tears.

I veered onto Greenville Grove and turned up the radio as a good song came on the station. I rolled down the windows, letting in the cool air. It brushed against our faces.

September smiled at me before moving to the opposite side of the car. She put her hand out the window, letting the air push against it and dance between her fingers. Her gaze fixed along the evergreens moving fast on either side of us.

She sat up on the seat and put her head out the window, closing her eyes and letting the wind run through her hair. I saw her smile grow wider.

I was caught off guard when she screamed into the dark, empty street, her voice carrying off in the wind. She looked back at me.

"Come on, Reed. You know you want to."

I shook my head and laughed. "No way."

"Have a little fun for once in your life. Go on. Let it all out."

I could feel her eyes on me as I leaned my arm on the window and stuck my head out. I took a deep breath and yelled as loudly as I could. She laughed, turning to do the same out her window. We screamed into the night, all our emotions melting and trailing away with the rushing winds. Our voices echoed down the empty street, fading in with the sounds of the brushing trees.

I did love September. I knew deep down that she was right; neither of us could handle the distance. I also knew that somewhere she felt something for me, too.

No matter how I felt, that would have to be enough for now.

13

the re-run of *i love lucy*

"She's ready," Tom said, opening the driver's side door and gesturing to it. "You want to drive her?"

"*Me?*"

"Do you see anyone else here?" He tossed me the keys, and I caught them with one hand before he rounded the car and moved towards the garage door button on the wall. "Pull her out of the garage, will you? The client should be here in a few minutes."

Tom hit the button, and the door started retracting upwards. I slid into the new leather seats, holding my breath as if a small breeze would break something. I gingerly slid the key into the ignition and started the car. It started up on the first turn, making a lovely purring sound.

Tom gave me a thumbs up. "She sounds great!" he yelled over the sound of the engine.

I shut the driver's side door and shifted gears. I inched the car forward out of the garage, not allowing myself to exhale until I cleared the doors and pulled out into the small parking lot. As soon as I was in a good position, I parked, cut the engine, and removed the keys. I was out of the driver's seat in a matter of seconds.

"That wasn't so bad," Tom said, walking out to the car.

"Speak for yourself." I folded my arms in, wrapping them around myself to preserve body heat. The garage was usually warm, meaning I always wore short sleeves when working on the cars. The temperature had stayed steady at 45 degrees for the past week, though, so my t-shirt did little to keep me warm.

Tom circled the car, admiring our work. "She looks good, yeah?"

"Yeah. Hopefully, he'll like her."

"He will. This car looks too good for him not to like her." He shoved his hands into his pockets to keep them warm. "Listen, after this guy gets his car, go on home. I don't want you to have to work the day before Thanksgiving, and neither do I. If you show up tomorrow, you're sitting outside the garage because I won't be here."

Wow. Thanksgiving snuck up on us.

Things had been so crazy that I hadn't even been paying attention to the calendar. I'd forgotten we were on break until September reminded me.

"Sounds good," I agreed.

I shifted on my feet, scanning the product of our handy work. Lucy really was a beautiful car. The body shone a brilliant, dark, midnight blue. The rims were polished, and the black leather on the interior was smooth and pristine. I even added a little tree air freshener for good measure. Lucy ranked pretty close to the top on the list of my favorite cars to roll through Tom's shop.

"Who did you say owns this car?" I asked Tom.

"I didn't."

"Well, who is it?"

He pointed to the road where a sleek, black Audi rolled its way up towards the shop. "He's right there."

My jaw dropped open as I recognized Jack's familiar car pull into the parking lot next to us. The engine turned off. Jack stepped out of the driver's side, and a man I had never seen before got out on the passenger side.

"Thomas O'Brien," the man said with a grin, slamming the door behind him and stepping forward to shake Tom's hand. "The car is beautiful. I could see it from up the road."

Jack stood solemnly on the opposite side of his Audi, leaning up against it onto his elbows. He avoided looking at me.

Tom shook his hand, slapping his shoulder before nodding his head towards me. "I had a lot of help, Greg. This is Reed Davis. He's been working with me since he was sixteen."

The man, Greg, turned to me and shook my hand, too. "Well done, kid. Lucy has never looked better."

I smiled politely and nodded. "Thank you, sir."

"Say, I've heard your name before. Have we met?"

"Reed goes to school with me," Jack interjected. "You don't know him."

Greg seemed so happy with the car that he couldn't bear not inspecting it any longer. He rounded the vehicle several times, his smile wide the entire time. He opened the doors, ran his hand over the upholstery, admired the paint; he looked like he'd been told he won the lottery.

"Can I drive her?" he asked, closing the passenger side doors.

"Your car," Tom pointed out. "Reed has the keys."

I held out Lucy's keys to Greg. He shook his head.

"How impolite of me," Greg said. "Reed, do you want to drive her? You worked so hard on this, I'd hate for you not to get to take her out for a spin."

I shook my head. "I'm fine, thank you."

"Oh, come on, now. You know you'd like to. I don't mind."

"I pulled her out of the garage, sir. That was enough for me. I don't want to take the chance of ruining something."

He shrugged. "If you insist."

Suddenly, he seemed to remember Jack still standing at his car silently. He waved him over to us. "Reed, are you and Jack friends?"

"No," Jack answered for me. "No, I don't know him."

I looked at Jack. He didn't look back.

I wanted to tell his uncle that we had met, just to spite him, but decided against it. I didn't want to have to pretend to be nice to him.

"Jack, you and Reed take Lucy out for a test drive," Greg said.

"You're trusting me with your car?"

"You're paying for it to be fixed if you mess it up, so yes, I'm trusting you with my car. Don't mess her up."

Jack took the keys from my still outstretched hand and moved towards the car. "I can drive it myself. I don't need a chaperone."

"Quit being moody and be nice, Jack." Greg ignored Jack's foul tone. "Make a friend. Reed's riding with you."

"It's really fine, sir," I interrupted.

"You boys just get in the car and go for a drive while I settle the cost with Thomas," he said, his tone leaving no room for argument. "Be back no earlier than 3:30."

I pulled my phone out of my pocket and checked the time. 3:10. My eyes shifted up to Tom who looked at me with a smug smile. I made a mental note to give him a good punch to the shoulder.

Great. Twenty minutes in a confined space with the kid who wants to put my head through a wall.

Begrudgingly, I got into the car on the passenger side and shut the door. Jack did the same, the car moving back and forth from the amount of force he put into slamming the door. His uncle flashed him a look through the windshield, but he ignored it and started the engine.

Jack swerved out of the parking lot quicker than I ever would have, not seeming to care how reckless his driving was. He pulled straight out onto the road and started driving at fifty miles an hour, ten miles over the speed limit, gripping the steering wheel so hard that his knuckles turned white.

"Slow down, speed demon," I muttered, looking out the window.

"Shut up," he said, his tone annoyed. "You don't talk to me, I won't talk to you, and we'll both get out of this car in one piece. Got it?"

I wanted to argue with him, but again, Marcus's advice kept running through my head. So instead of taking out all my anger on him for being such a jerk, I kept my mouth shut. I looked out the window and didn't do anything that would possibly make him angry.

Five minutes into the ride, he spoke.

"You're something, Reed Davis."

I looked over at him. He kept his eyes on the road. "So I've heard. What did I do?"

"That's just it. Shouldn't you have done something by now?"

"I'm not sure I know what you mean."

"You haven't made any comments. You haven't tried to get on my nerves. You haven't told me to pull over so you could punch me again. What's up with you?"

"You act like it's a bad thing."

"Not at all." He settled back into the driver's seat, his hands now more relaxed on the steering wheel. "I'm just wondering what strange angel-demon possessed you."

"I'm not possessed," I snapped. "I just talked to Marcus."

"So, you finally went to see him? What did he say?"

"Nothing interesting. He just reminded me of stuff I should've already known."

"Like?"

I shifted in my seat. "Why are you talking to me, man? I thought you were about to crash the car a few minutes ago, you were so mad."

"I'm still mad at you, but I want to know why you aren't whatever you were a few days ago."

"I'm still me. I'm just a slightly smarter version of me."

"Smarter isn't a good word. It's more like you grew a heart."

"Listen, I'm just trying really hard not to start any more fights. I'm trying to give you guys a break. It wasn't easy before, and you aren't making it any easier."

"By *guys*, you mean—"

"You and September, who else?"

I don't know if he realized it or not, but the car slowed down. I was glad I no longer had to worry about dying in a wreck.

Not that dying in a beautiful car like that one would be all that bad. I mean, come on. It was a nice car.

"Well," he said awkwardly, "good for you, Reed."

"Yeah," I muttered. "Good for me."

"Just... don't explode on anyone, okay?"

I raised my eyebrows. "Explode?"

"Yeah. Find an outlet or something. Don't let it all get pent up."

I rolled my eyes. "You just got angry at me for punching you when I was angry, and now that I've stopped you want me to find an outlet? Maybe you should go back to ignoring me. I think I'd take that over Dr. Phil."

"About that," he said, turning down a neighborhood street. "I'm kind of tired of being mad. It's a little exhausting."

"So?"

He shrugged. "What, do you expect me to apologize first? You threw the first punch, man."

"Are you seriously going to be like that?"

"I'm waiting for an apology, lover boy."

I almost choked. *"Lover boy?"*

He grinned. "Like it? I came up with it the day after you broke my nose."

"Whoa. Did I really break it?"

"Nah, I just said that to make you feel better. Now come on, apologize."

195

I sighed. "Are you serious?"

"Deadly."

"Fine," I snapped. "I'm sorry for punching you in the face."

"And?"

"Yelling at you."

"And?"

"Ignoring you."

"And?"

"And if you say *and* one more time, I'm grabbing the steering wheel and putting this car in a ditch."

"Fine," he said. "Apology accepted."

"Great."

For a few seconds, it grew quiet. I looked at him expectantly.

"Well?"

"Well what?" he asked.

"Aren't you going to apologize to me?"

"Oh, that. Sorry for breaking your face."

"You didn't break my face."

"You're right, I'm sorry. It looked like that before I beat you up."

Without warning, I jabbed him hard in the stomach, causing him to swerve a little into the opposite lane.

"Hey!" he exclaimed, holding his stomach. "I'm driving!"

"My bad. I didn't notice."

He exhaled hard, obviously a little aggravated at me. "Just be glad that we only have a few more minutes in here."

"How sad," I mocked. "I wanted to spend eternity in this car with you, Jack."

He groaned. "Shut up, already."

Jack maneuvered the car back into the parking lot a few minutes later. Tom and Greg were no longer standing around in the parking lot, so Jack cut the engine and we headed towards the garage door.

"How was Marcus?" he asked, as he approached the door. He stopped with his hand on the handle. "When you saw him. How was he?"

"Thin," I admitted. "But he's better than I expected him to be."

He nodded, as if he knew exactly what I was talking about. "Yeah. Apparently, one of the side effects of his medication is weight loss. It's kind of scary, isn't it?"

I remembered his tired, sunken face greeting me at the door after his long absence. "He doesn't look like himself."

"He does to me," Jack said. "Somehow, he looks like a healthier version of himself. Old Marcus wouldn't listen to any reason. It's like this whole experience has... I don't know, changed his outlook. The medication seems to be helping him feel better, though, and if it makes him feel better, I'm all for it."

He pushed open the door, and we were hit with a gust of warm air. The change in temperature made the ends of my fingers tingle as they warmed up.

The sound of Tom and Greg laughing echoed in the garage and resounded against the metal walls. Greg spotted us as we walked into the building.

"Reed." He waved me over. "How much do I owe you?"

"That's up to you, sir," I answered, weaving around several cars to stand beside them. They were waiting next to Charlotte, covered in a gray tarp.

"This car is yours, is she not?" he asked, gesturing to my car.

I nodded. "Yes, sir."

"And I understand there's a lot of repair work to be done to her."

"Yes, sir."

He pulled his checkbook and a pen out of his pocket, licking the tip of the pen before putting it to the paper. He scribbled out a number and showed me.

"This should cover your labor and just a little extra to help you finish your car. Is this enough?"

I couldn't pull my jaw up to meet my mouth. I wanted to say something, but the words wouldn't form in my mouth.

"That's very generous," Tom answered for me. "Thank you. Reed appreciates it; he's just in shock."

"The car is beautiful," he praised again, sliding two checks into an envelope he'd picked up off the work bench. "You two deserve every penny. I trust you'll find something good to spend your check on, Thomas."

Tom shrugged. "More car parts."

They laughed as Greg gestured for Jack to join us. "Jack, how did she run?"

"Great." He tossed Greg the keys. "Smooth."

"Good. I'm driving her home." He looked between Jack and me. "Will I be seeing more of you two hanging out together?"

"Believe me, sir," I said, finally finding words, "we'll be around each other a lot."

That seemed to satisfy him. "Great. I'm going to head on; make sure your parents know where you are, Jack."

"Will do."

With a playful salute and a slap to Tom's back, Greg moved back around the cars and out the front door. We listened as Lucy's engine roared to life then faded into the sounds of other cars on the road.

"It's been awhile, Jack," Tom said.

"Too long," he agreed.

"You aren't going on another long, depressing leave of absence, are you?" Tom flashed a look at me. "This one gets moody."

"Hey!"

"I'm probably not much better," Jack said.

"I beg to differ."

"I'm right here, Tom."

He shrugged. "I know."

Jack nodded towards the envelope in Tom's hand. "How much did my uncle pay you guys for the car?"

"More than Reed needs."

"Speak for yourself," I interjected. "I have a whole Scout II to rebuild."

Tom handed the envelope to Jack. "He gave Reed $3,000."

Jack raised his eyebrows. "You're joking. $3,000?"

"No, I'm not. Charlotte better be looking good by the time we're finished with her. We have a nice little budget to work off of to get her back onto the road."

Jack handed the envelope to me, which Tom then took out of my hands. "I don't trust him to hold the checks. He might fall and drop them in oil or something."

I rolled my eyes. "Whatever."

Tom pulled his check from the envelope and handed it back to me, folding his own in half and putting it in his pocket. "Didn't I tell you that you could go home after Greg got his car? What are you still doing here?"

"He only left, like, three minutes ago."

"You've been here three minutes too long, then. Get out. I want to go home."

"Quit complaining."

"Get out of my garage."

I held my hands up over my head and followed Jack to the door. We waved at Tom as we left.

"What are you doing this weekend?" Jack asked as we unlocked our cars.

"Stuffing my face with food," I said. "Mark would be proud."

"Besides that. Any plans on Saturday?"

I thought for a moment, then shook my head. "No, not that I know of. What's up?"

"Nothing, right now. It's just, well…" He ran a hand through his hair. "September leaves next week. I figured we should all try to make the most of the next few days, you know?"

Oh. Right.

Less than ten days.

"Yeah," I agreed. "Yeah, you're right. I'll text you and see if we can get something worked out."

"Sounds good," he said. "It's crazy how fast it snuck up on us."

"I know. We spent most of it at each other's throats, anyway."

He laughed a humorless laugh, leaning on his car. "I'm sure September has had a great last month. We sure made it easy."

"*I* sure made it easy. She's got to have a special place somewhere in her heart dedicated to strangling me."

"If she ever did, it's probably gone. You know she'd feel guilty for even thinking bad about any of us."

We laughed because we both knew he was right. September couldn't stand being mean to people. Even the snarky remarks she gave us took a while for us to coax out of her; she grew into sarcasm when she moved to Greenville. She wasn't always the outspoken, opinionated girl that she appeared to be.

I wondered what September would be like when she moved to England. Would she still be outspoken and cheerful? Would she still make jokes about us? Would she make friends easily?

"I'm going to head in," Jack said, interrupting my thoughts. "I'll text you later."

"Okay." He started to get into his car. I stopped him. "Hey, Jack?"

"Yeah?"

"Thanks for forgiving me. I was a real jerk to you."

He grinned. "It's all good. Besides, I really did put you on that skateboard just to watch you fall. I guess that makes us even."

Before I could say anything else, he slammed his car door and jammed his key in the ignition. He was out of the parking lot before I could even process what he'd said.

14
low quality pictures, high quality memories

September's parents called her early on Thanksgiving morning, apologizing profusely for not being there to spend Thanksgiving with her. Being the person she is, she told them not to worry and reassured them that she was fine. They also told her that they booked her plane ticket for December 1st—a whole week after Thanksgiving. They reminded her to pack up everything she could and get it ready to be shipped a few days before her flight.

She spent an hour on the phone, listening to her dad tell her all about Cambridge and how much she'd love it there. I could hear her pacing the upstairs hallway as she listened, laughing and agreeing with him where it was necessary. I tried not to be too hurt, but to tell you the truth, it was hard. She was leaving in one week.

Without me.

I could feel that anger that I'd been suppressing for the past couple of days fighting at my throat. Why did she have to leave? Why didn't she care? Why didn't she make an effort to stay?

I knew the answer to all of those questions, but my brain convinced me otherwise. I had an impulse that was telling me to hit something, yell at someone, do *something*.

But I didn't.

I pressed the boiling emotions back into my chest, forcing them down so that they wouldn't bubble over. I felt like I might explode, but I did my best to ignore it. I put on a smile, and when she came downstairs, politely asked her how her parents were. Seeing her smile as she talked about them and their new house and their new life was enough to make me forget about the pressure building in my ribs. At least, for a little while.

My parents made sure to set a place for September at our dinner table. My mom spent all day long in the kitchen working on dinner. September got up before me and had volunteered to help Mom out. Mom made sure to let me know (multiple times) what a great house guest September was.

As if I didn't already know.

Dad and I spent the day picking up extra groceries that Mom needed. We went in and out of the house several times that day, and every time I walked through the front door, the aroma got sweeter and sweeter.

"That smells amazing," I commented, helping Dad carry in grocery bags and set them on the counters. I put down my bags and pulled out the flowers we picked up while we were out, handing one bouquet to Mom and the other to September.

"How good of a house guest is September, Mom?" I asked as she took the flowers from my hands. She got teary eyed as she hugged me.

"She's still a better house guest than you," she joked, sniffing as she hugged me tight. "Thank you for my flowers. They're beautiful."

"Thanks, Reed," September added. "How did you know I liked Autumn Joys?"

"Lucky guess," I said, remembering the bushels of Autumn Joys her mom had planted outside of her house.

"That's the last of it." Dad put the last of the bags onto the countertop. "Anything I can do to help, ladies?"

"Nothing that I know of," Mom answered. "Grab something small for lunch to hold you over until supper. We'll eat early tonight."

"Sounds great. Smells even better." I rubbed my hands together and inhaled deeply, taking in the savory scent of turkey and dressing in the oven. "Thanks, Mom."

"Thank September, too. She did half the work."

I leaned over the island counter to September, raising my eyebrows. "Thanks, Em."

"You're welcome." She shoved a flower in my face. "Here's a token of my affection."

I spit out a flower petal, backing off of the counter. "Right."

"September," Mom said, untying her bright yellow apron, "take a break. I'm almost done in here. I'm going to finish up then we'll be good to go until suppertime."

"Sounds good, Mrs. D." September untied her apron and hung it on the pantry door. "Thank you for letting me spend Thanksgiving with you guys."

"Don't thank me. You're welcome any time."

Em's warm smile was so radiant that I could practically feel the kitchen get a few degrees hotter.

We wandered out of the kitchen and into the living room where I plopped down on the couch and searched for the remote. September stayed standing, frowning at me.

I looked up at her. "What?"

"Why are you watching TV?"

"Why not?"

"It's pretty outside, and it's Thanksgiving," she said. "You're going to spend all day in here watching TV?"

"I was planning on it."

"No, you aren't." September found the remote before I did, picking it up from the floor and putting it all the way on the stand next to the TV.

"Hey! Give it to me!"

"Get up and get it yourself."

I put my arm out and reached as hard as I could, but my arm wasn't long enough.

"It isn't working," I complained.

"What isn't working? Your legs?"

"The Force. It won't work."

She rolled her eyes. "You're not cool enough to have the Force, Davis. Come on. Let's go outside and do something productive."

"Like what?"

"I still have Cora's Polaroid camera," she offered. "Can we drive around Greenville so I can get pictures of the town?"

I looked at her for a long moment, my grin reducing to a sort of sad smile.

"Yeah," I answered, nodding slowly. "Yeah, we can go. Let me go grab a jacket from upstairs then we'll go."

"Thanks. Will you grab me one, too?"

I lifted myself from the couch. "Sure."

She stood in front of me, and when I stood up, I ended up a lot closer to her than planned. After a moment of trying to decide what to do, I cleared my throat and moved around her to the staircase. As I turned to scoot past her, I scanned her expression. She smiled at me.

Holy crap, she's beautiful.

She didn't drop her gaze even when I reached the stairs, and I could feel her eyes on me until I made it to the second floor.

Once out of sight, I leaned my back against the wall and took a second. September did something to me that I had no control over. It was unknown. Terrifying.

And for some reason, I couldn't get enough.

With oxygen in my lungs, I walked up the hallway to my bedroom. The door stood slightly ajar, inviting me in. I pushed it open and drifted to my closet, pulling out my winter coat and a hat. I combed the room for September's jacket, finding it laid across the neatly made bed.

I reached the bed in two strides and was ready to head back downstairs when something caught my eye. As I bent down to get her jacket, I spotted it on my desk.

The bucket list, written in Mark's messy handwriting on that worn, wrinkled napkin.

It wasn't that I thought she'd thrown it away. I hadn't. I knew she'd want to keep it—she had a thing for items with a story behind them. What surprised me the most was that she kept up with it. I could see where she had crossed off the ones we'd done. *Hiking, concert, drive-in, shopping, Homecoming*. The only leftover items in Mark's handwriting were *Waffle House*, which she wanted to do right before she left for England, and *movie marathon*.

Those weren't the only things on the list though. September had added one at the bottom.

Take pictures of Greenville.

Next to the list, stacked in a neat little pile, were all the Polaroid pictures she'd taken so far. I slid them over the surface of the table, scanning each one. There was one for everything we'd done so far; hiking, the concert, the drive-in, and even the fireworks in the field. There was one of September and me from before Homecoming, and I was so tempted to take it.

"Reed?" September called. "Are you coming?"

"Yeah. One second."

I stacked the photos back up and re-positioned them before going downstairs.

"What took so long?" she asked as I came into view.

"I just had to find your jacket." I held it up. "Found it."

"Thanks." She took it from me and I helped her put it on.

"Where do you want to go first?" I asked her, taking the keys from the hanger by the front door and holding the door open for her. The cold air blew in, burning my face as I closed the door behind us.

"I left the camera at my house," she said. "I want to get a picture of it, anyway."

I slipped on my jacket and pulled my beanie over my head before jogging down the front path to the truck and unlocking the doors. With the engine on and warming up, I turned the heat to the highest setting, rubbing my hands together to try and regain warmth in my fingers. September shivered as she slammed her door closed behind her.

"Cold, huh?" I asked. "Are you sure you want to do this today?"

"Yeah," she answered, pulling her seatbelt around her body and settling back into her seat. "I won't have time next week."

"Why not?"

"Packing. I've got to get stuff boxed and shipped to England."

"Oh. Right."

Once again, pulsing emotions overwhelmed me. They beat against the inside of my chest, begging me to let them out. I swallowed hard, trying to push them down and out of the way. This time proved harder than the last.

No, I told myself. *I won't hurt her anymore.*

"I hope it snows soon." She turned her head to the window. "It's still so gloomy. I wish the sky would just let it go already."

I hummed in agreement, shifting the truck into reverse and backing onto the road. September hummed quietly along with the radio as we rode. It was a comforting sound.

I realized that a lot of things about September made me feel just that—comfortable. She was familiar. It was easy to keep up with her. Her voice, her gestures, her habits—all of them were things that comforted me in one way or another.

I remembered how she brought up change in the car shop, and I shot her down. Thinking back on it, I felt really guilty. Maybe change wouldn't be such a bad thing. Something refreshing.

But change meant getting rid of things that were comfortable and familiar. It meant stepping into no-man's-land.

Was I ready to handle something like that?

September's still leaving. That's going to be a huge change.

I'm going to have to figure out how to deal with it.

The first thing I noticed as we rolled into September's driveway was that the Autumn Joy bushels in the front yard were wilted. The cold must've gotten to them.

"The Autumn Joys look sad," I commented.

"It's kind of pitiful, isn't it?" she asked. "Thank you for getting me some, by the way. They look much happier than these."

"No problem."

We sat for a moment in silence, listening to the radio, neither of us wanting to step back out into the cold air. I shifted in my seat.

"One of them is fake," I said.

"What?"

"The flowers. One of them is fake. You know... so you can take a little of your Greenville home with you. Put it in your room in England."

She didn't say much, just studied me for a few minutes. It was as if she had to process the words, like she didn't quite understand what I was saying. I got a little uncomfortable and stared out the front of the car.

"Thank you," she said finally. "That's amazing."

"Don't worry about it."

Before the air could get any more awkward, she jumped out of the car and jogged to her front step.

When I joined her in the house, I noted that while the sea of boxes had grown bigger than last time; there were still piles lying around that needed to be boxed up. Clothes, photos, dishes, bathroom supplies; each was organized into its own pile on the floor.

"Hey, Em," I yelled, nudging a box towards the wall so that I could walk, "when are you boxing the rest of this?"

"Next week," she yelled back from her room. "I've put it off so long that I'm going to have to pull a couple of all-nighters to get it finished."

"Do you need help?"

She slipped around the hallway and poked her head out. "I think I'm okay right now. I'll get as much done as I can while I'm here. I'm going to start staying the night here again after Thanksgiving."

"Are you well enough to stay by yourself?"

She laughed.

Oh, how I love her laugh.

"I'm fine. I haven't felt bad since last week."

I shrugged. "If you're sure."

I pushed back the pang of disappointment. I would miss watching movies and playing board games with her. I loved getting up in the morning and driving to school together. It made the early morning ride bearable.

September seemed to notice my expression change. She opened her mouth to speak but closed it again, changing her mind. She moved back into her room and searched for the camera.

A few minutes later, she emerged with the Polaroid in hand.

"Ready?" she asked, waving it at me in triumph.

Nodding, I followed her out the front door and back to the car. Instead of opening the door, she stepped out onto her yard and aimed the camera at her house.

"Just so I can remember what it looks like," she told me. She held her lip between her teeth as she lined up the camera and clicked the shutter button. The photo printed out and she took it with her fingers and waved it against her side until the paper changed color and the image was clear. Once she finished, she skipped back to the truck and jumped in, blowing warm air on her hands.

"Where to?" I asked.

"The school. I want to get a picture of it, too."

"Why?" I snorted. "That place isn't worth remembering."

"It is to me."

I backed out onto the road and headed towards the high school. September pulled out her phone and started playing Making Midnight's latest album.

She got two pictures of the high school when we arrived, and then we set off again.

The parking lot was empty when we rolled up to the car shop. Tom's familiar blue truck was nowhere to be seen. I hoped that he was home with his wife; he'd been working so hard to get cars done by their deadlines that he'd started staying overtime.

After unlocking the shop door, stepping inside, and closing it securely behind us again, September pulled her jacket off her shoulders and put it on the workbench. The sound of her footsteps echoed in the garage, bouncing off the walls and the smooth surfaces of the cars. She weaved between the array of colors that littered the concrete floor, fingering the trigger on her camera. I lingered at the front of the garage, just watching her, just waiting.

We didn't talk. She stopped in front of Tom's Impala, hovering her fingers over the surface as if she were afraid to touch it. The body had been sanded down, and the dents patched. The surface was a smooth but patchy gray.

"I always liked it in here," she said after a moment. Her voice echoed lightly against the metal garage doors. "It's so... comfortable." She allowed her fingers to touch the surface of the car, then a few moments later, her whole hand.

"It's my second home." I joined her in the center of the garage, shoving my hands into my pockets.

The corner of her mouth quirked when she looked at me. Then she turned her head toward the misshapen pile in the corner of the garage. It was still covered with a tarp.

Her gaze panned between me and the tarp. Her steps were hesitant, nervous.

Her hand found the fabric. Her fingers ran along the edges before latching on and pulling the tarp away.

Underneath, Charlotte was starting to look like her old self again. The body appeared straight for the most part, with just a few dents here and there. The broken glass was gone and replaced with new, crystal clear panes. New tires, rims, and bumpers drew attention away from the mangled paint job, making her seem much more alive.

September's modest smile grew into a grin. "She's almost back to normal."

"Almost," I agreed. "She'll be able to drive by next week. We've been working on her nonstop."

"Good. I'd love to ride in her again before I leave."

She moved around to the passenger side and opened the patchy—but no longer pancaked—door. She scanned the interior as if it were something completely foreign.

I held my hand out. "Let me have the camera."

She raised an eyebrow but didn't question me. The strap went over her head, and I stretched over the hood and took the camera from her before pointing it in her direction.

She leaned her head onto her arms against Charlotte's door. She looked so comfortable that she could sleep there.

I clicked the shutter button to snap the photo and waited for the picture to print. I handed the camera back to her and tucked it behind my back.

"Don't I get to see it?" she asked.

I shrugged. "Maybe. I'm keeping it, though."

She rolled her eyes before hiding her face behind the camera. "Smile, Davis."

I shifted my weight and put it all on Charlotte, looking directly at the camera. She took the photo before I had time to smile properly. The photo printed, and she too pocketed the paper without letting me see.

"I don't get to see it?" I asked.

"Maybe," she mocked me.

I rolled my eyes at her before moving to Charlotte's open window. I leaned over the edge, peering into the cab. "You can hardly tell she wrecked, can you?"

"Besides the paint," she agreed, "no, you can't."

"Tom worked on it a lot," I told her. "He did a lot of it while I wasn't here. He said that he owed it to me."

"That was nice of him."

I nodded. "Yeah. I was a little disappointed, but he saved some of the body work for me." I ran my hand along the rough panels on the door, giving them a little pat. "I'm glad he agreed to help me rebuild her. My dad would've scrapped her."

She shut her door and leaned her elbows onto the hood. She propped her head on her arms. "I can't imagine you without Charlotte."

"Me either."

September exhaled and stood up straight, stretching her arms above her head before stepping in front of the car. "Are you ready to go?"

I nodded.

She raised the camera one more time, this time taking a picture of Charlotte alone. Once the picture had printed, we walked back down the garage to the door. I helped September put on her coat, took one last look at the garage, and got on the road again.

We stopped at the town square next where she took pictures of our tiny stone courthouse. We drove by the movie theatre where she snapped a quick picture and then moved on back towards my side of town. We came to that same back road surrounded with evergreens. She surprised me and asked me to pull over here, too. She waited until the cars moved past us then ran out into the middle of the road and took a picture. Once we were back on the road, she took a picture of us in the truck.

"Did you get all the ones you wanted?" I asked, driving back towards my neighborhood. She shuffled through all the photos.

"Not quite."

"What do you lack?"

"Your house. And Waffle House. But I want that one when all of us can be there."

I smiled, but didn't say anything.

We pulled back into my house just as the sun was setting. As I stepped into the foyer, the warm aromas of turkey, pie, and cider sent chills up my spine.

"That smells amazing," September commented as I helped her out of her jacket.

"I'm glad," Mom said, meeting us at the door. "You helped make it." She hugged September and kissed my cheek.

"Can I help set the table?" I asked her.

"It's done," she answered. "You came just in time to eat."

"Sorry we cut it close," Em apologized. "We were out taking pictures."

"I didn't picture Reed as the modeling type." Mom nudged my shoulder with hers and laughed.

We followed her into the dining room where Dad met us with the turkey on a platter. He nodded hello to the two of us and we all took our places at the table.

"Reed," Dad said once we were all settled, "will you say the blessing, please?"

I nodded, awkwardly shooting a glance at September. She didn't seem to mind. My parents linked hands and reached out to September and me to do the same. They closed their eyes. September smiled at me and closed hers too.

"Dear God," I began, fidgeting in my seat, "thank you for everything you've blessed us with. Thank you for this food. Thank you for allowing us all to be here today. Thank you for keeping me and September safe on the road."

My mother squeezed my hand.

"Please continue to heal us. Please continue to heal Marcus and Jack."

September squeezed my hand. I gulped.

"Be with September as she moves across the world," I said, and I meant it. "Help the move to be as smooth and easy as possible. Please keep her safe in England. Amen."

"Amen," said my parents.

"Amen," said September.

My mom let go of my hand. September's lingered in mine for a moment before she let go too.

I knew this Thanksgiving would be one I'd remember. Not just because September was there but also because I felt thankful to be alive. Turns out, near death scenarios can kind of change your perspective.

As I listened to my parents tell stories of their Thanksgivings as kids and September laugh at the photos we took earlier that day, I wondered if September would remember it, too. I thanked God that September had moved to our tiny little town of Greenville, that I had the pleasure of knowing her. And although I didn't want her to leave, I knew she'd be okay in England.

She'll find her way.
She always does.

15
friendsgiving

The next morning, I found myself disappointed. It was quiet.

Too quiet.

September had spent the first night back at her house—meaning that the kitchen sat cold and motionless the next morning. I'd grown so used to getting up and having a cup of coffee with her before school. We'd play music and sit at the bar and sip our steaming drinks until we had to leave. She never ceased to amaze me, waking up bright and early with a smile across her face. She was an early bird if I ever saw one.

In the two short weeks she stayed with me, we'd created a new normal. Our morning routines shifted to fit in our little coffee chats. I couldn't lie; I loved it. And although I hated to admit it, I forgot that it would have to end.

So that morning, I woke up early, my subconscious fooling me into thinking Em would be waiting for me downstairs. The now familiar pang of disappointment settled into my stomach when I found the kitchen empty. I couldn't go back to sleep—I was wide awake by now—so I paced, lost at what to do. I found a note from my parents telling me that they'd gone Black Friday shopping and wouldn't be back until late that night, meaning I'd be on my own.

I started by making myself a cup of coffee. It wasn't as good as September's, but it was good enough for me to finish.

Funny thing: September didn't even like coffee. But man, she could make a great cup of the stuff.

"Coffee is bitter," she'd complain. "Like your soul."

She probably wasn't all that wrong about that.

I finished one cup of coffee, then another. I watched TV for a while then got bored. I showered, got dressed, made breakfast, ate. I resisted calling September. I considered calling Jack but figured he'd probably be hanging out with Cora. I almost called Marcus but decided not to bother him. Then I almost called September again but decided against that, too. I'd spent the last two weeks with her. The girl probably needed a break from me. Still, I ached to hear her voice again.

My time with her drew closer to the end. Every time I thought about it, my chest tightened. It was unpleasant to think about. Though I'd felt like I'd finally got my anger under control, shoved back into its little cage that resided just below my throat, it was as if it kept trying to pick the lock—trying to make me say something that I would regret.

The news of September leaving had brought out the absolute worst in me, a side I didn't know I had. The first time it appeared, back at the beginning of the month, it scared the crap out of me. How do you learn to cope with something like that? How do you cope with anger so strong it's almost violent?

It made me antsy, thinking about it. Marcus didn't cope with it, and look what happened to him.

September had become my own personal drug. I couldn't get enough of her. I had an addiction. The separation, even if for just a morning, made me antsy. The

215

mention of her departure set my teeth on edge. I'd forced myself to spend every moment with her, to savor the days before she left, and all I'd really done was shove all my emotions onto her. I'd become dependent—in fact, so dependent that I'd forgotten what it was like to be alone.

The more I thought about it, the more I realized that being alone might be a good thing. I'd spent so much time with September that month that I hadn't had any time to just chill on my own. Maybe some separation would do me good. Maybe it would help me clear my head.

And then the phone rang.

And that thought went out the window.

"Hey, Reed!" September's voice radiated so much pep that I could've sworn she was trying to shove it at me through the phone. "How's your morning going?"

"Fine," I answered, making a conscious effort to keep my voice level in lieu of my excitement. "What about you?"

"Great!" She started rambling, talking so fast that I couldn't understand a word she said.

I blinked. "What?"

"Ithinkthisyearweshouldallgetogetherandsincewehave n'tseeneachotherinalongtimeorhungoutitwouldbeagoodopp ortunityandwecanhavefoodandwatchmoviesandMarcuscanf inallybethereandwecanhave—"

"Em, breathe. Complete sentences. What are you talking about?"

"Friendsgiving," she huffed through the phone. I could hear the smile in her voice. "We haven't all been together since the wreck. We should get together and have a party. You know—food, drinks, movies—just have fun. Be thankful to be alive."

I groaned at the sound of food. "Em, I don't have the capacity to even think about food right now. Last night's dinner is still in my stomach."

"TMI," she said. "Give it a few hours. You'll be starving soon enough; you're a bottomless pit."

I laughed, mostly because she was right.

"Besides," she added, "I want us all to spend more time together. I leave at the end of next week, and I still have one or two things left on the bucket list."

And just like that, my good mood went down the drain. I'd learned my lesson, though—I wasn't going to let her see it. I'd been destroying her with my terrible attitude for weeks. I couldn't do it anymore.

I held in the anger. I fought against my instincts. Why had my temper grown shorter in just a month? I never used to get angry. It seemed the thought of September leaving had driven my mind into a dark hole, one I couldn't get out of.

What had she done to me?

I was angry at her, but I wasn't angry at *her*; I was angry at the adventurous side of her that made moving across the world so appealing and I was angry at her father for taking a job there. I hated that my world was so small compared to hers, that she could see so much farther than I could.

And then I scolded my brain for being so selfish. Could I really be so heartless that I would choose my happiness over hers?

Maybe, the darker side of my mind hissed from the cage.

No, I argued back. *No, I'm not.*

"Reed?"

I snapped myself back to reality. What were we talking about?

"Yeah, that sounds good," I said. "Make sure you call Cora. She's in town for Thanksgiving weekend."

"Oh yeah, you're right. Thanks." I could hear her shuffling around through the phone—most likely because she was packing. "Anyway, I'm about to call up Jack and Cora and Marcus. How does 3 p.m. sound to you?"

I nodded, then realized she couldn't see me. "Yeah. Sounds great."

"Good." I could picture her grinning. "You can bring the popcorn... and Red Bull. Lots of Red Bull."

"Red Bull?"

"For the movie marathon," she answered, as if it were obvious. "How else do you expect us to make it through all eight of the Harry Potter movies?"

"*All eight?*"

"Well, maybe not you and Jack and Mark, but Cora and I will stay up all night. If you guys start getting sleepy, you have to go home. You can't sleep at my house."

"Why not?"

"That shouldn't even be a question, Reed. Anyway, call up Marcus for me, won't you? I'll call Cora and Jack, and we can all meet at my house at three."

"Sounds good."

"Bye!"

I chuckled to myself when the line went dead, shaking my head slightly. How she harnessed so much happy energy all the time was beyond me.

I caught a glimpse of the clock. It was only 10 o'clock. I was tired of wandering the house, so when I called Marcus to tell him about September's "Friendsgiving," I asked if I could come over.

"Of course," he said. "Why are you even asking?"

Luckily, my parents rode together to go shopping, so my dad's truck still sat in the driveway. I found his keys on the hook, threw on a jacket, shot my parents a quick text, and bounded out the door. Marcus didn't live far from me—ten minutes tops—but I drove much slower than usual. The sky still cast a dreary gray on the world. The morning dew froze in the cold weather and looked like glimmering dust on the brown grass. Ice had crept up onto the edges of the pitch-black asphalt.

Marcus already had the door unlocked when I got to his house, so I let myself in. His parents were gone—Black Friday shopping, too—so he had the house to himself.

I could hear his TV from the hallway playing the familiar background music of James Bond. I knocked twice.

"It's open."

I nudged the door with my foot. Mark sat in one of two new giant red bean bags on his floor.

"007?" I asked, tossing my keys onto the TV stand and plopping down into the one next to him. "The newest one is so much better."

"Remind me why I'm friends with you again?" he asked. "The first one is always best, as a general rule."

I rolled my eyes. "It's the day after Thanksgiving, and you're at home watching movies. Why aren't you doing anything productive?"

"Reed, Mr. Jackson has been standing over my shoulder for two weeks, and I'm sick of being productive."

"Who's Mr. Jackson?"

His nose wrinkled as though he'd smelled something putrid.

"My tutor. He's old and smells like gym socks. I would know—he stands right in front of me while I work on my online classes. His favorite phrase is, *Hurry up, boy.*"

I kicked off my shoes and settled back into my seat. "September is super excited about all of us getting together."

Marcus grinned. "I know. She called me about a minute after I hung up with you. She could barely make complete sentences."

I grinned. "She's something, all right."

"I'm excited, too. I don't think we've ever gone this long without being together. You, Jack, and me, at least. We were all joined at the hip freshman year."

"I remember that," I agreed. "We were lucky we didn't get pummeled by the football players for being so soft."

"Nah, Jack was in pretty good with some of them. The worst they would have done is shoved us into lockers—which if you think about it, isn't that bad. I'd take a locker over a tutor any day."

"You hate it that much?"

"Of course I hate it. I'm a social butterfly, man. This is driving me insane."

"That really sucks. I'm sorry."

He shrugged off my apology. "Don't apologize. You gotta do what you gotta do."

"How are things going with your new medication?" I asked.

"It was terrible the first few days. I had mood swings like nobody's business. But now I'm kind of adjusted to it. It's helping me keep my anger under control. I haven't punched a wall in a whole week, so I assume that's good."

My eyes found the white patches on Marcus's bedroom walls. I laughed humorlessly. "Maybe I need to take some of that."

He didn't say anything, but I could feel his eyes on me.

I turned to him. "What?"

"I don't think your problem is chemical, Reed," Mark said. "I think you just haven't figured out how to handle emotions at this magnitude yet."

"What's that supposed to mean?"

"You never acted like this before September told you she was leaving," he pointed out. "And you've never had to deal with any trauma in your life."

Trauma? "So? I hardly consider this trauma."

"*So*, my guess is that your brain just doesn't know what to do with all of these emotions. Now, when you get angry, it's like you're an entirely different person. You used to be so level-headed and you rarely got upset. At least, not as upset as you do now. I think you're just so attached to September that this has *become* traumatic for you."

I looked away. The whole conversation made me uncomfortable. "I don't know how else to handle it."

"Exactly. I think you just need a better outlet."

"Like what? Anytime I try to get rid of the anger, I end up hurting somebody."

"I don't know, man, but the longer you hold it in, the worse it's going to get. I suggest finding some sort of release—one that doesn't involve punching somebody—before you have a come apart."

That's easier said than done.

I didn't answer. We watched the rest of the movie quietly for about a half hour before it ended. Things grew awkwardly silent while Marcus searched through Netflix for another movie. I cleared my throat, eager to break the silence.

"What are you bringing to September's?"

"She asked me to bring my Harry Potter collection. Apparently hers is already packed."

"She told me to bring Red Bull," I said with a suggestive smirk.

His eyes went wide, and he cracked a smile. "Do you remember the last time Em had a Red Bull?"

I grinned. "The night we went to that double feature showing at the movie theater. Yeah, I remember."

"She wouldn't sleep for hours after we'd gone home." He laughed, leaning back to put his hands behind his head. "She blew up my phone until 3 a.m."

"Same here. Remember how she had that flat tire before the movie started and almost missed it?"

"Do I? She wouldn't let either of us come help her change it. She literally called us while she was changing it herself."

"She loves being independent."

"Bless whoever she marries," Marcus joked. "She's not going to let him help her with anything."

"I can't imagine her asking for help unless she's tried something a hundred times on her own, and even then, she wouldn't want to do it."

"That's her problem, I think. It's not that she doesn't need help; it's that she doesn't want to ask for help. She's very much a fixer, isn't she?"

I blinked. "You know, Marcus, being shut up in your house for a couple weeks has done you some good. You're very insightful."

He smirked triumphantly. "Thank you."

"Where'd you get your instant wisdom, hmm?"

"Yoda," he answered without missing a beat. "I watched all the Star Wars movies in my free time. I'm practically a fully trained Jedi."

"Mind using the Force to bring me my car keys? Because you obviously need to get outside. When's the last time you got in a car?"

He shrugged. "I don't know. Probably a couple weeks."

"You're joking. That long?"

"I haven't exactly had anywhere to go. Besides, it's not like I'm just jumping for joy at the idea of getting inside another metal box that I could potentially crash."

"What if I'm driving?"

He shrugged. "I'm sure I could find a way to crash it again. Speaking of which, how's Charlotte?"

"Almost road ready," I said confidently. "I'll probably have her on the road in a few days."

"That's great. Sorry again, man."

I shook my head. "Don't sweat it. Everyone's fine."

"*Almost* everyone."

"Hey, it's all gonna work out. You'll be back at school in January."

"How do you know?"

"I just know. Come on, let's go pick up that Red Bull."

I stood to my feet, reaching over to grab my keys off his dresser. He looked at my keys with uncertainty.

"If it makes you feel better, you can ride in the back seat," I offered.

He swallowed hard then stood up. "No, I'm fine. Let's go."

When we got outside to the truck, I opened the backseat door. Marcus looked at it for a second, as if it was foreign to him. Then, with a slight head shake, he shut it and circled the truck. Hesitantly, he slid into the passenger seat.

I raised my eyebrows. "Wow."

He didn't look at me but instead adjusted his seat and examined the seatbelt as if he was looking for something wrong with it. "Shut up and get in the car."

I got in next to him and shut my door. He immediately fastened his seatbelt, and his right hand reached up to grip the ceiling handle, his left still cradled at his chest.

When I started the car, I saw Marcus flinch in the corner of my eye. He didn't say a thing, but I let the car idle for a minute, pretending to check my phone. I texted September and asked if she had anything else for me to pick up on my way to her house. Marcus stared out of his window. I waited until he looked back to me before I put the car into gear and slowly backed out of the driveway.

"Can we put on some music?" he asked.

"Sure."

Marcus didn't make a move towards the radio, so I reached over and flipped it on. I scanned until I found a station playing good music then made sure it was loud enough to drown out some of the car noise. He rode quietly in the passenger seat with his fingers curled around the ceiling handle.

We dropped by the convenience store around the corner, picking up a case of Red Bull (that Marcus insisted be sugar-free) and a couple of different packs of sodas. This time, Marcus jumped into the car with more confidence. He seemed much more comfortable on the ride to September's.

When we rolled into the driveway, Marcus hopped out of the car first, eager to hit stable ground. I gathered our grocery bags and locked down the truck before following him up to the door. It opened as he raised his hand to knock.

"Marcus!"

September hit Marcus like a train, knocking him backwards into the door. I evaded them just in time, slipping around Marcus before September could nail me into the wall.

Marcus's laugh boomed in the half-empty house. "How've you been, Em?"

"Much better now that you're here," she said over his shoulder, her arms tightening around his neck.

"I could say the same." He patted her back. His voice changed to a lower, strained pitch. "You're kind of suffocating me, though."

"Oh, sorry." Em pulled back to give him air, but the glow on her face didn't falter. "How're you doing?"

"Great." It seemed as though the anxiety that had been riding on his shoulders on the drive there had disappeared. In its place, his bright, vibrant attitude shined through—almost like nothing had changed. "I missed you."

"We missed you, too." She reached down and squeezed his hand before letting it drop. She made her way back down the hallway towards the kitchen. "Jack and Cora are on their way. Did you bring the Red Bull?"

Marcus and I exchanged a look as we followed her.

"Yeah." I stifled a smile. "Marcus brought his movies, too."

"He better have. I would've made you turn around and go get them if you'd forgotten."

I lifted the bags onto the counter where September delved into them. She pulled the box of Red Bull from the plastic and wrinkled her nose.

"Are you serious? *Sugar-free?* Who do you think I am?"

"Come on, Em," Marcus chided. "We all know you can't hold your energy drinks."

"This is disgusting. I'm offended." She dug through the other bags and produced an assortment of sodas. "At least you got the good kind of pop."

I scoffed. "Are you kidding? I don't buy the cheap stuff."

She hummed in disapproval. "Mhmmm."

"I don't!"

The doorbell rang down the hallway. September grinned again.

"They're here!" She cupped her hands around her mouth. "Come in!"

The door swung open. In stepped Cora, carrying a stack of pizza boxes and Jack, behind her, carrying a bright duffel bag.

"Marcus!" Cora exclaimed. Her sneakers thudded against the hardwood floor as she scrambled to put down the boxes and throw her arms around Marcus's neck. "How are you?"

"If you had visited him, you'd know," Jack taunted, putting down the duffel and throwing an arm around Marcus's shoulders.

"I was at college!" she defended.

Jack yawned. "Excuses, excuses."

Marcus interjected before Cora could argue. "It's good to see you, Cora."

The frown disappeared from her face, and she smiled back at him. "It's good to see you, too."

I looked at September who looked fondly at Marcus. Her gaze flicked between Marcus, Jack, and Cora before meeting my eyes. Her smile grew.

"This is the first time we've all been in the same room since the wreck," Marcus said. "Strange, isn't it?"

"What?" Jack asked. "That we haven't all been together in a few weeks or that you wrecked a car as massive as Charlotte?"

Mark laughed. "Shut up, Evans."

"You first, Holmes."

"Alright, guys," September interrupted. "Let's eat. I'll start a movie." She paused for a moment, looking at all of us again. "I'm so glad we all got to be here; you have *no* idea. I'm so thankful to be your friend, and I'm thankful that we all have each other. Happy Friendsgiving!"

The corner of Marcus's lips turned up, and he outstretched his arms to Em, enveloping her in a hug. After a moment, Cora hugged them both and then Jack, until they were all in a little group hug.

"Come on, Reed," Marcus called. "Get in here."

"Ew, gross." I waved them off. "This is all too mushy gushy."

"Says the guy who cries at *Titanic* and loves every minute of it."

"That's totally unrelated," I defended. "Everyone cries at that movie."

"Reed," September groaned. "Don't be lame."

I sighed playfully, rolling my eyes before outstretching my arms and joining the group hug. After about thirty seconds of silence, September pushed everyone out of the way and broke the circle.

"Everyone get food!"

"Gladly," Jack chimed.

"What movies are we watching?" Cora asked.

"Harry Potter," September answered, her eyes glimmering with excitement.

Cora frowned. "Whose idea was that? Harry Potter is lame."

September blinked. "It was *mine.*"

She tried to cover it up with a cough. "Oh... Never mind."

Em narrowed her eyes at Cora. "*You're* lame."

She snorted. "Original."

Once we'd all finished getting our pizza, September turned on the TV in her living room and put in the first movie. Her couch and the TV stand were the only pieces of furniture left in the living room. The Leaning Tower of Never-ending Boxes still stood strong, but it looked exactly the same as it had the last time I'd been there. There were no more boxes added to the collection. In fact, it looked like those boxes hadn't been touched at all for weeks, like they were just left there to collect dust. It seemed as if she hadn't done any packing in a while; the tower of boxes was big but definitely not big enough to be all the trinkets in her house.

Jack helped her with the assortment of large blankets, pillows, and quilts she'd pulled from the linen closet. They laid some out on the floor and the rest onto the couch. When everything was ready and the movie had started playing, she settled onto her spot on the quilt pile on the floor.

We spent the entire first movie just commenting on the poor special effects. While Jack and Marcus argued over what effects in the films were best, Cora, September, and I cracked jokes on the young actors. By the time the first movie had finished, it was just past six o'clock. Marcus and Jack retreated to the kitchen for seconds on pizza, and September downed her first Red Bull, despite our warnings.

Movies two and three went by just as quickly. This time, we picked on the characters we didn't like and even went as far as to debate which characters were the absolute worst. I argued Lockhart, but September insisted that Umbridge beat out any villain ever. By the time they'd finished, all of us had started to drift, except September. We took a break to stretch our legs and drink caffeine.

When our break concluded, we all reconvened in the living room with new plates of pizza and cups full of soda. We got so wrapped up in conversation we didn't start another movie.

"So, Jack," September cooed, "are you and Hannah Stephens a thing?"

"What do you mean?"

Cora nudged his shoulder. "You have a girlfriend? And you didn't tell me?"

"We've just been on a few dates."

"Are you sure?" Em asked. "I saw you walking her to class. It really was sweet, Jack. I didn't know you had it in you."

"Hey, I can be romantic if I want to be," he defended, a grin spreading across his face. "But my parents won't let me take her out until my grades come up anyway. I'm struggling."

"You? Struggling?" I asked.

He shrugged. "It's not that hard to believe."

I looked at Marcus. "What about you, man?"

"What do you mean?"

"A girl. You talking to anyone?"

He shook his head. "Do I seem like the kind of person to be in a relationship right now? I can barely keep things in my head stable. How do you think I'd do in a serious relationship?"

I shrugged. "You never know."

"How's homeschool?" September asked.

Cora frowned. "You're homeschooled now? Why?"

Immediately, the air grew silent and thick with tension. All our eyes shifted from Cora to Marcus, who acted like there was nothing awkward about the question.

"My parents decided it would be good for me," he answered, shrugging. "They put me on a new antidepressant. They were afraid that the side effects would make school harder. Really, though, they just wanted me to have some space. Decompress."

"Side effects?" Cora inquired.

"Nothing out of the ordinary. Mood swings, nausea, insomnia. They said the first couple of weeks would be rough, but all the side effects started passing after the first week. I feel fine now, really."

"How long have you had it?" she asked. "You know… Depression?"

"You know, I'm not really sure. The way they explained it to me, it's rooted from a 'severe build-up of stress.'"

Jack let out a little chuckle. "You did a really good job of hiding it. You never seemed stressed to me until this month."

The corner of Marcus's lip turned up. "Thanks."

September's eyebrows drew together, and her mouth formed a neat little frown. "I wish you'd have told us. We could've tried to ease your load."

"It was nothing you could have fixed."

She rolled her eyes. "What can't be fixed?"

He rubbed his right hand against his knee before he spoke again. "My parents are divorcing," he stated.

Silence.

"It's not just that." Marcus looked between us and then down at his hands again. "It was everything. My parents separating, September moving. I worried about college. My grades dropped, and I was kicked off the basketball team. I got fired." He looked at me. "That's why I was out drinking when you had to come get me, man. I was fed up. After that, I felt even worse, too—like you were all disappointed in me. I wrecked Charlotte and handled the situation terribly."

"I'm sorry you felt that way," September said, breaking the silence.

"It's okay, really. I'm doing a whole lot better. Honest. Being around you guys makes me feel the best I have since it all happened."

We were all quiet.

September broke the silence with a soft chuckle. "We're just a mess, aren't we?" she asked. "All of us. Mark's sick, I haven't packed half of my house, Jack's grades are dropping, and Reed's in an emotional crisis."

"Hey, I've been doing good," I protested. "And what about Cora?"

She frowned. "What about me?"

"You aren't a mess?"

"Are you joking?" She flipped her hair over her shoulder. "I'm *fabulous*."

"Actually," Jack interrupted, "I overheard my parents talking about her. She's struggling with her grades, too."

Cora hissed. "Jerk."

"The point is," September said, "we all have problems. We've got your back, Mark."

He smiled a real, genuine, feel-good kind of smile. "Thanks, guys."

"If it makes you feel better, I still don't know where I'm going to college, either," Jack added. "Not a clue."

We all joined in, saying the same thing. September didn't say anything.

"I've thought about Portland," Marcus said. "Not too far away from home but far enough to have some separation. The drive isn't bad—all this assuming I get my grades up and get accepted. I still have to find some scholarships, too."

"California is looking good," said Jack. "I'd like to see the sun for once in my life."

"What about you, Reed?" Cora asked. I shrugged.

"I don't know. Probably not here, but I don't think I'll go too far. Maybe Seattle?"

We talked about college for another minute or two. It was sad to think we were all going to split up; from the looks of it, we'd all be pretty far from each other.

September especially.

September broke up the conversation when it hit a lull. "Let's watch the next movie. We gotta keep going if we're gonna get through all of them."

This time, we didn't talk over the movie. We all paid close attention to the film, inserting comments where we felt best. It wasn't until September pulled out the Polaroid camera that things livened up a little bit. She made sure to take plenty of pictures with Marcus—making up for lost time, I supposed. She even made a point of pulling out her creased, frayed paper napkin from Waffle House.

Her bucket list.

"That's almost everything," she gloated, dragging her pen across the words *movie marathon*. "I'm so happy we got to make everything happen."

"What are you missing?" Jack asked.

"Just Waffle House the morning I leave," she responded. "Then that should be it."

We weren't even an hour into the fifth movie by the time everyone started falling asleep. September kept chugging Red Bull, which had quite obviously affected her. She couldn't sit still and bounced in her seat.

At about 3:30 a.m., Jack, Marcus, and I tapped out on the movie marathon and packed up to leave. We left the Red Bull with the ladies (but not before instructing Cora to keep it away from Em). Jack went out to his car first, saying he'd meet us at my house. I stood by the door and waited for Mark.

September stopped him on his way out and handed him a little rectangular Polaroid photo. They hugged for what seemed like a very long time. A part of me wanted to feel jealous, but it was beat out by the part that valued my friendship with Marcus. The man had been through hell and back, and I wanted to have a pity party?

As if.

"We all love you, Marcus," she said as he approached the door.

He grinned at her. "I know. I love you guys, too."

Her smile was content as she waved us out the door. "Text me when you get home, okay?"

When we'd gotten into my dad's truck and started pulling out of the driveway, she stood at the front door and waved until we couldn't see her anymore.

We stayed quiet in the car on the way home. We were both tired and ready to sleep, but I made sure to stay alert. I couldn't help wondering about Marcus's confession.

"I didn't know you had all that stuff on your plate," I told Marcus. "All that stress you were telling us about."

"It's not as big a deal now as it was," he said. "Now it all looks a whole lot smaller than it did in the moment."

"I'm sorry about your parents."

He shrugged off my apology. "It's okay. I still see them both all the time. Instead of making me move from house to house, they're taking turns staying with me at home until they get everything figured out. They haven't decided the living situation or even signed the papers and it's already complicated. I feel bad."

"They love you."

"I know. And, believe it or not, it made me feel better to see them putting in effort for me. You know how every kid that goes through having their parents' divorce feels like they have to blame themselves? I used to think that was an overreaction, but it really is true. Now it feels good to see that either way they still want to take care of me."

I nodded in understanding. We pulled into my driveway, and I cut the engine.

"Thanks for bringing me, Reed. I appreciate it."

"Don't thank me. All I did was give you a ride."

"It means a lot. Really."

I rolled my eyes. "Come on, dude. Don't go all super soft on me."

He grinned. "Wouldn't dream of it."

We got out of the car and went into the house where Jack had already made himself at home and started watching TV in the living room. We sat down on either side of him on the couch.

"Hello, gentlemen," Jack said, obviously more awake and flipping channels. "Anyone up for finishing the Harry Potter movies? We still have three and a half to go."

Marcus and I exchanged glances. He shrugged.

"You were half-asleep at September's house," he pointed out. "Where did the energy come from?"

He shrugged. "What can I say? The boys are back in town. We gotta make up for lost time."

16
intervention

None of us heard from September at all for the next few days.

I take that back. I got *one* text. I'd asked her if she wanted to hang out, and all I got back was, "packing." I asked if she needed help but got no response. Saturday, Sunday, Monday, and Tuesday all passed without another peep from her. She didn't show up to school. She didn't try to contact any of us.

It struck me as odd that September had put off packing until the week she had to fly out. She was normally the more organized one of the group; while she had a terrible habit of being late to stuff, she hated waiting until the last minute to get things done. I'd thought that she'd have the packing done by the second week of November, yet now, just a few days before leaving the country, she spent the rest of her time packing up her belongings.

I wanted so badly to spend time with September before she left, but I also didn't want to bother her. If she was trying to get anything done, I'd probably end up being a distraction.

After school on Monday and Tuesday, I went to work on Charlotte. I swept out the inside, did some tuning on the engine, and when Tom was free, hammered out dents in the body. We spent a few hours of each day just fixing up other little things that needed to be done before we could put her back on the road.

Wednesday, Jack and I picked up Marcus and took him out to eat after school. When we got to his house, he came outside with his previously healthy hand wrapped up in a thin layer of gauze. I looked at him and then shifted my eyes down to his hand as he hopped in the car.

"I'm fine," he said. "Just had a little moment."

Jack and I exchanged glances but let him be. After all, it was nothing compared to the bulky cast on the other hand.

On Thursday, I woke up well before I needed to be awake. I got ready in a hurry and drove straight to the car shop before the sun even came up. The cold didn't bother me one bit; I was far too excited to care.

Charlotte was ready.

As I pulled into the parking lot, Tom raised the garage door. He'd moved the cars around and made a clear path to the back of the garage where she sat under that gray tarp. I jumped out of the car, slung my backpack over my shoulder, and jogged towards it, my hands gripping the fabric as soon as I could feel it. In one swift move, I pulled the tarp from the car and dropped it to the ground.

Tom stopped at my shoulder and tossed the keys at me. "Get her out of here."

I grinned. "With pleasure."

With the tarp out of the way, I opened the door and hopped into Charlotte's driver's side seat. I slammed the door shut again and buckled my seatbelt before inserting the key into the ignition.

The sound of Charlotte roaring again almost sent chills down my spine. It was like nothing had changed. The seats and steering wheel had brand new covers, but the interior still smelled like that comforting, warm cigar smoke mixed with new leather. The brand-new windshield sparkled, no spot in sight. Tom even surprised me by installing a new stereo system.

I put the car into gear and steered it out of the garage. The steering wheel turned easily, just like I remembered. Tom helped me maneuver around the other cars and out into the parking lot. When I'd successfully made it in the clear, I killed the engine.

"She's looking good," Tom praised. "Let's give her a quick wipe-down and then you can drive her to school."

As I rounded the car back towards the garage, I admired our handiwork. The body was almost perfectly smooth, give or take a few spots that Tom and I still had to sand down. While patchy, the faded red paint job still shone through the places where we had puttied the dents, hammered out creases, and sanded down rough spots.

Tom stepped into the garage for a moment and emerged again with a couple of rags. He tossed one to me, and we wiped down the outside of the car to get rid of the dirt and dust. When we finished, the sun was breaking over the horizon.

"You've got plenty of time before school." He took back the rag and moved towards the garage. I followed him. "You could drive her out to September's and pick her up."

"September isn't going to school today," I said.

"I didn't pin her as the skipping type."

"She's not. She's packing. She flies out on Saturday."

He frowned at me before turning to the workbench and throwing the tools scattered across the top into bins. "Still packing? I thought she'd have had that done weeks ago."

"Me, too."

"Have you offered to go help her?"

"Of course I have, but you know her. She hates asking for help."

"So you're just going to let her do it by herself?"

"I don't want to stress her out."

"How much worse could you possibly make it?" he asked. "She's already packing her house up by herself. I think a little bit of help would be good for her. You could even offer to take her out for dinner or something to help her relax."

I thought about it for a moment. "Maybe."

"Oh, come on."

"What?" I asked in defense. "I've spent most of the month with her. Don't you think that she deserves a little space?"

"Maybe. Or maybe you should forget about the whole 'space' thing and go help the girl finish packing. Do you want her to miss her flight because she's still packing?" I opened my mouth to answer, but he cut me off. "Don't answer that."

He spun on his heel and strode back out to the parking lot. I followed close behind him.

"Get to class, Reed. You can leave your dad's keys here, and he can pick up his truck when he gets the time. Give me a call if Charlotte has any problems."

I fished Dad's keys from my pocket and handed them over to Tom. "Thanks."

"Be careful, okay? She's still in recovery. Take it easy."

I pulled the door open once again and slid into my seat. "I will."

With the door shut, and the engine fired up once again, I pulled out onto the road towards the school.

I didn't bother pushing Charlotte on speed that morning. She hadn't been on the road in almost three weeks. Luckily it was too early for most teenagers to be out and about and on their way to school, so the roads were mostly deserted. I could ride as slow as I wanted until Charlotte warmed up to the movement. When I neared the school, I gave her a little more gas and sped up just slightly. Her familiar purr reached my ears and grew louder with more pressure on the pedal.

I pulled into my regular parking spot well before school started. The lot was empty except for a few teachers' cars. I turned on the new stereo and sat back in my seat to listen until other people arrived. Leaning my head back and closing my eyes, I let myself drift.

I woke to the sound of someone beating on my window. Jack beamed at me from outside, his infectious grin causing me to grin even wider. I rolled down the window.

"Nice ride." He leaned onto the window on his elbows. "Where'd you get it?"

"Fresh out of the shop," I answered proudly. "Isn't she beautiful?"

"A sight for sore eyes."

"Yes, she is." I opened the door and rolled up the window before cutting the engine. Then I grabbed my backpack from the passenger seat and stepped onto the pavement, slinging the strap onto my shoulder.

Jack started moving towards the school, tossing his keys up and down in his hand as he went. "We'll have to drive by and show Marcus after school."

"We will. I've got to show Em at some point, too."

His face dropped ever so slightly, but he recovered. "How's she doing?"

"I don't know, man. She hasn't talked to me either."

"Do you think she's okay?" His voice had a hint of worry, but he did a good job of keeping it under control. "I mean, you'd think she'd at least check in. She's by herself in that house."

I grimaced. "If we haven't heard anything from her by this afternoon, I'll go see her."

That didn't ease our consciences much, though. All day, I couldn't focus. I fidgeted in my seat, reread sentences over and over, and eventually gave up trying to pay attention. It'd been five days since any of us had heard from September. Far longer than any of us were comfortable with.

After the last bell rang and ended my unproductive agony, I shot a text to September.

You okay?

It wasn't until I got back to my car and had been lingering in the parking lot talking to Jack for a while that my phone buzzed.

Fine.

"That her?" Jack pushed himself away from his car so that he stood straight up.

"Yeah. She says she's fine."

I quickly messaged her back.

Need help?

She answered immediately.

No.

Sighing, I nodded towards Jack. "Let's run by Mark's house."

"Are you going to go see September?" he asked.

"I don't know. Are you?"

"Probably not." He walked around his car to the driver's side door. "I don't know that she'd want more than one of us over there. Who knows how much more she's got to do? I'd just get in the way."

I turned my phone over in my hand before pocketing it and opening my car door. "I'll think about it. See you at Mark's."

He nodded at me and got into his car.

A few minutes later, we pulled into Mark's driveway. Jack went up to the door ahead of me, and I hung back by Charlotte, leaning against her hood while I waited for Mark to come out.

Jack rapped his knuckles against the door and didn't stop until the door pulled away from his hand. He beamed up at Marcus before gesturing to me and Charlotte behind him.

Marcus frowned at him before following his pointing finger. His mouth dropped open.

"Is that… Charlotte?"

"Fresh from the doctor." Jack jumped off the porch steps and led Marcus to the car. "Isn't she a beauty?"

Marcus didn't answer. He'd stopped advancing before he even made it off the lawn. He looked almost afraid of the car. His eyes scanned the length of it, searching for the imperfections that the wreck had caused.

"She won't bite," I said.

"I will."

"Come on, man," Jack urged. "Come get a good look."

"I can see just fine from here. She looks great, Reed."

I shifted my weight from one foot to the other. "You won't break her, if that's what you're thinking."

He looked from the car to me and then back to the car. "I don't want to take a chance. I'm good. I don't want to break *me*, either."

Jack and I exchanged a look.

With a clap of his hands and an unnecessarily long exhale, Jack jogged back to Marcus and stood behind him, pushing against his back with his hands until he couldn't stand still anymore. No matter how hard he resisted, he couldn't overpower Jack's determined shove towards the car. Once they stood in front of it, Jack didn't let him go.

"Touch it," he said.

"No!" Marcus cried.

"Reed, get over here," Jack demanded. "This is an intervention."

"I don't need an intervention!"

"You can't be scared of this car. It's a *car*."

"I'm not scared of it!"

"Prove it!"

I shrugged, watching the two struggle against each other. "What do you need me to do?"

"I want you to open the passenger side door and help me get little Marcus here into the seat."

"NO!" he cried louder. "Seriously, guys, this isn't funny!"

"Of course it isn't. We're trying to help you out here, Mark."

I rounded the car and opened the passenger side door then helped Jack put a squirming Marcus into the seat. Once he finally made it in, we let go of him and stood in front of the open passenger side door.

Mark stopped and looked up at us, huffing as he regained his breath. His hands gripped the fabric on his pants, like they just needed something to hold onto.

"See?" Jack asked. "This isn't so bad. You don't need to develop an irrational fear of this old piece of junk." I shot him a look. He flashed a guilty smile. "Sorry, Reed."

Our friend didn't answer. He scrutinized the inside of the car through heaving breaths.

"Mark?"

He looked at me, closed his mouth, and swallowed.

"It looks good, Reed," he said.

I nodded nonchalantly. "Thanks."

"No problem. Can I get out now?"

Jack and I moved out of the way and let Marcus out of the car. He jumped to the ground, dusted himself off, and moved back off the driveway into the yard.

"I'll get back into the car on my own time, okay, guys?" he said over his shoulder. "Thanks for trying to help and all, but that was a lot more painful than it needed to be."

Jack choked on his own breath. I slapped his back as he wiped the drool from his mouth. "Sorry, man."

Marcus seemed satisfied. "Don't worry about it. Can I go finish my work now?"

Jack was still recovering from Mark's sudden bluntness, so I answered for him. "No problem. See ya, Mark."

He grinned. "Bye, guys."

Laughing hysterically (more at Jack's reaction than Mark's), I steered Jack back to his car. The sun had already set, despite it being 4:30 in the afternoon.

Stupid winter.

Once he was safely in his car and back on the road, I got back into Charlotte and sat in the driver's seat. I stared at my phone, wishing I'd get another text from Em, a call, anything—but nothing came through. I debated about calling her but didn't want to disturb her.

I eventually decided that Tom was right. I would go see her anyway.

I made the drive to her house in less time than it really should have taken. When I rolled into her driveway, I could see every light in the house illuminated. September's tiny car still sat in the driveway with the FOR SALE sign in the window. It had been collecting dust all month.

After getting out the car and checking my reflection in the side view mirrors, I jogged up to her front door. I knocked once and waited a few seconds.

Nothing.

I knocked again with a little more force.

Nothing. Not even a sound from the other side.

Frowning, I jiggled the door handle. It was locked.

I knew she kept a spare key on the porch somewhere, so I searched around under different pots until I found it. After getting it unlocked, I pushed it open cautiously.

"September?" I called from the porch. Still, I heard nothing.

Hesitantly, I stepped inside, one foot at a time, listening for her, waiting for her to come jog around the corner, but she didn't. Worry set in.

It wasn't until I reached the hallway outside of September's room that I heard any noise. The soft rustling of packing paper eased my nerves, and I breathed a sigh of relief. I pushed open the door with my foot.

September stood on the far end of the room with a stack of books in her arms. As the door swung open to reveal me standing there in the hallway, she let out a scream, dropping all the books to the floor.

"Reed!" she gasped, supporting herself against the bed as she tried to regain her breath. "You scared the crap out of me! What are you doing here?"

I held my hands out, making sure she wouldn't fall. "Sorry. You had me worried for a while."

She frowned at me and crouched to the floor to restack her books. "I told you—I'm fine. You can go now."

My eyebrows furrowed. "Don't you need help?"

She shook her head. "I'm fine."

Turning my head side to side, I scanned the area. Her room was a maze of boxes, clothes, books, and empty hangers. "Are you sure about that?"

She groaned. "I said I'm fine!" she exclaimed curtly. "Are you done?"

My eyes met hers in wide disbelief. In the year we'd been friends, she'd never been curt with me. It wasn't like her to lash out unprovoked.

She looked right back into my eyes, her stare hard. After a moment, I held my hands up in surrender, not breaking eye contact with her. "Sorry."

Her eyes softened for a split second. "Look, I'm sorry for being so rude, but I have a lot to do. Is there something you really needed?"

I shrugged, shoving my hands into my pockets. "I was going to see if you needed a break. Charlotte is on the road again."

"That's great, Reed. I'm happy for you, but I don't have time for a break. Just go on home; there's nothing you can help me with."

I nodded but didn't move. She turned back to her books and began wrapping them individually with paper and putting them into a box.

September loved her books. I wouldn't take the time to wrap each of my books individually—I don't care that much about them—but September looked determined.

Eventually, I moved over to her bookshelf and began removing books from it. I sat in the floor and stacked them neatly in a pile next to me. When they were all off the shelf, I started wrapping the books and putting them into a box like hers.

I felt her look at me, but she didn't say anything. She continued packing.

Once finished with all the books, I stood up and dusted off my hands. "What's next?"

"I really don't need any more help," Em insisted. I waved her off as I looked at the pile of clothes to be packed. A stack of unassembled boxes laid on the floor surrounded by assembled ones.

"Where can I take those?" I asked, pointing to the boxes of books. I reached around her to grab a tape gun and began taping my box. She looked between me and the boxes and then around the room.

"I'm... not really sure yet. Give me a second to think about it." She ran a hand over her ponytail, scanning the piles. "I think getting this bookshelf out of here is the next best thing? Maybe?"

"Or we could do furniture last," I suggested, trying to be helpful.

"Okay," she said weakly. "Then maybe clothes?"

I nodded. "Do you have everything out that you need for the flight?"

She shook her head.

I scanned her expression, noting how overwhelmed she looked. Her eyes were red—something I hadn't caught when I walked in—and her gaze kept shifting between all the things not yet packed. She looked at me, then at the floor, then at her boxes, then to her piles of clothes, and back at me. She spun in a circle, looking at everything she still had left to accomplish.

Her breathing changed from a slow, steady pace to a frantic, uneasy gasp for air. It sounded like she was winded, like she couldn't find any oxygen.

"Just, um, put the—we'll do the, um..."

Her fingers gripped at her hair, and her head turned rapidly in different directions. I could see her hands shaking.

"September." I reached a hand out to her.

"I'm fine." Her voice trembled. "I just need to—we can just—"

I stepped towards her. Immediately, she retreated back.

"I'm *fine.*" She moved straight past me, dragging her hand along the wall for support as she moved towards the living room. I followed close behind, almost afraid to see what she was doing.

She got to the living room in a panic, her chest heaving up and down as her eyes scanned everything lying around. The bare walls and the stacks of boxes caught her eye, and she ran her hands over her face.

"Em," I insisted, "you need to sit down. Breathe."

"No!" she yelled, holding a hand up to stop me from coming closer. She backed up until her back hit a wall. "No, *don't.*"

I stayed right where I was. She looked into my eyes, and I watched as the tears fell. She slid to the ground, buried her face into her arms, and cried.

Cried.

As I drew nearer, I could hear her mumbling to herself, trying to calm down. The only phrase I could understand was *don't move.*

I slid down the wall next to her and just sat with my knees pulled to my chest like hers were. She either didn't hear me or didn't care because she didn't flinch.

Slowly, I put a hand on her arm. "It's okay."

"No, it's *not* okay." She raised her head to look at me. The tears streamed her makeup down her face, and her eyes had turned a darker shade of bloodshot red. The purple circles under her eyes almost looked painful. "Am I making the wrong decision? Am I going to regret making this move? Is it worth all this stress?"

My heart stopped in my chest. Was she really asking *me*? The one who had fought against her leaving for so long?

The little monster living in the cage under my throat began rattling his bars. It was the perfect opportunity to change her mind. September was a strong girl, but here, where she was most vulnerable, I was almost positive that if I asked her to stay, she would have.

I had an opportunity to manipulate the girl I loved into staying with me. I hated that this was how I thought, but I couldn't help it. I just wanted her here. I could've used any method to persuade her, and at this point, it probably would've worked. I could've changed all of her plans.

But... I just couldn't.

I realized that, contrary to my own beliefs, I didn't have it in me to ruin her dreams. I couldn't take away her chance at living the dream life, her chance to reach her goals and cross things off her bucket list. I couldn't manipulate her into thinking that staying was best for her when in reality it was just me looking out for my selfish needs. I couldn't do that to her.

I loved her far too much.

And that was why I had to let her go.

"It's worth it," I answered quietly. "It's so worth it."

"H-how do you know?"

"I just know. You're not going to regret going."

Her chest heaved, and sobs racked her body as she tried to control her voice. She bit her lip to hold back a hiccup, drawing her eyebrows together at the same time. "Then why d-does it hurt s-so bad? Why is it so hard t-to let g-go of this place?"

"Because it's home. No matter where you go, you'll always have a home here. I think we'd all be a little worried if it wasn't hard for you to leave," I joked lightly, swallowing down my sadness. "You can just leave a part of your heart here with us and take the rest with you to England."

She closed her eyes and leaned her head back against the wall, shoulders shaking and tears falling. I'd never seen September, someone so strong, confident, and driven, reduced to something so hopeless and broken. It scared me. I was terrified for her.

And in the silence of her vast, empty, lonely house, the sounds of her heart breaking into two pieces broke mine into a million.

"I love y-you," she said, still trying to get her crying under control. "Thank you for e-everyt-thing."

"Shhh."

She leaned her head onto my shoulder. Her tears turned spots of my light gray shirt a dark gray. "I love you too, Em." I raised my arm and put it around her, and she buried her face into my shirt. I kissed the top of her head. "I love you, too," I whispered.

She'd grown too tired to hold herself together. It was my turn to carry some of her burden, my turn to keep her from falling apart—so I just let her cry. She deserved at the least that much from me—time to be honest. Time to tell me exactly what she thought without me ruining her excitement. Time to tell me her fears and have me listen without suggesting something that would benefit me and me only.

A few tears dropped down the front of my shirt, and it took me a second to realize they were mine. I wiped them away.

Who knew how long September had been carrying around all this anxiety? She wouldn't tell anyone. She loved being independent. For her, that meant keeping her dark thoughts to herself. It meant destroying herself from the inside out. It meant that she never asked for help, even if she knew she needed it. It meant she was ashamed of her own thoughts.

I leaned my head back against the wall and ran my hand up and down September's back. It didn't matter now.

Once she recovered from this, she'd come back stronger than ever. I was sure of it.

And though that cage rattled and my anger struggled to break free, I knew I would let September go in the end. I'd drive her to the airport myself.

September was leaving. That was final.

And I was done standing in her way.

17
why is she always right?

I didn't leave September's house until late that night. I just let her cry. My shoulder was soaked by the time she'd regained her composure, but in all honesty, I didn't care. I knew that breakdown had probably been a long time coming.

We sat in her floor for a while, just talking. We hadn't done that in a long time. It was good to feel like nothing had changed, even if only for a little while.

We spent at least two hours sorting things into piles and another three boxing things up. Once we'd gotten all we could get, we deconstructed furniture that needed to be taken apart and moved everything else towards the front of the house for the movers to get on Friday. By the time we'd finished, we had the walls bare, the rugs rolled up, the rest of the furniture moved to one room, and the Leaning Tower of Never-Ending Boxes had plenty of new additions. I got home close to midnight.

Charlotte finally had her spot back in my garage. Tom promised that we'd get to paint her and do final touch ups in a few weeks; he'd gained two new clients that week that wanted total flips done on their cars. He told me to take the rest of the week off and help September get ready to leave.

September was busy right after school though, so I went home and worked on Charlotte a little more.

Tomorrow morning, September will be on a plane to England.

And no matter what, I'm going to be supportive of her. I'm going to drive her to the airport myself.

I wiped my arm across my forehead, drying the drops of sweat that dripped from my toboggan. Lying on my back under the car, I rolled around on my cheap, off-balance creeper, tightening the last nut into place before gliding back out from under it. I heard the house door open and close.

"How's it look under there?" Dad asked, his footsteps echoing against the metal walls.

"She's running again," I answered, grabbing a rag from the workbench against the wall and wiping my hands. "I think she had a loose bolt or something. She rattled a bit earlier today."

I opened the driver's side door and turned the key. Charlotte started up with a satisfying purr.

"Sounds great," he said.

"She *is* great." I cut the engine and tossed the rag to the bench. "I'm going to get her painted soon. I'm also looking into new interior carpet; it's trashed from the wreck, and the parts that aren't trashed from *that* are trashed from all the food Marcus eats in my car."

"Holds a lot of memories, though." He opened the passenger side door and leaned inside.

"Sure does."

He smiled, admiring it a moment before speaking.

"She leaves tomorrow, doesn't she?"

I didn't have to ask who she was talking about. I leaned against the driver's side of the car, propping myself up with my forearm and exhaling heavily.

"I don't want to talk about it, if that's okay with you."

"I think you need to talk about it. You've been kind of quiet, lately, Reed. I'm worried that all these pent up emotions will hurt you."

"I'm fine. Honest, I'm fine."

"I'm sure you are. Just promise me that you'll make sure to not let anything get out of control, okay? Find an outlet. Take care of yourself. Just because you're trying to control your composure doesn't mean you aren't allowed to express what you feel."

It was the same things Jack and Marcus had told me. I nodded. "Yes, sir."

He seemed surprised at how easily I agreed but satisfied nonetheless. "Good." He closed the passenger door and walked back to the door. "By the way, Jack called. Something about Cora's car and a party."

"I'll call him. Thanks, Dad."

"No problem. Be careful, okay?"

I nodded. "Always am."

"I mean it. Make smart decisions. I trust you."

"Yes, sir."

The door closed. My phone buzzed against the wooden workbench. I stretched over to the workbench to retrieve it before sitting in the driver's seat.

"Hey," Jack said. "I called you twice. Ended up calling your dad."

"I was working on Charlotte. Must not have heard it. My bad."

"It's all good. I was just wondering… are you free right now?"

"What, aren't you going to get to know me before you ask me on a date?"

"Real funny," he said. "Actually, Cora's car won't start, and she has to drive back this weekend. Could you come take a look at it?"

"Sure. Be there in ten."

————

"Thanks for coming," Jack said as I slammed my car door. "I can't figure out why it wasn't starting. I'm not a car junkie like you."

"I prefer the term mechanical enthusiast," I joked.

He led me to Cora's car, which he had parked in the middle of the driveway. I raised an eyebrow when I saw it.

"When did she get a new car?"

"Mom and dad got it for her a few months ago," he explained. "Her old one had issues."

"Should've had me take it to the shop. I liked that car," I mumbled.

Where Cora's old, white, 2000 convertible Mustang used to be sat a shiny gray BMW.

"What year is it?"

"2005. They found it used online."

I walked around to the driver's side, opening the door and sitting in the driver's seat. Jack pulled the keys from his pocket and tossed them to me. I put the key in the ignition and started up the engine. The engine didn't even turn over.

"When did this start?" I asked.

"A couple hours ago," he answered, leaning against the car. "She had to take my car instead when she went to go run errands."

"Sounds like it may need a new battery. I can jump start it for now though."

"How quickly can you do that?"

"Jump the battery? Like, two seconds."

"No—how quickly can you change it?"

"It'll literally take fifteen minutes, if that," I said. "Don't worry about it. Give me a little while to get Tom on the phone, and I'll come change it tomorrow. It'll be done before she has to leave. Promise."

Jack wasn't much of a worrier but boy did he worry over Cora. Despite the two-year difference, he always made sure she was taken care of. They were as close as siblings could get.

"Great. Thanks, man."

"No problem." I stood up, walking back to my car and reaching under the seat for jumper cables. I popped the hood and connected the cables to my car while he popped Cora's hood and followed suit. It took only a second before we had Cora's car running again.

"Let me know if it dies again," I said. "I'll look for a battery."

"Sounds good." He shoved his hands into his pockets and shifted his weight. "I forgot to mention—there's a party tonight at nine. Do you want to go?"

"You're going to a party tonight?"

"I'm thinking about it," he admitted. "September will be going to bed early so that she gets enough sleep for the flight, and I don't have anything else to do tonight."

"Where is it?"

"Some varsity football player's house. I think his name is Dean. I got a text from Hannah a couple hours ago, and she asked for a ride."

I shook my head. "I've never heard of him."

He shrugged his shoulders. "I think he's in calculus with us. Anyway, I just don't want to be there alone. I'm supposed to be Hannah's designated driver."

"You're going to let her drink?"

"No, but if she drinks something by accident, I don't want her to get stuck there or get into a wreck. I couldn't talk her out of going, and I sure wasn't letting her go by herself. I don't trust our class—or anybody at our high school, for that matter." He exhaled, running a swift hand through his hair and shoving it back into his pocket. "She's trying to convince me that going to this party will help her fit in. I don't understand why she needs to fit in though; are the friends she has now not enough?" He laughed a short, humorless laugh. "My opinion doesn't matter as much to her as I'd like it to."

"Sorry, man." I clapped a hand on his shoulder. "That sucks."

He shrugged. "Nothing you can do. You coming?"

I thought about it for a moment. "Yeah, I could use a break. I'll go with you."

"What about Mark? Do you think we should ask him, too?"

"I'll ask, but I don't know if he'll want to go. I wouldn't blame him if he didn't." My hand delved into my pocket and found my phone. I pulled it out and dialed September's number. "I'll ask Em, too."

"She hates parties," he reminded me. "And she's leaving early tomorrow morning, remember?"

"I'll ask anyway. Maybe she'll want to end her last night with a bang."

"I doubt it," Jack murmured. "She's not the partying type."

"Neither are we," I responded, a smile tugging at my lips. "We haven't been to a party since sophomore year."

"Worst night ever," he recalled. He laughed. "That night was a disaster."

During sophomore year, Jack, Marcus and I were invited to a party with the varsity football team. So many people had gotten into trouble with the police that night that we decided that parties weren't worth the trouble. That was the first time—and only time—any of us had tasted alcohol. At least, it was the only time for Jack and me.

I'd hated it; it smelled foul and burned my throat like I'd swallowed a fireball. I had no interest in trying it ever again. It made me feel like I wasn't myself—like I was some slow motion, sickly version of myself.

I held the phone to my ear and listened to it ring until September picked up.

"Hello?"

"Hey. Quick question, do you want to go to a party tonight?"

Silence, and then:

"Why on earth would I want to go to a party?"

"Just thought I'd ask. Jack and I are going."

"You know that's a bad idea, Reed."

"Don't worry; it'll be fine. We're just going to hang out for a while and then we'll probably go back to my house."

"Reed, parties like that never end well."

"There's a first for everything. Besides, how do you know it's that kind of party?"

"Because no one you know throws parties that *aren't* that kind of party—besides me, that is. And you know where I am."

"Come on, Em."

"Reed." Her voice took on a sharp tone. "Be smart about this."

"I'll be fine. I promise I won't drink anything, and I'll stick close to Jack. We'll drop by and then leave."

"Why are you even going? You haven't been to a party since I moved here."

"Hannah is going," I responded. "Jack doesn't want her to go alone, and he doesn't want to go babysit her the entire time either."

She scoffed. "Here's an idea; take Hannah somewhere else."

I shrugged, although she couldn't see me. "He said she's persistent."

"*I'm* persistent. Just listen to me on this one, Reed."

"I'm listening, and I'm telling you we'll be fine. We're big boys. We can handle ourselves."

She paused a moment as if she wanted to argue back but changed her mind.

"Whatever, Davis. Just pay attention, alright?"

"I will. I'll pick you up in the morning?"

"Bright and early. I'll be ready."

I shook my head as I pocketed my phone. September could act like my mother sometimes.

"That sounded rough," Jack commented.

"She didn't approve."

"Told you so."

"Whatever, man. Listen, I don't feel comfortable taking Charlotte out to that cesspool of drunk teenagers. Mind if I ride with you?"

"So my car can get destroyed by drunk teenagers?" he joked. "Sure. You can just leave your car here, and we can stay here tonight."

A few hours later, I'd showered and changed from my torn up shop jeans into a pair of long black running pants. It was freezing out, but I didn't feel like lugging a big winter coat around with me, so I settled with a thin sweatshirt. I threw a gray beanie over my wet hair and laced up my sneakers before I left.

When I rolled into Jack's driveway, he and Hannah were just coming down the front steps of the house. I could barely see them; the sun had gone down hours ago and the only light came from the front porch and the dim streetlights. I cut the engine and hopped out of the car.

Hannah gave me a small wave. I nodded back.

"Did you call Marcus?" I asked. Jack shrugged his shoulders.

"I did, but he doesn't want to come. He said to be careful."

I quirked an eyebrow. "Of course."

He walked around the car and opened Hannah's door for her. She thanked him quietly and got in before he shut the door.

"She doesn't talk much, does she?" I asked, nodding towards the car. "I never noticed."

"She's more talkative around people she likes."

I looked at him. "*She's* the one who suggested going to a party?"

He nodded. "She wants to be more social. I told her that a high school party wasn't really the ideal place for that, but she insisted. She told me she'd go one way or the other."

"Wow. Feisty."

"She can be." The corner of his mouth turned up. "Speaking of which, she can't do your homework anymore, buddy. She no longer needs your wingman services."

I laughed. "What? Why not?"

He seemed proud of himself. "She's taken."

We hopped in the car and ended up about fifteen minutes outside of town on a very large piece of land with a very large house sitting in the dead center. Evergreen trees dominated the back part of the land.

"So, Jack," I said, after we'd pulled onto the driveway, "when were you going to tell me this kid was super rich?"

He shrugged. "When it became relevant. Oh, by the way," he added, turning around, "this kid is super rich."

I grimaced. "Thanks."

He grinned. "My pleasure."

We all exited the car, slamming the doors shut behind us. I could hear the music blaring from outside.

This will be a long few hours.

Hannah spotted a friend and jogged ahead of Jack towards the door, a smile blooming on her face. She threw her arms around another girl who almost spilled her drink in the process.

"Let's make a deal," Jack said as we walked very slowly towards the door. "After two hours, I drag Hannah back to the car and we bail. I don't want to stay here longer than need be."

I nodded. "Agreed."

When we got to the porch, Jack put an arm protectively around Hannah's waist and guided her away from the girls with the solo cups. He opened the door, and we stepped inside.

Immediately, we were hit with a thick wall of smoke. I coughed, waving it all away from my face. I didn't smoke. None of us did; Marcus hadn't even tried a cigarette. Not only were we underage, but also, I hated the smell. Once, I gave Marcus a ride home from a friend's house while his car was in the shop. His "friend" smoked a pack a day; he smelled so much like cigarettes that I made him sit in the back of Charlotte so he wouldn't stink up the cab.

No one messes with Charlotte.

We pushed through people, trying to find a room where we could breathe. Someone had plugged up an electronic disco ball or two, and the lights were off, making it impossible for us to see exactly where we were going. Glass crunched under my sneakers—probably an empty beer bottle.

I almost veered into the room on my left before I noticed four or five girls strewn over the couches with bottles in hand. Stopping dead in my tracks, I turned on my heel and headed the opposite direction.

The cheerleaders.

That was a bear I didn't want to poke tonight.

I turned back to Jack, yelling over the music.

"Why did we think this was a good idea?"

He shook his head. "Sorry," he yelled back.

I pushed past more people into one of the rooms on the right with Jack and Hannah at my heels. From what I could see, it was a den. The furniture was pushed against the walls and people were dancing. Someone dipped out drinks at a bar across the room. I hoped that they weren't all alcoholic.

I didn't drink, either. In my opinion, it was a waste of time and money—money I could have been putting towards Charlotte or college or September. Jack had his own reasons for not taking up the bottle; he thought it was just plain stupid. He was convinced it could ruin a person's life; I can't say I'd argue with him on it, either. Jack was probably the most responsible of any of us.

"Hey, bro," someone yelled, tapping me on the shoulder. I turned around to find a tall, red-headed guy staring back at me. From his jersey, I assumed this was his house.

What was his name? Dean?

"Glad you could make it," he gushed. "I wasn't sure if you would come."

"Well, I'm still trying to decide whether I'm happy I came," I replied dryly.

He laughed nervously. "Listen, I have a couple of girls in the other room asking if you're here. If they find you, make sure to mention something about how I invited you, okay?"

I snorted. "What for?"

"Well, since you let them trail behind you, I guess someone has to make them feel like they're worth something," he replied smoothly. Jack laughed, reaching over and shaking Dean's hand.

"Thank you. That was beautiful."

Hannah laughed behind him, covering her mouth with her hand.

I growled through gritted teeth. "Shut up, Jack." I pointed at the ginger. "And you, get lost. I'm not interested in sending desperate girls your way."

He shot me a glare. I ignored him.

Turning away and heading towards the bar in a foul mood, I leaned against the granite and sighed. Jack followed, laughing hysterically.

"Man." He wiped imaginary tears from his eyes. "I never knew you could get burned so badly by someone like him."

"Well," I muttered, "there's plenty of alcohol for the flame in this room."

I turned to the teenager behind the bar, asking for water. Seconds later, he sat a red solo cup down next to my arm on the counter.

One large gulp, and my throat burned like fire.

"What the crap, man?" I asked, throwing the empty cup against the wall and holding my head. "What was that?"

Jack made a face. "I believe that was vodka. I can smell it from over here."

I turned around, ready to teach the kid a lesson, but he'd disappeared. I cursed under my breath, feeling unstable where I stood.

"Here," Jack said, handing me a cup. "Try this one."

I accepted the cup from him, this time smelling it first. I handed it back. "That's alcohol. Don't these people drink anything else?"

"I doubt it."

He looked around, raising his hand to point across the room. "It looks like they have water and punch over there. You could see if that's any better."

I pushed myself up to stand upright, leaning as I steadied myself on my feet.

I hate alcohol.

I dragged my feet across the room, bumping into dancing drunks and other intoxicated teenagers. Jack and Hannah disappeared behind me in the crowd.

How did I end up here?

My hand reached over to the wall for support as the room started leaning. I used it to help me make the rest of the stretch to the table at the far wall.

There were two drink dispensers. One held a blood red drink that I assumed was punch, and the other was a large, clear water tank. At least, I thought it was water. My throat still burned, and the room all of a sudden grew twenty degrees hotter. I filled a clean cup to the brim.

A couple of gulps later, the burn in my throat set in stronger and my head buzzed. I slung the liquid out of the cup and onto the floor.

You've got to be kidding me.

I pushed my cup under the dispenser containing the punch, releasing some until my cup was about half-full. I smelled it and tasted a sip, making sure there was no alcohol in it. I didn't taste any, so I assumed it was fine and filled my cup to the brim, anxious to get the burning sensation out of my throat.

Taking another swig of the overly sweet liquid and looking up, I realized that I'd lost Jack.

My vision blurred at the edges, and the room was much too hot. I pulled at the collar of my sweatshirt and struggled to find an exit to the room—I desperately needed air. My head hurt so bad it felt like it could roll off. The punch started tasting sour in my mouth.

This was such a bad idea. Why did I think a party would be better the second time around?

And why did I have to drink the punch? That's like, the golden rule of partying—don't drink the punch. I feel worse than I did before.

Pushing my way through the endless throng of teenagers, I finally made it to the hallway, shoving people aside to reach the front door. I swung it open and reveled in the cold air, plopping down on the front steps to wait for Jack.

No way was I going back in there.

"Feeling rough?" someone asked me. I took another sip of my drink, eager to get the bad taste out of my mouth. It only got worse.

"Little bit." I wiped my mouth. I turned around to see who was talking to me.

A thin, freckled, blonde girl with glasses crouched down next to me. She seemed familiar, but I couldn't remember where I'd seen her.

Probably in one of my classes.

She reached over and snatched my cup from my hand, looking at it before tossing the liquid out onto the lawn.

"Hey!" I lunged at the cup. She tossed it behind her and sat down next to me.

"Are you really that stupid?" she asked. "Haven't you ever heard that you're not supposed to drink the punch at a party like this?"

I wanted to argue, but my head was spinning. I groaned, pulling both hands up to hold my head. "What was in that?"

I felt her hand push the back of my head so that my head was between my knees. "Someone spiked it, doofus. Funny—I figured you'd be the kind to enjoy intoxication, but you seem miserable."

"I *hate* alcohol," I moaned.

"Well, that makes two of us. You're a lightweight if I ever saw one."

Taking deep breaths, I sat up and leaned my back against the posts on the railing.

"If you hate alcohol, why are you here?" I asked weakly.

"I was forced by a few of my friends. I'm the designated driver. If I had my way, I would've bailed a long time ago, but I couldn't change their minds and I don't trust anyone here to drive them home if they pass out."

"Sounds fun." The ground started to tremble. I felt like throwing up.

She patted my back. "Good luck. I'd offer you a ride, but my car is full of four hormonal teenage girls high on life and so intoxicated they can't remember each other's names. Not to mention, you don't appear to be worth my time."

"I'm sorry?"

She exhaled sharply. "Why doesn't it surprise me that you don't recognize me?"

"In my defense, I can't really see anything clearly."

"Whatever. I should probably thank you; you did me a favor by brushing me off that day in the hall. Er, your friend did, actually. September. That's her name, right?"

I lifted my head but immediately hung it again. The weight was crushing.

"Anyway, she talked some sense into me. Gave me some confidence. Thank her for me next time you see her, will you?" She stood up, brushing herself off. "I've got to get these girls away from the alcohol and into the car."

"Don't let them near a flame," I mumbled.

She snorted, turning and climbing the stairs back into the house. I never even got her name.

I wanted to feel guilty—after all, I really couldn't remember who she was or what I did, but I'm sure it wasn't good—but I felt too sick to pay much attention to what she'd said to me.

I pulled myself up, desperate to lie down in the car. As soon as I stood, the bile rose in my throat. I bent over, my stomach contorting in my abdomen as everything I'd just drank came up.

My phone buzzed in my pocket. I was vaguely aware of it but not enough to answer.

I decided to go find Hannah and Jack and tell them to take me home. This was a terrible idea, and I knew it; I'd never been so sick in my life.

I thought about what September would do when she found out. In a way, I was more afraid of September being disappointed in me than I was my parents. Believe me, I hated disappointing my parents, but nothing compared to the look on September's face when one of us did something we knew we weren't supposed to do. The image sent a chill down my spine.

I tried to make it up the stairs back into the house, but my vision started going black. I sat back down and leaned against the railing again. My phone buzzed in my pocket once more, but I closed my eyes and fell asleep before I could get to it.

———

"Reed?"

My head throbbed against the ground. I tried to lift it, but it felt heavy like lead.

"Reed, can you hear me? Are you okay?"

I realized that I was laying down instead of sitting up, like I remembered. Though my eyelids were heavy, I forced them open. My vision was clearing, and the music seemed to fade back into my ears. When my eyes focused, I recognized September standing over me.

"Em?" I squinted, unsure if it was really her. "What are you doing here?"

"You didn't answer your phone," she explained, crouching and helping me sit up. I had been lying on the grass in front of the house.

Someone must've moved me.

"So you came to check on me?" I joked weakly.

She frowned. "You've been here for three hours, Reed."

"Three hours?"

She ignored my question and looked towards the house. "Where are Jack and Hannah?"

I shrugged. "Inside somewhere. I lost them about half an hour in."

"Geez, Reed, you really can't stay out of trouble, can you?"

I grimaced. "Apparently not."

She handed me a water bottle. "Drink this. I'm going to go find Jack and Hannah and make sure they aren't unconscious somewhere like you were. When you feel better, go wait by the car."

Something random occurred to me. I looked at her. "Hey, aren't you supposed to be asleep?"

She rolled her eyes. "I'll be back in a second."

Em stood up and jogged toward the house to find our friends. I opened the bottle of water and started chugging, feeling a little better with each gulp. Believe me, I still felt terrible, but I felt a little less like absolute death.

When I felt well enough, I stood. The ground still wobbled under my feet but not near as bad. I slowly made my way to September's car and leaned against it.

One minute turned into five minutes and five turned into ten.

That's a long time to be getting Jack and Hannah. The house is big, but it's not that big.

Ten minutes.

Fifteen minutes.

I decided that if she hadn't found them then maybe two people would have a better chance of finding them. I ventured back into the house to help search.

As soon as I entered the front door, I could hear yelling. Not like party-hard kind of yelling either—more urgent, more violent.

I followed the sounds back into the room with the drinks. It sounded like a fight. I had to push past what seemed like a billion people to be able to see, but when I did, I couldn't see anything else in the room. Everything in my mind went dead silent. I could see mouths moving, but no sound came out.

September stood in the middle of the circle, struggling against Dean's grip. She kicked at his legs, but he easily dodged it, laughing as he slung liquid from his cup onto the floor. Some of it splashed onto September, and she looked disgusted. She elbowed him in the stomach, and he flinched before gripping her tighter and swinging her in a different direction.

Jack was across the way from her, pushing people to the ground. Dean's friends came at him one by one, and he dodged them, getting a good punch in at a few of them. One of the boys came behind him and had him pinned behind the back while another punched him square in the face. Hannah screamed, trying to pull one of the boys off of him. They shoved her to the ground. Anger welled up in my throat. I felt like I was vibrating where I stood, so overwhelmed with fury.

I don't remember what happened next; I blinked and the room changed.

The room grew silent and everyone stared at me. I saw mouths hanging open no matter which way I turned. Dean's friends were leaning against walls for support and sprawled on the floor. He himself was holding his face with one hand and pushing himself away from me on the floor with the other. His eyes were alarmed and wide.

Hannah was on the floor with Jack kneeling at her side. A shadow of a bruise started to form on one side of his face. September was on the floor in front of me, just watching me with wide eyes. She almost looked... scared.

Scared of me.

I felt an ache in my hands. I looked down at them and found them bruised and red with blood.

I reached a hand down and helped her up. Once September, Jack, and Hannah were all on their feet, I pinned Dean with an unforgiving stare.

"Touch them again and I'll do more than break your nose."

I turned on my heel and stumbled through the people back outside. September grabbed my hand behind me, and I pulled her towards the car. Jack and Hannah followed at our heels.

The adrenaline rush combined with the alcohol in my system made me feel strange. As soon as we got to September's car, I opened the driver's side door for her and then rounded the car and hopped in the passenger side without a word. Jack and Hannah went to their own car, and we pulled out of the driveway back towards town.

We didn't speak. I stared out the windshield at the road and didn't look at her. She did the same. After a few minutes, she said two simple words.

"Thank you."

I knew that wasn't all she wanted to say. When I decided I'd calmed down enough to talk normally, I spoke quietly.

"I know you're disappointed in me."

She didn't say anything.

"You don't have to say it. I can tell. You're angry with me."

She exhaled quietly. "I just... you're better than this, Reed."

"We've been through this. I'm not as good as you think I am."

"But you *are*. You haven't been yourself all month. It's like the move has made you into a totally different person. You never used to get angry or get into fights or *ever* raise your voice at me."

"People change."

"Not like this. Not all of a sudden. This isn't a change in character; this is a change in choice. You're *choosing* to act insufferable, which is what has me so confused. I don't understand why you feel the need."

We pulled into Jack's driveway. He hadn't made it back from Hannah's yet, so we sat in the car.

"Why did you go to that party in the first place?" she asked.

"I needed a break. I needed to forget."

"Forget what? That I'm leaving? And you thought that a party would do that for you?"

"It did."

"You passed out on the front porch, Reed. I fail to see how that's a break."

The emotions had built up again, and this time, tired of holding them back, I let slip what I *really* thought. "And I fail to see how you think moving across the world is going to be a good thing for you."

Her eyebrows furrowed. "What do you mean by that?"

"Just what I said. You can't handle a city that big. How do you know you'll make any friends?"

I knew that the remnants of alcohol influenced my words, but it felt good to say things like that. I had kept everything in for few weeks, and it had become almost unbearable. I felt like a ticking time bomb, just waiting to explode.

"If you're saying this just because you want me to stay, I'm sorry Reed, but I'm going. I know you're afraid I won't be here for you. I'll always be here to help, whatever you need."

"No, you won't," I bit back. "You're leaving."

"That doesn't mean I can't be your support. You can call on me no matter where I am."

The anger started to settle in my chest. It felt artificial, like something conjured up from the leftover alcohol in my system.

"You'll be across the ocean. Gone. We'll never hear from you again. How are we supposed to lean on when you're across the world?"

"Alright, that's enough," she said. "You're just being dramatic now."

"No, it's not enough," I replied angrily. "We're never enough. If we were enough, you wouldn't be leaving. Tell me, September, why are you really leaving?"

Her knuckles turned white as she gripped the steering wheel. She clenched her jaw.

"Shut up."

"No. You need to hear this."

"I've heard enough."

"What? Are you afraid of the truth? You know it's all true. You don't want to leave. You told me so, remember? You're afraid that you're making the wrong decision. Well guess what? *You are.*"

"That's *enough.*" She ripped her seatbelt off and jerked the door open, stepping outside onto the driveway. I pulled my seatbelt off and followed.

"Is this what it takes for you to talk to me?" she demanded. "Getting hammered at some stupid high school party? You go weeks of being good and being supportive and then all of a sudden you have an earful for me. You're an honest drunk, you know that?"

I stepped closer to her, my hands clenched at my sides. "If you'd listened to me back at the beginning, I wouldn't have to be doing this now. If you'd have just—"

"If I hadn't decided to move?" she spat. "Excuse me, Reed, but I didn't know I needed your permission to make decisions that affect my future. I thought you were past this." She pushed at me hard once, then twice, and then three times. I lost my balance and fell back onto the grass.

"This affects all of our futures, Em," I barked at her. "You're so *selfish.*"

"*I'm* selfish?" she asked, raising her voice to a yell. "No, Reed, *you're* selfish. Did it ever occur to you that I *want* to move? That I *want* to travel the world? That I *want* to live in another country? That I've been dreaming of this my *entire life?* Do you know what kind of an opportunity this is? I know that we're close, *believe me,* I know, but I assumed that you'd want what's best for me. Obviously, I was wrong."

"Maybe I thought that I was best for you." I could feel myself sobering up, feel my head getting clearer and my thoughts coherent, but I kept talking. I knew that now I could get everything off my chest—everything I had been thinking for the past few weeks, everything that I'd wanted to say since she broke the news that she was leaving. The anger had grown more powerful than me, the monster had broken the lock on its cage, and there wasn't anything I was going to do to try and resist it.

"You don't get a say in my life, Reed. And after the way you've acted this month, I don't think you qualify as 'good for me.'"

"I thought you cared what we thought," I retorted. "I thought your friends mattered to you."

"This isn't about my friends. This is about *you.* Don't lie, and don't change the subject. You're the *only one* with a problem. Why is it so hard for you to *let go?*"

"I *won't* give up on you." My chest heaved, my eyes burned livid.

She didn't back down but instead stepped right up to my face. She uttered a simple sentence.

"Letting me go isn't the same as giving up on me."

That phrase stopped me in my tracks. I couldn't stop the next thing that fell from my lips.

"You want me to let you go?"

Her eyebrows furrowed, then her eyes widened as she made sense of everything. "That's what this is about?"

She stared for a moment as if she were running my words through her head again and again. After a moment, her eyes met mine.

"All this time, I thought you were just worried that things were going to change," she said quietly, a small breath escaping her mouth.

"Did you know that taking you on a date has been a goal since the day I met you?" I joked lightly. The corner of her lips twitched.

"All you had to do was ask, Davis."

"How could I? You always shot down my hints. It was luck that Jack couldn't go to the movies the night we finally went on a date."

"Your flirting methods are lame. You need something original."

"Yeah, I guess I do."

We stood quietly for a moment, the conversation lulling. She shook her head, a sad smile crossing her mouth as she offered me a hand and helped me stand up.

"Reed, you know that I love you, don't you?"

I shrugged, turning away from her to the street. I could clearly see small snowflakes falling in the light of the lamps on the sidewalk.

The first snow of November.

"You don't love me the same way that I love you," I said. "I know that."

"That doesn't mean I feel less towards you than you do towards me. Right now they're just different kinds of love."

"Is there anything I can say?" I asked.

"Well, you can start with an apology. You've been a jerk this month."

"I'm sorry. I'm an idiot."

The corner of her mouth turned up, and she ruffled my hair. "I know you are. Just try to embrace reality; this move is happening whether you like it or not. I'd hate to part ways tomorrow on bad terms."

"Reality sucks," I mumbled.

"I know."

I sighed, my breath turning into a frozen fog. In all of our arguing, I didn't realize how cold I'd gotten. My thin sweatshirt wasn't doing much for me. I looked over September's attire: a pair of jeans and a sweater under a winter coat. Her cheeks and nose were pink.

"You should get back in the car. It's cold."

"You too," she said. "You'll freeze."

"No, Jack will be here soon. I'll go on in. You should go home and get some sleep."

She gave me a wary glance. "Are you sure?"

I nodded. "Listen, I'm sorry for what I said. I'd blame it all on the alcohol, but I think that's mostly worn off." I shifted where I stood, extremely uncomfortable. "I do support you, I swear—this was just a shock to my system."

"I know," she said, "but at least you were telling me the truth."

Without warning, she wrapped her arms around my waist and hugged me tight, leaning her head against my chest. "I would apologize, but I'm not sorry for anything I said."

"I know."

She pulled away and flashed me a smile before opening her car door, sliding in, and starting the ignition. "I'll see you tomorrow morning."

"Be careful. Get some sleep."

She waved at me one last time before pulling out and driving away. I watched her drive down the street until I couldn't see her car anymore.

18

every day is leg day when you're running from your problems

I waited until she turned the corner to take off running down the road. I didn't look back.

My feet couldn't feel a thing as they pounded the pavement. My throat burned, dry from the cold air. The snow made my hair wet, and it hung down in front of my eyes.

Down the middle of the empty road is where I left all of my thoughts. I ran harder than I ever had, and I knew that it eventually would hurt. I didn't focus on it though. I didn't focus on anything. My mind went blank. My heart hurt in my chest. My lungs heaved for air.

But I kept running.

The snow melted on the road, creating puddles that I didn't take the time to avoid. It felt good to not *feel*, to not *care*. September was leaving, and *I didn't care*.

One more step, one more breath, one more beat. It wasn't until I reached my street that I realized how far I'd gone. My phone buzzed in my pocket. I ignored it, slowing to a breathless walk as I took my time strolling down the cold, wet, empty street. My eyes scanned the houses before mine, adorned with early Christmas decorations. I watched a cat scamper across the street and disappear into a dog

271

door. I felt the cold soak into my shoes, through my clothes, and against my face. I heard the deafening silence.

A few more steps up the road, I came to stand in front of my house. The soft lights of dawn peeked over the horizon. Birds chirped. Almost as if someone knew I was there, the light in my parents' bedroom window flickered on. Carefully, I watched as my father drew back the curtains and looked through the glass.

If he could see me, he didn't acknowledge me. It must've still been too dark or his eyes were adjusting to the light or he was simply too tired to notice. He looked back and forth—probably looking for me—before turning away from the window and disappearing from view.

I should've gone inside and told them I was okay. I should've gone in and apologized for the total jerk I'd been. I should've apologized for the stress I'd put on them. For making things complicated.

But I didn't. I turned and ran.

Running from your problems. That's a new low, even for you.

Once again, I sprinted at full speed. Daylight grew brighter with every minute. September would be on a plane in a few hours. My parents would be disappointed in me. We'd all be graduating and separating in a few short months.

My life was a mess. I was a mess.

I am a mess.

All at once, several things hit me.

One, I had a lot of crap on my mind that had been festering for a month, and it was eating me alive. Guilt for treating September so badly, grief that she was leaving, confusion on what I felt. It was poisonous.

Two, my lungs were fighting against me. It seemed like they couldn't handle any more pressure.

Three, I had issues. *Real* issues.

Don't ask me how I ended up at the evergreen-lined highway because I don't know. When I hit the tree line, I stopped, falling forward onto all fours as I forced air into my chest and forced it out again.

I had no clue what was happening. This had never happened to me before, and I didn't know how to handle it.

I pushed my back against a tree, forcing my head between my knees as my heart pounded in my throat and I struggled to breathe.

I don't know how long I sat there, trying to calm myself, trying to force air down my dry throat. I know that I was there long enough for the sun to rise over the trees and the cars to start moving down the road. My phone buzzed in my pocket again, but I couldn't bring myself to answer it—partly because I didn't have the air to speak. My eyes fell shut, and I counted numbers in my head, trying to do something to calm myself down.

"Reed?"

Slowly, my eyes opened, focusing on the image of September crouched in front of me. Her cheeks were red from the cold. Jack's car sat on the side of the road behind her, humming quietly.

Oh.

"Reed, what happened? Are you hurt?"

I shook my head, taking in another heavy breath and trying to swallow.

"I don't know." My voice came out hoarse.

Her eyebrows drew together with worry. "Just... breathe for a sec. We've been looking for you for the past two hours. Your parents are freaking out."

"He looks like he's just had a panic attack," came Jack's voice. He stepped into view, frowning as he looked down at me. "Geez, man. Are you okay?"

"Panic attack?" September looked from Jack back to me. "Why didn't you tell me you have panic attacks?"

I shrugged, my eyelids growing heavy. The adrenaline was wearing off, and I could feel the sting of the cold on my skin. "I don't."

Her eyebrows furrowed, and she pursed her lips. "Where did you go?"

"I ran."

"You ran? Ran from what?"

My tongue rolled over my lips, trying to make it easier to talk. After trying to clear my throat, I spoke. "You."

"Me?" She seemed like she wanted to add something but changed her mind. "Let's get you warm, okay?"

She stood up. Jack helped her get me on my feet then they both threw an arm under my shoulders for support. Jack smirked at me. "How're you holding up, Reed?"

I breathed out what was supposed to be a laugh. "What does it look like?"

He shook his head in response, laughing as he helped me back towards the main road where Jack's car was waiting. September opened the door to the back seat while Jack helped me in.

"So," she said once we were all in the car, "you didn't go to Jack's last night."

"Not right now, September," Jack cut in. "The guy's had a rough night. Let's cut him a little slack."

"No, it's fine," I answered.

"Are you sure?" She looked at me from the front seat. "Jack is right. I'm too hard on you sometimes. I'm sorry."

"I deserve it. No, I didn't go to Jack's last night."

"You didn't go home, either."

"How did you...?" I began, before it clicked. "Mom called you."

She offered me a weak smile. "She was worried. I called Jack, and we came out to look for you."

I didn't respond.

Her eyebrows furrowed, worry overtaking her expression. "Have you ever had a panic attack before?"

I shook my head. "What do I have to panic about?"

"Sometimes it's not a specific thing. Sometimes it's just all your emotions catching up to you at once."

I remembered the day I helped September pack, the day she broke down in her empty living room. I remembered how broken she was... and how helpless I felt.

"Thank you. For finding me, I mean."

"Don't worry about it. Jack here was worried that the love of his life was dead."

Jack nudged September's arm playfully, and she swatted him away. "If Reed dies, who am I going to harass you with?"

She laughed. It was music to my ears.

"What time does your plane leave, Em?" Jack asked.

Oh yeah. That.

"Ten," she said, looking over at the clock on the radio. "Four hours from now."

"Yeah, by the way—thanks for making me get up at six to come find you, Reed," Jack complained. "It's been *lovely.*"

"No problem. I'd feel sorry for you, but you got more sleep than I did." I slumped down in my seat, the exhaustion catching up with me. My muscles ached and my face burned from the cold wind. I couldn't stop shivering. "Where are we going?"

"Your house," September answered, "so you can apologize to your parents. After that, we're going to Jack's to pick up Charlotte then to my house to get my bags."

"Didn't you want to go to Waffle House on your last morning?" Jack reminded her.

"If we have time."

"We'll make time," I said. "Call Marcus. Have him meet us there."

———

September drove Charlotte to Waffle House, partly because I still shivered pretty violently and partly because she just wanted to drive it one last time. Our booth, as usual, sat empty when we got there. As we settled in,

Terra handed September a five-dollar bill with a wink and a smile.

"Pick something good, hon," she said. "All of the favorites."

She offered a radiant smile in return. "Thanks, Terra."

September popped up out of her seat, her good mood evident in her peppy attitude and body language. She all but skipped to the jukebox, taking her time picking her playlist. The sound of music faded into the restaurant speakers, and September made her way back to the booth, sliding into her spot next to me.

"Pick anything good?" Jack asked.

"Is that even a question?"

My lips turned up into a smile. It felt good, to *genuinely smile* and to be *happy*.

The bell above the door rang, and we all turned to see Marcus stroll into the restaurant. He slid into the booth. "Morning, guys."

"Good morning," September chirped. I knew she couldn't have gotten much sleep last night, but she didn't show it.

We ordered our food. Her feet swung back and forth under the table as we ate and talked over the past year, all of us nostalgic. Terra paid for us one more time, saying it was her treat for our last meal as a group.

Before we left, September asked Terra to take a picture of the four of us. She handed her the Polaroid camera.

"Do I have to?" Jack groaned.

"Grow up." September nudged his foot under the table. "Can you just smile for two seconds?"

Jack smiled. "I'm counting."

Terra took the photo and handed it all back to September. When the image became clear, September laughed.

I looked over her shoulder. September was the only one looking at the camera. Jack had a deep, silly frown on his face. Marcus had crossed his eyes. I was smiling at September.

September looked at it and smiled. "This is my favorite."

"Send me a copy of it, will ya?" I asked. Jack and Marcus chimed in and asked for one, too. She told us that she would be sure to do that. Then she gave Jack Cora's Polaroid and asked him to return it for her.

We all filed outside and got ready to head to the airport. Jack decided to ride with Marcus, saying that they had catching up to do. I silently thanked him.

I drove Charlotte to the airport. We didn't speak, but I could tell September was happy. She was savoring the comfortable silence.

I would miss it, too.

"I really am sorry, Em."

"It's done," she said. "I'm past it."

"No, really. I feel terrible. I've treated you awful this past month."

"I'm serious, Reed." She looked at me, smiling genuinely. "I'm not mad at you. It's over and we've moved on. All it took was a little... waking up," she said, "but I promise, we're good now. I just want to enjoy my last few minutes in Charlotte, with you, okay?"

September never ceases to amaze me. How can she move on from something like that so quickly?

I didn't deserve it, and I knew that, but I decided that I didn't want to make her last hour a pity party. So I nodded thankfully and focused on the road. Making Midnight played softly on the radio until we pulled into the airport parking lot. We sat in the car for a few minutes, just listening. She leaned back against the seat and closed her eyes.

When Jack and Marcus got there, they jumped out to get September's bags. Together, the four of us walked through the airport. September reached down and grabbed my hand, and I entwined our fingers.

The terminal was full of people, but we managed to find four seats together to await her plane's arrival.

"Do you remember the Making Midnight concert we went to together?" Marcus asked after a moment. Jack and I exchanged a look, nodding.

"I'm glad we survived that one," September teased.

He grinned. "Me too."

"What about hiking?" Jack asked. "That was terrible."

September snorted. "You loved it. Don't lie."

"Until you fell into a hole," he added.

Marcus laughed. "The movie marathon may be the only thing that didn't go wrong."

"The conversation got deep," she said. "It was actually kind of nice."

All too soon, our reminiscing was interrupted by the loudspeaker, calling out boarding for September's flight and dropping us into silence. We all exchanged looks. September looked at me and offered a comforting smile. My throat grew tight.

"That's me," she murmured, rising. Jack and I grabbed her bags while she hugged Marcus.

"Keep your nose clean, Marcus." She kissed his cheek. "I don't want any calls telling me that you're in jail or something."

"Don't worry," he said, a ghost of a smile on his lips. "I've learned my lesson."

She offered him a smile and turned towards Jack and me. Together, the three of us walked to the gate while Marcus hung back.

"Thanks, guys," she told us. "For everything."

"Don't thank us." Jack shook his head. "We have more to thank you for than you do us."

Jack sat September's bags down, wrapping his arms around her and hugging her tight. "Love you, Em."

"Love you, too." She reached up and kissed his cheek like she did Marcus. "Keep these lunatics in line, won't you?"

"Of course." He grinned, kissing the top of her head. "Call us, alright?"

"I will," she answered.

Jack flashed her one last smile before walking back towards Marcus.

Just the two of us now, I met September's eyes, offering her a weak smile. "So this is it, huh?"

"You act like it's forever," she said. "I'll visit."

"I hope so," I said.

"Reed, I want you to promise me something."

I nodded. "Anything."

"Promise me that you'll move on." Her eyes were honest, and she pressed my hands into hers. "Promise me that you're going to be happy."

I looked away as tears sprang to my eyes.

Don't cry, Reed. If you cry, I swear—

"Reed?"

My eyes met hers, and I could see her on the brink of tears, too.

I cleared my throat, making sure my voice was steady before I answered. "I promise."

She offered a weak smile. "Good. I want to see you smile when I visit."

I wrapped my arms around her, hugging her as tight as I could. She returned the favor, reaching on her toes to kiss my cheek. I kissed the top of her head.

"Take care." She let go of me and grabbed her suitcase. She slung a backpack over her shoulders. "I'll call you when I land."

I mustered half a smile, waving at her.

September waved back, turning towards her gate, but she hesitated then stopped.

"Hey, Reed?"

I raised an eyebrow. "Yeah?"

In one unexpected motion, her lips met mine. She seemed surprised in herself, and for a moment, I thought she would pull away but instead her hands came to the side of my face. I kissed her back, hugging her close. When we pulled away, September kept her eyes closed.

"I had to at least one more time," she said quietly, laughing a little.

"Me too," I agreed.

"I love you, Reed Davis. I really do." One of her hands found mine, and I felt her press something soft into the palm of my hand.

"I love you, too," I breathed, my smile turning into a grin. I hugged her tight one more time before letting her go. She turned and walked towards the gate door. As she walked away, I noticed a single flower poking out of her backpack. It was an Autumn Joy, one of the flowers I'd given her. She turned and waved one last time before disappearing behind the gate.

I looked down at my palm, finding a crumpled napkin, folded into a small square. I unfolded it, finding September's bucket list scribbled across the paper. At the top, she'd crossed Waffle House out. At the end, September had penned in the words *kiss Reed goodbye* and circled them. My gaze lifted, looking back towards the gate where she'd left, even though she was already gone.

The three of us sat on the bench facing the window where we could see her plane readying for take-off. None of us said a word. When the plane finally lifted from the tarmac, we watched it disappear into the sky. Mark and Jack got up, but I stayed where I was, staring at the smoke trail it left behind.

Jack slapped my back with his hand.

"Man, if that kiss was your first with September, that's *really* disappointing. I shipped you two *hardcore*."

"You know what else is disappointing?" I asked. "Finding out that your best friend uses words like *ship*."

Before he could react, I turned and slugged him hard across the arm.

"*OUCH*," he said, rubbing his arm. "What was that for?"

"You're turning into a fan girl," Marcus said as I stood up. "That's embarrassing."

I slugged Marcus across the arm, too.

"What was *that one* for?" he asked, rubbing his arm like Jack.

"You used the term *fan girl*," I said. "You guys are going soft. Toughen up."

"*We're* going soft?" Jack asked. "Which one of us keeps looking over at the gate? Her plane took off three minutes ago."

I realized how long I'd been standing there, just staring at the gate, like I expected her to come back through the door any second.

Marcus patted my back. "She'll be back before you know it, man."

"Yeah." Jack pivoted away from the gate, "and then you can kiss her better than you did a few minutes ago. I mean, *come on*—that was the first one?"

I turned from the gate, shoving my hands into my pockets as we walked back towards the exit. "For your information, it wasn't the first. Besides, you can't talk; you haven't even had your first kiss yet."

"Says who?"

"No way," Marcus marveled, "you haven't had your first kiss yet?"

"Why do I tell you idiots these things?" Jack groaned. "It always comes back to bite me in the butt."

Marcus and Jack kept walking as I slowed down. I looked back at the gate over my shoulder one more time before following them out of the airport.

"So, that's it," Marcus said. "September's gone."

"She was just passing through anyway," Jack said, waving him off. "We all knew she wouldn't stay in a small town like this for too long. Her dreams are bigger than all of ours combined. She's always wanted to go to England, and now she's seized the opportunity."

"It's a good thing she left then, isn't it?" I asked. Marcus raised an eyebrow. "We would've held her down. None of us have the drive that she does."

"You do," Jack teased. "Your dream was to marry the girl."

I shrugged. "I promised her I would move on, so I will."

Both my friends stopped, turning to look at me with wide eyes.

"You're joking, right?" Marcus asked. "*You're* going to move on?"

I pushed past them, walking towards Charlotte and swinging her door open. "Don't sound so surprised, Marcus."

"He's right," Jack said. "Have a little faith."

Charlotte's engine roared to life and settled into a familiar low purr. It was comforting, knowing that some things never change. Jack crossed in front of my car, swinging the passenger side open and hopping in before closing it behind him.

"See you tomorrow." Marcus fished his keys from his pocket and waved before turning away to find his car.

When I jumped in the car, I noticed something stuck to the dashboard behind the steering wheel. I pulled it out and held it up so I could see it.

It was one of September's Polaroids, the one of us sitting in Charlotte. At the bottom, in September's scrawled handwriting were the words *September and Reed.*

I reached into the glove box and pulled out another photo, the one of her with Charlotte in the shop. I put it next to hers on the dash.

My door slammed shut, and I pulled out of the parking lot, headed back down the road towards Greenville. Neither of us spoke as we watched the airport grow smaller behind us. I found myself wondering what Charlotte would look like when September visited.

"Will she be red?" Jack asked.

I shrugged. "Maybe not."

He seemed surprised but didn't say anything.

"Are you sure you're going to be okay?" Jack asked after a while. "I know she meant a lot to you."

"She meant a lot to all of us, but yeah, I'll be fine."

He nodded, seeming satisfied. "A lot of things are going to change around here."

I shrugged. "Guess so."

"And you're fine with that?"

"You aren't?"

He chuckled, turning towards the window. "I've never had a problem with change. The way I see it, we're just going back to the way we were before September moved here."

"It won't be exactly the same." I kept my eyes on the road. "I don't think that Marcus will go out drinking any time soon."

Jack let out a laugh. "I don't think so either."

I laughed with him. It felt good to be happy after being depressed for so long.

"All joking aside," I said, "I'm sad to see her go, but she was pretty clear that she wanted us to be happy."

"You're right," he agreed. "Besides, if we moped around for months, she'd show up at our doors to slap us across the face and tell us to get a grip."

A smile twisted across my lips as the image formed in my head. He was right, no doubt about it; September would be upset if she found out we had hung onto her departure for so long.

I decided that September was good for me. Maybe Jack was right; she came, she stayed, then she left, and that happened to be what I needed. No more taking things—or people—for granted.

In a way, I was glad she had left. It was a new chapter of my life that I needed to start with a new perspective and see where it led me. She'd changed my outlook on life, and I needed to experience it without her for a while.

I knew that her life would be different and maybe even a little scary, but I wasn't worried about her. She was probably happy that she didn't have to worry about us for once; she was free to go make new friends that she wouldn't have to keep in line. She was strong—stronger than me. She'd find her way.

She always did.

epilogue

"How are you?" she asked. "Nervous?"

I shrugged, though I knew she couldn't see me through the phone. "Not really."

"Funny. I'd be terrified. I'd probably throw up."

Laughing, I imagined September nervously pacing the hallways in a graduation gown. "Good thing you aren't here, then. Graduation gowns are probably expensive to dry clean."

Her laugh made me grin. "Probably."

I dodged people in the crowd, making my way to the left side of the stadium to join my class. It was tradition for our school's graduation ceremony to be held on the football field, not to mention our auditorium couldn't accommodate the amount of people that attend every year. When I finally spotted the sea of black and green, I ran to my spot in line.

"Why are you breathing so heavy?" September asked. "Are you running?"

"Cutting it a little close," I said, catching my breath. "I forgot my cap at home and had to go back and get it."

I could almost *hear* the eye roll through the phone. "Typical."

Our principal tapped the microphone, checking to make sure it was on before starting his welcome speech. The roar of the conversations in the stadium died down to barely a whisper as he introduced the staff and congratulated the senior class.

"I hear the speech," she said. "Call me later?"

"Will do."

"Good luck!"

The grin on my face felt like it'd never go away. I loved Em's calls; she always sounded so happy. Based on what she'd told me about England so far, I could see why; she had easily made friends with her father's students and had gotten involved in the community already. The town she lived in, according to her, was a perfect fit.

I pocketed my phone and looked around at the scene, taking in my last moments as a senior. *In a few minutes, I'll be an alumnus. How crazy is that?*

I caught the eye of one particular blonde-haired, freckled, glasses-wearing girl. She smiled and waved at me. I waved back.

After the whole party incident, I ran into her at school. I apologized for being a jerk to her. From then on, instead of asking Hannah for my homework, I went to her after school for tutoring in calculus. Turned out, we had a lot in common; we both planned to attend the same college in the fall, too.

I finally learned her name. It's Emily.

It seemed like forever before they started calling names and even longer before they got to me on the list. When they did call my name and I heard it echo against the stone stadium and saw my family cheering for me, I *felt* it. A rush of pride, a pang of sadness, and a breath of the future, all at once crowding my system. *I did it.*

I took the steps on the stage to the podium two at a time. When the principal handed me my diploma and shook my hand, I beamed, closing one chapter of my life and beginning another with every step back down to the grass. Adrenaline propelled me to my seat and had me on my feet cheering when Jack crossed the stage with a grin and a fist pump. We both yelled from our seats when Marcus walked across stage, having finished the fall semester online and rejoined us back at school in the spring. It was a rocky semester, but he pulled through, and Jack and I were there for everything.

All three of us had our diplomas. It felt surreal to be graduated after spending so long in one place.

I vaguely paid attention to the names called after Mark's. I was so excited, so ready to celebrate that I almost missed it.

"September Jones."

My head snapped back towards the stage at the name. *A mistake, that's what it was. They just forgot to take her name off the roster.*

She couldn't possibly be here.

At least, that's what I thought before I saw her.

Her auburn hair was longer, but that was the extent of the difference from the last time I saw her. She walked with confidence up the steps of the stage, catching my gaze and sending a wink my way. I was convinced she was a daydream, a mirage, until Jack called my name from a few rows back and asked for confirmation.

"Is that Em?" he asked, his smile growing. "I'm not dreaming, right?"

"If you are, we're dreaming the same dream," I said, watching her receive her diploma and shake the principal's hand. The entire student body screamed for her success. As she crossed the other side of the stage, Marcus, Jack, and I got up to meet her at the bottom of the steps. No one tried to stop us.

"Hello, boys," she said as her feet hit the grass. Her smile was bright; she glowed with life. "Surprise."

"You flew all the way here for graduation?" Marcus asked with a smirk.

She snorted. "Well, I wasn't going to Skype in. How lame would that be?"

"Not as lame as you calling me beforehand to tell me you wish you could've been here," I pointed out. "Sneaky, Jones."

She beamed with pride. "You believed it, Davis. Now, come here. Everyone's staring and I haven't hugged any of you in six months."

I was the first to throw my arms around her, then Jack and Marcus around the both of us. To my surprise, our class behind us began to cheer again.

"Enough cheese for one moment." Marcus wrinkled his nose as we walked back to our seats. Luckily, our classmates moved down to allow us to sit together. We took four seats in the front row: me, then Em, then Marcus, then Jack. She clasped my hand when we sat down, giving it a tight squeeze. *I missed you*, it said.

I squeezed back. *I missed you, too.*

We sat through the rest of our class graduation together, side by side like things used to be. It felt like everything fell back into place; our group was complete again.

"Congratulations to this year's graduating class," our principal said into the microphone. "We congratulate you on your accomplishments, and we're all looking forward to seeing what your future holds. You may move your tassels."

We all moved our tassels, and within seconds, caps were in the air. The collective cheer and the rain of graduation caps brought forth applause from our audience of family and friends. I saw more than a few people crying.

September found her cap in the grass and put it back on her head, holding out a hand for me once I'd found mine. "Catch me up. What did I miss?"

"Mark's got a girl!" Jack dodged a punch from Marcus.

September's mouth formed an O shape. "A girl? You're dating?"

"She lives in Portland," he answered sheepishly. "Met her on a college visit and kept in touch."

"Three months," I added. "Mark thinks she's the best thing since sliced bread."

"That's because she is," Mark defended.

I jerked my head towards Jack. "He's still dating Hannah."

"*Still?*"

"Don't look so surprised," Jack said. "It's kind of offensive. She's nice, and I like her. We get along well.

"Jack Evans, keeping up a relationship for longer than a week. Geez, I leave for a few months and the world ends."

Jack grinned. "Face it, Em. You left and missed all the action."

"Apparently so. I move countries and suddenly you leave me out of the loop. Thanks, guys. I feel loved."

"You're only living five thousand miles away," Mark commented.

"That's no excuse!"

"That's enough, children," I interrupted, my smile betraying my tone. "September, you have to stay long enough for us to go out on a triple date."

"Triple date?"

"I just remembered," Jack mumbled, grabbing Marcus by the elbow and pulling him away, "we've got a thing—" He didn't finish before they'd already cleared the area. September looked on at their retreat, frowning with suspicion.

I raised my eyebrows at her. "So…"

Her eyes moved to me. "So?"

"How's England? Found a boy I need to beat up?" I cracked my knuckles. "I got pretty good at that during the fall."

"Jack doesn't count as someone you beat up; *he* beat *you.*"

"Did not!"

"Does this have a point, Reed?"

"Yeah. How long will you be here?"

She shrugged like it wasn't a big deal, but she struggled to suppress her smile. "A week. Why?"

Impulsively, I reached down and took her hand, interlocking our fingers. "Mind if I take you out on a date?"

Her mouth formed a perfect 'O' as the shock set in. "Reed, that was actually polite!"

"I know how to be polite, Em."

She ignored me, holding up our hands for me to see. "What's gotten into you? You're like, a different person."

"You did."

She blinked. "Me?"

"I learned a lot of things from you while you were here."

Her eyebrows raised. "Wow. Well, I'm glad I could do something useful."

"I went to counseling, too, thanks to you. The first week was the most awkward week of my life." I cringed at the thought. "But I've been working on emotional management."

Making the decision to go to a counselor proved to be one of the hardest I ever had to make, but I ended up glad I did it. Once I set my pride aside and opened up about my problems, they became so much easier to manage. The counselor was a pretty cool guy, too; our sessions ended with Black Ops on the PlayStation he kept hidden under his desk. I wasn't really sure how Black Ops would help me manage my anger, but I didn't question it. Besides, it only lasted a couple months, and as much as I hate to say it, I was kind of sad when it ended.

Em's eyes went wide. "Wow, Reed… That's great. I'm proud of you."

"Thanks, me too. So, about that date?"

She thought for a moment. "Depends. Are you going to run away and hide in the woods if I say no?"

"It's possible."

She bit her lip, looking at me for a long moment before nodding. "Yeah. I'd love to go on a date with you."

"Great," I said, grinning.

We spotted Jack and Marcus making their way back towards us from the crowd.

"This has been fun and all, but I'm starving," Jack said. "Can we go eat now?"

"People keep trying to talk to me," Mark complained, his lips pulled into a grimace. "I don't *know* half these people."

"Let me go see my family but then we can go," I said. "We've got to leave soon if we want our booth at Waffle House; people suddenly think it's a cool place to eat."

"It *is* a cool place to eat," September defended.

"Well, yeah, but we don't want other people to know that. Geez, Em. Keep up."

Her hand came out to swat my arm, but I dodged it with a laugh. Her eye roll carried me back to the many, many, *many* times she'd done the same gesture at me in the past.

"I'll meet you guys in the parking lot then," Jack said. Mark followed him away from us and towards the gate to leave the field. I gestured for Em to go first, and we started towards the stands where my parents were talking with hers.

"My parents will be so happy to see you," I commented. "My mom thinks you're the best thing to ever happen to Greenville." She tried to hide her blush, but I squeezed her hand. "She's right, you know."

"I was worried about you," she admitted.

"We managed. It was tough not having you home, though."

She squeezed my hand back. "I love you, Reed. After everything that happened and the thousands of miles between here and England, I still do. I hope you know that."

"I love you, too."

She dropped my hand, hugging me tight before standing on her tiptoes to kiss my cheek. "Come on; our parents are waiting."

She started on without me, and I watched her climb the steps and open her arms to hug my mom. My dad welcomed her back before looking down and catching my eye. He shot me a wink before reaching over to clap her dad on the back. Her father looked on at her with pride.

I had imagined it would be hard seeing her again. I thought I would relapse, fall back into the pit, and drown myself.

But then I *did* see her—after so many months of *trying* to be happy, after all that I did to try and be *better*—and I saw that smile. That one Making Midnight song started playing from nowhere but my own mind, and all my friends were in one place again, and for a moment, it was like nothing had changed.

I knew everything would be okay. I was home, and so was September. Even though we were all going our separate ways for college, we'd find our way back here eventually. This wasn't the end; it was just the beginning of a new chapter for our friendship.

That's what September was—family. I'd never recover from the year she spent in Greenville, and I didn't care. I learned too much from her to forget.

I became a better person because of her—not perfect in any sense of the word—but better. I'd never been more thankful to be rejected in my entire life because it made me realize how much of an idiot I'd been. She changed my outlook on everything, and all I wanted was her happiness—whether that was in England or in our little evergreen Oregon town. I'd enjoy her while she was home, and I'd be okay when she left again. She'd find another person, and I'd support her, given he treated her right. I'd take everything she taught me to the next relationship and start fresh.

It still seemed impossible, the fact that one person could change my entire perspective—me, a stubborn, stuck up, excessively proud idiot—but it happened. Besides, she wasn't just *any* person.

She was warm and kind and compassionate. She was the beginning of a great change, a whirlwind of energy and potential and excitement. She left an impression. She was September, and when September passed through, everything changed for the better.

acknowledgements

September contrasts my first book in so many ways—the genre, the characters, and the overall aesthetic and feel of the book are all different. One thing that is the same, however, is the overwhelming support I had while writing and publishing. I have a support system like you wouldn't believe. I'm so thankful to everyone who has pushed me follow my dreams and to hone my skills.

First, to God be all the glory. He's given me a creative mind and hands to write. He's given me a family that loves me and a church that supports me. He's given me so many opportunities and brought so many people into my life that I will cherish forever. No words can describe the amount of love and joy and thankfulness I hold for my Creator. Thank you, God.

Meredith—you read *September* as I finished each chapter, so I have to thank you for sticking with it through the rough drafts and messy bits of the manuscript. I'm thankful for a friend like you that is so supportive of my writing. I've been looking forward to giving you a physical copy of this book for a *long* time.

To my parents: thank you for supporting me in everything I pursue. Whether it's performing, writing, or leading worship, you always have my back and push me to be better. I love you.

A huge thank you to Mrs. Willis for once again proof reading a 300 page manuscript in addition to all of her other amazing work as a teacher. I'm so grateful.

To Noah, my brother: I'm sorry for making you stand out in the freezing cold on top of a mountain just so that I could get a picture. It turned out pretty cool, though, huh?

Thank you to Stacy Juba, my editor, who was constructive but encouraging in helping me improve my writing.

Lastly, to my readers: I was overwhelmed by the response I received from my first book and even more surprised to hear the excitement for my next one. You motivate me to finish things I've started and to improve my writing. You've made a dream of mine come true. For that, I'm so eternally grateful. I hope you loved *September* as much as I did... and I hope you're ready for Keeper, book two. Hold on a little longer!

Until the next one, loves.

About the Author

K. M. Higginbotham is a young writer from a small town in North Alabama. When she's not writing, she's enjoying a hot cup of black tea, reading, longingly planning her future trips across the world, or making music with her family.

Kate published her first fantasy novel, *Keeper: The Book of Aon*, in 2016, and her second novel, *September*, was published in 2018. She plans to extend the *Keeper* series into a trilogy.

For news and information on upcoming books, go to **kmhigginbotham.com** or like the Facebook page at **https://www.facebook.com/kmhigginbothambooks/**